The wa̲[...] Sand̲[...]
s̲[...] [...]ne
pretty blonde crying over there.
Where'd a woman so quiet and tin[...]
get such a core of steel?

Mason's eyebrow shot up as Miss Sanders got th[...]
children's attention and gathered them into a group.

"It's time to be calm and quiet. We're safe, and
things will be all right from here. Everyone have all
their fingers and toes?" The voice was sensible and
cheerful, as if it didn't belong to the same woman
who'd just stood over Arlington's body. "My town is
just over that hill, and you'll all get to visit tonight.
You'll get some supper, too. But we've lots to do to
make that happen, so I'll need everyone's help."

As Mason stood watching this small woman
accomplish this very large feat, the train conductor
came up with an equally stunned look on his face.

"Who is that?" he asked Mason as both men stared.

"That," Mason said, not bothering to hide the
respect in his voice, "is Holly Sanders."

ORPHAN TRAIN:
Heading west to new families and forever love

Family Lessons—Allie Pleiter, April 2013
The Marriage Barter—Christine Johnson, May 2013
The Baby Compromise—Linda Ford, June 2013

ALLIE PLEITER

Enthusiastic but slightly untidy mother of two, RITA® Award finalist Allie Pleiter writes both fiction and non-fiction. An avid knitter and unreformed chocoholic, she spends her days writing books, drinking coffee and finding new ways to avoid housework. Allie grew up in Connecticut, holds a B.S. in speech from Northwestern University and spent fifteen years in the field of profes-sional fund-raising. She lives with her husband, chil-dren and a Havanese dog named Bella in the suburbs of Chicago, Illinois.

Family Lessons

ALLIE PLEITER

◆HARLEQUIN® LOVE INSPIRED® HISTORICAL

Special thanks and acknowledgment to Allie Pleiter for her contribution to the Orphan Train miniseries.

Recycling programs
for this product may
not exist in your area.

™ LOVE INSPIRED BOOKS

ISBN-13: 978-0-373-82960-6

FAMILY LESSONS

www.LoveInspiredBooks.com

Printed in U.S.A.

Blessed are those whose transgressions are forgiven, whose sins are covered. Blessed is the one whose sin the Lord will never count against them.
—*Romans* 4:7–8

To Angie, because when she claps,
children really do listen

Chapter One

Nebraska, April 1875

Holly Sanders now knew two things for sure.

She knew that she was smart enough to convince the Prairie Trust Bank of Nebraska to loan rebuilding funds to her flood-stricken hometown. That was a fine victory.

She also knew that any such victory could be wiped out in the split second it took the man behind her to cock the hammer of his pistol.

"Afternoon, ma'am," sneered the greasy-haired bandit, his breath hot on Holly's neck. "Seems to me a smart gal like yourself ought to know you'd best do *exactly* as we say right now." He addressed the entire railroad car in which Holly currently stood. "Y'all shush up and no one will get hurt."

The woman in front of Holly, the pretty one who had just introduced herself as Rebecca Sterling, let out a terrified whimper. The girl sitting beside Miss Sterling— one of the several orphans Miss Sterling had said she was escorting to nearby Greenville—started to cry. For a moment, the schoolteacher in Holly was mortified. Children shouldn't have to witness the man's threats. It seemed an oddly logical thought for someone with a gun barrel poked into their shoulder blade, but then again, Holly had always been the sensible type.

The grimy man stepped up and glared at Holly with a look that made her skin crawl. "Where's that man?" She'd never heard a voice so sinister. Where had he come from? Had he been hiding in wait on the back railing of the car this whole time?

He couldn't possibly be asking about Curtis Brooks, the bank representative who had insisted on escorting her and the bank's loan of two thousand dollars' worth of gold back to Evans Grove. How could this thief know about the banker, or the loan? It took her a second or two to find her voice. "What man?"

The bandit leered over her, close and foul. "The one what was with you back in Newfield. Mr. Fancypants Banker." He nudged her with the tip of his gun, pushing Holly down into her seat.

Her brain scrambled to assemble the facts, to get a grip on what couldn't possibly be happening. He knew who she was and what she had. *Dear Lord, save me!* "He's not here."

This clearly wasn't the answer the bandit wanted. "I know he ain't here!" He nodded to his partner—a second man Holly hadn't even seen until just now—who dashed down the train aisle to peer through the door to the next car. The first bandit leaned in closer to Holly. "Where is he? He went for it, didn't he?"

There would be no victory. Her town's future, the precious funds she'd labored to secure, the funds to rebuild Evans Grove after a storm and flood had nearly wiped it out—all was being thieved right out from underneath her. She'd return to Evans Grove empty-handed—if she returned at all. These men looked like the kind who wouldn't think twice to kill for whatever they wanted.

Too frightened to lie, she grappled for the safest truth: "He said he had…business in another car, so he took one of the antsier boys with him." Mr. Brooks had told Miss Sterling's partner agent that he was going up to the express car "to check on something," and had invited him and a boy named Liam as a diversion to the long ride. Of course, Holly knew he'd gone up to check on the safe where the gold was stored, but she wouldn't tell that to these horrible men.

"Business, hmm? As if you don't know what *kind* of business." The bandit grabbed her arm with one hand while he brandished the gun around, sending the orphan boys in the car ducking into their seats, and the little girls into tears. "Where is he? Which car?"

"There are children aboard!" Holly pleaded as he wrenched her arm.

A second little girl across from Holly began to sob. "The mail car!" one boy yelped, pointing to the door Mr. Brooks, the other orphan escort called Mr. Arlington and Liam had gone through. At that moment, two more men burst into the car behind the first bandit. Mercy, how many of them were there?

"Go get him, boys!" shouted the leader, nodding his head in the direction the boy had pointed. "And don't forget to mention how many *precious little lives* are at stake."

"You wouldn't!" Miss Sterling suddenly found her voice.

The bandit's glare silenced her. "Don't try me, missy."

Just then, the train slowed with a shuddering lurch, wheels squealing. Someone had thrown the brake, and bags and boxes flew from seats and shelves as the train slowed far too quickly. Shouts rose up from the cars ahead. Holly startled as the sharp sound of pistol fire split the warm afternoon, feeling as if the breath had been ripped from her lungs. Miss Sterling yelped and even the boys now looked close to tears.

"What's going on?" an old woman from the far end of the railcar cried. A storm of falling and tumbling belongings raged as the car lurched, surged forward, and then lurched again. Holly was held firmly in place by the bandit's iron grip. Once the car finally stopped—which seemed to take forever—whimpers and groans filled the air. Still, none of the passengers dared to move, even to pick up the things that had fallen.

"Is anyone hurt?" Holly said as calmly as she could manage with the bandit's glare so close. While everyone was frightened and upset, she was glad no one replied that they were injured.

"I am an agent of the Orphan Salvation Society, sir. May I stand and see to the children?" Miss Sterling asked.

"No." The bandit's voice was low and cruel. "Everyone just said they's fine, didn't they?"

"We are, ma'am," came one of the boys' voices. The attempted calm in the poor lad's tone twisted Holly's heart. "But I don't know about Liam."

This sent one of the girls into crying again. "Where's Liam?"

"He went with Mr. Arlington and that other man," Miss Sterling whispered. "Just hush up now."

A second later the far door pushed open and a burly hand shoved Liam and Mr. Arlington into the car. The older agent looked roughed up while Liam had a nasty bruise above his left eye. "Keep this feisty one outta my way while the banker man gets the safe opened."

"Why'd we stop?" The bandit next to Holly squeezed her arm so tight she winced.

"This little rat." The second bandit nodded at Liam. "He ran to the engine car and told 'em to pull the brake."

"We ain't at Evans Grove yet." The leader's comment made Holly look out the window, trying to judge where they were.

"We're close enough," the second man said, and Holly guessed him to be right. Their awareness made Holly's stomach drop. Usually, no one paid much mind to tiny Evans Grove. It wasn't even large enough to have a rail station. Today's train was only "whistle-stopping" there at the request of Curtis Brooks. The bandits couldn't know that—unless they'd seen the wire she sent this morning telling of her change in travel plans. Holly's stomach dropped further.

"If we're close enough, then stick to the plan," came the leader's voice, now pitched with frustration. "Why ain't it open yet?"

"We cain't get it open."

The safe. Of course.

The leader cursed, making Miss Sterling cover the ears of the little girl in her lap. "It takes two seconds to open one of those, and he must have the key so don't you let him tell you otherwise." He turned to peer at Holly. "Unlessen you have a key, too?"

Holly wasn't used to people paying her any mind. Small and "mousy" as Mama used to say, she mostly went unnoticed. Would that she'd gone unnoticed today, instead of finding herself at the center of a crime. A crime in front of children, no less. "I don't know anything."

The bandit cocked his gun again, demonstrating his disbelief. Holly flinched and fought for breath.

"Stop threatening her!" Mr. Arlington, a rather bookish gentleman in his fifties from the looks of it, was attempting to sound commanding but failed miserably.

The bandit all but ignored him, still looking straight at Holly. "You know how much gold is in there. You know what kind of 'business' he has, and how much. That ain't hard to figure."

Holly shut her eyes, wrestling the panic that threatened to swallow her. "There's two thousand dollars. It's a loan for my town. To rebuild after the flood."

"Ain't that sweet." His voice taunted. "Y'all will have to find another way."

The thought of everything this man was stealing—money, hope, a chance to rebuild—burned the fear in Holly's chest into a growing anger. He knew exactly what he was taking from good people, and seemed to enjoy it. Any jury in the county would send him to the gallows for such crimes, and all her good Christian charity wouldn't give her enough compassion to object.

A second bandit ducked his head into the car. "Boss, we still can't get it open."

"What do you mean you can't get it open? It's a safe, he has the key, you have the gun. *Make him open it.*"

The new bandit, obviously the muscle of the operation rather than the brains, scratched his chin. "Something fell against the safe. A big crate hit the lever and twisted it."

"So move the big crate. It's a safe, Earl. You can't break a safe." He looked around again. "Why ain't we there yet?"

Liam pulled away from the two men. "Not too smart, these two. I reckon your gold isn't going anywhere." Holly had only been in the boy's company half an hour and Liam had already proven to have a mouth that often ran ahead of his sense.

The ill-timed insult sent the leader off Holly's arm to lunge at the boy. Before she could get out a warning, the man backhanded Liam so hard he fell against Mr. Arlington. "You," the bandit barked, "need to shut your yap or die yelping." He looked as if his anger would boil over any second, his fingers working the hammer of his gun with an irritated twitch. "Get over there with her." He pointed back to Holly. "You keep him in line."

Liam pulled himself up out of the seat and came to sit next to Holly. His lip was already swelling and his face burned as crimson as his red scraggly hair. He breathed hard, and Holly placed a calming palm over his fisted hands, praying he'd know enough to keep quiet from here on in.

"You," said the leader, pointing to the beefy man who'd shoved Liam into the car, "stay here and make sure no one gets any ideas. I'm going up to the express car to see if I cain't—" he cocked the pistol again "—hurry up the fetchin'."

"We're finished," Miss Sterling moaned, gathering the children around her. "Stranded in the middle of nowhere at the hands of bandits."

"They're not very smart bandits, ma'am," Liam whispered. "I watched 'em up in the express car. We're not so finished as you think." He looked out the window, making Holly wonder what kind of life the orphan boy had known to stay so remarkably calm and cocky under such rough treatment. "Where are we?"

Holly looked out the window again. Evans Grove had nothing more than a sad little platform built alongside the spot in the tracks where the train occasionally stopped. She could see that sad platform just beyond the next outcropping of rocks. They were very nearly at Evans Grove. Someone small and fast could get to town and bring help.

"Liam," Holly whispered with her eye on their enormous captor, "how fast can you run?"

"Sheriff! Sheriff Wright, did you hear what I just said?"

Mason Wright pinched the bridge of his nose and longed for patience. When he envisioned breaking up feuds and brawls in the tiny town of Evans Grove, he hadn't pictured the combatants wearing bonnets.

"Yes, I heard you clear." He glanced over at the door of his office, still swinging open from Beatrice Ward's blustering entrance, and thought it might be time to make up a "Closed" sign to hang in the window. "But, Miss Ward, I don't have to tell you times are tight all over these parts. I don't see how requiring curtains is going to solve much of anything. People have more important places to put their time and money."

Miss Ward puffed herself up like a fussing hen. The way that woman clucked, it wasn't hard to draw the connection. "Ephraim always said, 'appearance is everything.'" Beatrice was forever quoting "wisdom" Mason had never seen the spinster's late brother display. "If we look respectable and civilized, why then we behave respectable and civilized."

Mason didn't see much he'd call respectable and civilized in the "basic privacy of curtains" battle Beatrice Ward had launched at this week's town meeting. He'd seen less contentious hound fights. Honestly, the woman had been on a righteous tirade ever since the storm took the roof off her house. Always proud of her fussy little cottage on Second Street—or what she liked to call "the high side of town"—Miss Ward took her home's destruction as a personal insult, as if no one else in town had ever lost their home or kin. Truth was, far too many had lost homes and kin when the storm burst a nearby dam last month. Most especially the Widow Evans, Beatrice's current opponent in the room. He offered Pauline Evans a sympathetic glance before saying, "I have to agree with Mayor Evans. I can't enforce this."

"*Acting* Mayor Evans," Beatrice corrected, casting a derisive glance at the other woman. Some days Beatrice treated Pauline Evans as if she had stolen the title off her late husband's still-warm body instead of the sad inheritance it was.

Robert Evans had been a fine man and a huge loss to the town, and Mason had to give Pauline credit for setting aside her grief to uphold her husband's office. If the widow never did anything else for Evans Grove, her decision to step in kept Beatrice Ward from declaring herself mayor. Beatrice always acted as if chairing the Evans Grove Ladies' Society—which merely consisted of eight grandmothers who met weekly in the church parlor for tea and criticism—gave her supreme authority.

"We've sent off for funds as it is, Beatrice." Mayor

Evans—Mason refused to think of her or address her as "acting mayor" no matter what Miss Ward insisted—squared her shoulders and jutted her chin in defiance. "We need to rebuild, not redecorate."

"One fuels the other," Miss Ward preached. "Who'd want to invest in a drab little town?"

"The Prairie Trust Bank of Nebraska, if you both remember. Miss Sanders wired yesterday to say she'd be on this morning's train to Greenfield and taking the stage back here this afternoon."

"Why on earth doesn't the train stop here regularly? We have a station," the spinster declared with undue pride.

"We only have a *platform,* and you know we can always get a whistle-stop if we ask a day ahead of time," Mason felt compelled to correct. "What matters is that Miss Sanders will be on that stage from Greenfield today with important promissory papers, and I intend to be waiting to meet her. But before then, I got a pile of paperwork to tend to, a bag of government mail left over from the flood and two complaints about Vern Hicks out yelling down by the saloon again last night. Can you see that I might have more important things to tend to at the moment?"

Mason had hoped that the mention of Vern Hicks, who spent far more time with a bottle than his wife, might throw righteous Miss Ward off her present course. It only seemed to deepen the woman's ever-present scowl.

Truth to tell, Mason felt a little like scowling himself. Miss Sanders was a sensible sort, but he didn't like the idea of her traveling alone on the train. He would have been much more satisfied with Miss Sanders on yesterday's train with an Evans Grove whistle-stop, but she'd wired to say the meetings took longer than expected. Mason wasn't much for changing plans last minute with so much at stake, but who was he to tell a banker how long it takes to get business done? No one asked him if it was wiser to wait one more day so they could request a whistle-stop right here in Evans Grove. No, that banker had gone right ahead and put her on to-day's train that went on through to Greenfield. It may get her home today, but he liked the idea of a woman alone on an open stagecoach from Greenfield even less than a train.

"Do you think Miss Sanders is traveling with any funds right away?" Mayor Evans asked, evidently glad for a change of subject.

"We won't know. The bank could send a small start-up fund, but I told her not to make any mention of it if they did. If she's traveling with any gold at all, the fewer people who hear about it, the better. No offense, but I'd hope the Prairie Trust Bank would know better than to send even one brick of gold with a tiny little thing like Holly Sanders."

"Well, I should hope—" Miss Ward's declaration was cut off by the sound of yelling in the street.

"Sheriff!" Shouts and the sound of galloping horse hooves sent Mason to the door in a flash. Ned Minor was coming up the street at full speed yelling "Sheriff Wright!" as his horse kicked up a cloud of dust. The young hotel clerk was a dozen yards away when a scraggly boy lunged off the back of the horse to run full tilt at Mason.

"It's the train," the boy yelped, pointing back toward

the tracks. "Gunmen. Miss Sanders had Miss Sterling fake the vapors so I could…sneak off and get help."

Holly Sanders? Here? Now?

Ned pulled up his horse behind the boy. "Robbers!" Mason was already untying his horse. "The train Miss Sanders is on is stopped just down the tracks. Bandits…"

Mason had one foot in the stirrup and the safety off his gun. Turning his horse south, Mason barked to Ned, "Get every man you can and meet me at Whitson's Rock. Get Bucky Wyler first—he's a good shot." He'd swallowed a bad feeling in his gut all yesterday, a twist that had been there ever since the wire from Holly Sanders. *I had a hunch and I ignored it.* Tamping down the chill such thoughts sent down his spine, Mason reached down to the lad and hoisted him into the saddle behind him. "Tell me everything you know while we ride." Looking to Ned, he called, "Be fast and quiet." The thought of tiny Holly Sanders under the gun of some lawless bandit drove Mason's boot heels into Ace's flanks and his gut down through the soles of his feet. If any harm came to her, he'd feel even more doomed than he already did.

Chapter Two

"Mercy!" Miss Sterling fanned herself, clutching her chest as she draped herself against a rock. "I believe I was going to faint without some air."

Holly mused that the woman could have had a career in the theater. Miss Sterling was a stunning beauty, and had quite the gift for producing a fit of the vapors on command. It had only helped matters when one of the little girls yelped out a need to "use the necessary." Within minutes all the children "needed" to get off the train and relieve themselves, giving Holly—and Liam—the perfect opportunity.

"Just get them kiddies done with their business and get back on the train, lady." Their beefy captor was annoyed but clearly in no mood to deal with the mess ignoring the children would have brought.

"This is the last one," Holly called to him, holding the hand of a little girl named Lizzie while Mr. Arlington pretended to be watching over Liam's ministrations. He had led the boys as a group to the edge of the clearing on the pretense of tending to their needs. Rebecca was to send up just enough of a fuss to keep the robbers from counting heads as the children filed back into the passenger car. Trying not to stare at the scraggly bush behind which Liam disappeared, Holly said a desperate prayer. *Father, let him reach town in time. Guide his steps along the directions I gave. Send help. Save us from these men!*

Holly caught the eyes of Rebecca and Mr. Arlington as they filed back into the car as casually as possible. How awful and odd to be so close to home and in such a spot. When the brutal storm hit Evans Grove last month, she'd thought that the low point. When the subsequent flood washed mercilessly through the low parts of town, she'd thought then that things had looked their worst. As Holly stood on the rocky soil, casting a worried gaze toward the express car where the banging noises had now stopped, she couldn't help but wonder if the worst was still to come. Had they gotten the safe open? What of Mr. Brooks? Even if he should be all right, the funds were surely gone by now. If the bank wouldn't replace them, Holly worried Evans Grove wouldn't survive this final blow.

A volley of sharp yells echoed across the clearing. After a loud clang, Holly saw the doors of the express car slide open and a pair of hands push Mr. Brooks down out of the car. He'd barely regained his footing from the leap when a large black box crashed to the ground at his feet. He was nearly crushed by the metal cabinet, which made a strange, chinging sound as it tumbled to settle heavily onto the ground. *The safe.* Mr. Brooks's jacket was off. He looked as if he'd been roughed up, but he was remarkably calm.

"I told you it wouldn't work!" The bandit leader's voice pitched in frustration as he followed Mr. Brooks out of the express car, gun trained on the banker. "More n' likely you've busted up the mechanism and we'll never get it open now."

The third and fourth bandits climbed from the car. "Do we go get the horses now? Time to take the safe and run?"

Holly was tempted to point out that one does not just take a safe and run, but kept her mouth shut in remembrance of the backhanding Liam had endured. Short of a wagon or a stick of dynamite, that safe was not going anywhere. Nor did it look as if it would open. Taking a step toward Mr. Brooks, Holly scanned the area and tried to think of where she would hide horses nearby.

"Time," sneered the leader as he raised the gun to Mr. Brooks's temple, "to up the ante. You're making me wonder, bankerman, if you ain't hiding the real key."

"Stop it!" Holly cried before she could think better of interfering. "Give him our money, Mr. Brooks. Nothing is worth a life."

"I assure you, Miss Sanders," Mr. Brooks said, his voice winding tighter with every passing second, "I am doing my level best to do just that." He held the key up to his captor. "Look at the numbers on this key." He was trying to make the bandit see reason, but it only seemed to anger the man. "They match the markings on the safe. This is the right key, but it won't work. Have sense, man. All your gun pointing can't change the fact that this key will not unlock a damaged mechanism."

Holly heard Mr. Arlington's voice behind her. She turned to find him holding out a hat filled with watches, wallets and the fine beaded reticule she'd seen on Miss Sterling. "Take what we've got and let us be. There are children here, for goodness' sake. We've no way to pursue you. Why don't you just leave?"

Holly heard a horse's whinny off to her right. Was it the robbers' accomplice or had Liam been even faster than she'd hoped? *Father, protect us!*

The leader turned to Mr. Arlington, eyes blazing in fury. "Howsabout you just shut your mouth?" he yelled loudly. Then to Holly's great horror, the bandit raised his pistol and fired.

She heard the terrible sound. She saw the dust rise up as the hat full of loot hit the ground. She felt the impact as if it sucked the air from her lungs. Someone screamed. A woman, a child, or perhaps it was both. It couldn't have been her—she had no voice, no breath. The entire world boiled down to the smell of gunpowder and the red stain blossoming under Mr. Arlington's hand as he clutched his chest. The look of shock in his eyes as he tilted forward turned Holly's heart to ice.

Nothing. They'd shot him for nothing. Who would they shoot next and for what?

The sound of the gunshot pounded in Mason's chest, and he urged Ace faster toward the spot on the railway line just east of town Liam had described. The boy had told him enough to chill his blood. If they were the clever kind, who knew what these men were capable of, what lengths they would go to succeed? "Give me a dim-witted thief any day," he said to himself as he swung down off his saddle, glad to see townsfolk coming a half mile behind him.

"You might get your wish," Liam commented as he slid off the saddle and they scrambled up the rock outcropping that gave both of them a view down onto the track clearing. "They didn't seem too smart to— Oh, no!" Liam gasped, covering his mouth in horror as he saw what Mason saw: Holly Sanders and two other people crouched in panic over a bleeding man. "They shot Mr. Arlington!" His voice was a whispered yell, full of shock and fear. He looked up to Mason with panicked eyes. "How could they have shot Mr. Arlington like that? Mr. Brooks had the key to the safe. Mr. Arlington didn't know nothin'!"

Mason didn't know what to say. His brain was churning through options, working furiously to find some way out of this. One thing was clear from the chaos below: these men weren't killing by plan, they were killing by panic. Panic was far more dangerous than clever, and from the looks of the safe dumped out on the packed earth just a few yards away, and the yelling going on between the bandits, things had gotten out of hand.

Within minutes, Bucky Wyler came up crouching behind Mason, rifle ready in his hand. "Aw criminey," he muttered as he took in the scene, "what now?"

"Act fast. Too much longer, and things will go from bad to worse." Mason looked over his shoulder at the four other men coming up the path, motioning for them to come closer but to keep down.

"Worse already, if you're asking me." Bucky settled onto his stomach and pulled his rifle up to rest on the rock. "What do we do? There's too many of 'em down there to shoot."

"You can't shoot." Mason grabbed Bucky's arm. "There's young'uns down there."

Bucky palmed his hat off his head. "Kids?"

"Orphans. Handful of 'em. That's one of the agents on the ground."

"Mr. Arlington's not dead, is he? We gotta get down there." Liam looked as if he'd burst down into the clearing in two seconds if Mason didn't do something. He scanned the scene again, grasping for any tactic.

"Bucky, can you shoot the safe?"

The man squinted through his gunsight. "Yep, but it's not likely to do much."

"It'll be distraction enough."

Just then, in the worst possible timing, the children came piling out of the car. There was an old woman trying to hold them back from the gruesome scene, but the orphans were too wild with panic for one old woman to keep them corralled. Mason swore under his breath. Even Bucky's sharpshooting was too much of a risk with all those youngsters about.

"Get back in the car!" The woman with Holly Sanders stood up and waved the children off. When the youngsters only rushed at her, she moved as quickly as she could away from the injured man. Thankfully, they followed, putting a bit of distance between themselves and the bickering robbers, who were now circled around the safe.

It didn't take long to figure out who was in charge. The other three were clearly muscle; only one of them seemed to be shouting commands. "There's our man," Mason said as he pointed to the leader. "If we could take him out…A shot in the leg ought to do the trick."

Bucky settled in to line up his shot, following Mason's thinking. "Then we can pick off the rest."

"Just do something! Mr. Arlington's bleeding bad." Liam was growing frantic.

Mason was out of options. He looked at Bucky and gestured back toward the now dozen armed men behind them. "Give each of them a target—wounding only, no killing in front of those youngsters. Understood?"

As Mason started to move, Liam grabbed his leg. "What about me?"

"You stay here. You've been brave enough already."

"No!"

Mason couldn't say he was surprised, and he didn't have time to argue. "Are you good at sneaking?"

"The best."

Mason pointed to the most likely spot for some accomplice to be hiding horses. "Head on over there and look for horses." He tossed the lad the bosun's whistle from his vest pocket. He used it for shooing away stray dogs, and the thing always made Ace crazy. Maybe it would rile up the bandits' horses if they had any. "Blow this all around to spook them and then run back here but be careful. Someone's bound to be guarding them."

The boy caught the whistle with one hand. "Got it."

Mason picked his way down between the rocks toward the rail line, still unsure how he was going to draw the men. He was almost in range when the biggest of them said, "How about I go get the horses and we haul that safe outta here?"

Not a lot of brains there, Mason thought to himself as he imagined the robbers attempting a getaway while dragging a heavy safe through the Nebraska countryside. Their lack of speed would be compounded by the obvious tracks.

The leader surprised him by consenting. "Just go get the horses. Jake," he shouted, pointing at another man, "get that hat full of loot, and fer Pete's sake get Miss Prissy and them brats back in the car."

Mason waited until the last possible moment, weighing every stride the big man took toward the horses—and Liam—with every child who stepped back onto the train. Bucky must have followed his thinking, for just as Mason cocked his pistol Bucky's shot rang out, pinging loudly against the safe to ricochet into the woods over Mason's left shoulder. From behind him the bosun's whistle sounded; Liam had found the horses. *Run, kid.* Mason sent him a mental message as shouts went up from all corners of the clearing and from other passengers who'd had enough sense to stay inside the railcars. The leader turned in the direction of the shot long enough for Mason to burst from behind the rock cropping, shouting himself.

In the two seconds it took the leader to turn, Mason fired. The bullet tore into the man's pant leg just above the knee, sending him to the ground. Half a dozen shots came from the ridge above, sending the place into a frenzy. Hoping Bucky was as good a shot as usual, Mason sprinted across the clearing to grab Holly Sanders by the waist and nearly haul her into the railcar behind the other woman and children. The fallen robbers managed a small volley of return fire, but even a sharpshooter would have a hard time hitting the men hid up in the rocks. When the bosun's whistle echoed again from the safety of the rock outcropping, Mason let out the breath he'd been holding for the boy.

There was a moment of stunned stillness. The robbers had used up their ammunition. Bucky and the others were surely trained on each of the fallen men, ready to fire if one of them made a move. Mason left

Miss Sanders at the railcar with the children—most of whom were screaming by now along with half the passengers—and rushed to crouch at the still body of Mr. Arlington.

One hand on the man's bloody chest told Mason nothing could be done. "Rest in peace, Arlington."

Holly watched in horror as Sheriff Wright took off his jacket and laid it carefully over Mr. Arlington's face. The man was dead. Shot for the crime of trying to let the bandits go, for trying to save the children from harm. The cruelty of it seemed to pummel Holly's lungs, and her steps wobbled as she made her way toward the sheriff.

"Lord have mercy on poor Mr. Arlington. Lord have mercy on all of us." Even as she felt relief that the gunfight was over, sorrow made her tears hard to fight back.

One of the things Holly most admired about Sheriff Wright was his quiet passion for justice and safety. Today held no justice and precious little safety. She would not have thought it possible for Mason Wright to look more stoic, but he straightened from the body with such a weary, pained effort that she felt it constrict her heart. He felt the crime—the *murder*—as sharply as she, even though neither of them knew the slain man.

There was a selfish corner of her heart that insisted this could have been prevented if Mason Wright had accompanied her to Newfield. He'd raised a lukewarm objection, saying he wasn't in favor of her going at all, but eventually consented to letting her travel alone. That hurt. A childish part of her wanted to think today wouldn't have happened if Mason Wright had been her protector.

But today *had* happened, and while she heard the old woman and several others flutter in panicked concern over a crying Miss Sterling behind her, no one steadied her as she stood over the body. Now, as always, she was the last one anyone thought to protect. Quiet, competent, invisible—even in this. All yesterday's sense of accomplishment evaporated just as quietly as Mr. Arlington's blood seeped into the sod. No comfort would be coming her way. That meant that it was time—as usual—for her to look past herself and see to comforting others.

"You saved us," she said, as she moved toward Sheriff Wright. Holly needed to keep speaking, to hear her voice fight the sense that she was evaporating into the sod herself.

He looked at her, his blue eyes brittle and hollow. She so rarely viewed those eyes—downcast as they often were or hidden in the shadow of his hat brim—that they never ceased to startle her when he stared. "No." He raised the single syllable like a knight's shield.

"But it is true." The sheriff seemed so very tall as she ventured another step toward him. Mason Wright was the kind of man who would take Arlington's loss as a personal failure, ignoring all the lives—including hers—he had just saved, and she hated that. Hated that she'd fail in this attempt just as she failed in *every* attempt to make him see his worth because he never looked at her long enough to notice.

He held her gaze just then, doubt icing his eyes until Holly felt a shiver run down her back. "No," he repeated, but only a little softer. Holly hadn't even realized she'd been holding her breath until Sheriff Wright broke his stare and looked down at the body shrouded in his own coat. Her practical nature wondered if his coat would be stained beyond repair, or if he would even care.

The shift in Sheriff Wright's attitude was physically visible. Whatever emotion had bubbled to the surface was resolutely put down with a deep breath and squared shoulders. His attention spread out beyond her and the body to take in the whole of the clearing and the larger crisis at hand. Everything about him said "enough of that, now to business," and Holly wondered if she would see that side of him up close ever again.

Even his voice changed. "Is she the other agent?" He nodded toward Rebecca Sterling and the upset children, now surrounded by the few other railcar passengers. "Liam mentioned a Miss…"

"Sterling, yes, that's her. Liam!" Holly suddenly remembered the brave boy who'd run off to get help. "Is Liam all right?"

"Shaken, but fine. Clever boy."

"I was so worried, sending him off." She scanned the clearing for signs of his red hair. "How foolish of me to gamble dangerously with a boy's life like that."

"Not at all." He looked at her again, this time with something she could almost fool herself into thinking was admiration. "It was quick and clever. If anyone saved the day here, it was you."

Holly blinked. From Mason Wright, that was akin to a complimentary gush. "It was the only thing I could think of to do." A murderous crisis was no time to get flustered, but she felt her blood rush to her cheeks just the same. She hadn't realized just how much she needed someone to affirm she'd done the right thing. The relief threatened a new wave of tears, and she fought them off with a deep breath.

A child's cry turned them both toward the bedlam surrounding Miss Sterling. The children were understandably out of control with fear and shock, and Miss Sterling didn't seem to be in any shape to take things in hand. Who would be in such a situation?

She would, that's who. Holly was an excellent teacher with a full bag of tricks at her disposal to wrangle unruly children. With one more deep breath, she strode off to save the day a second time.

Mason wiped his forehead with the back of his hand. Usually, when Holly Sanders's eyes tripped him up, he kept his mouth shut and steered clear. Sure, he'd worried about her in Newfield, but he'd worried more about how her wide eyes and meek smile would force him to get all close and protective of her if he went along on the trip. Mason always fought an urge to protect the tiny schoolteacher, and that urge could not be allowed. Ordinarily, Miss Sanders kept to the sideline of things, so it was easier to fight the urge, to not let himself be drawn in by her admiration. Staying away from Holly Sanders ensured he'd never again risk the kind of failure he'd already known.

Only that strategy had blown up in his face, for today she'd been stronger than he knew. Far stronger, and that truth was mighty hard to swallow. As a matter of fact, the shock of her strength had turned him stupid. *If anyone saved the day here it was you?* What kind of fool remark was that? He'd lost his control. Only for a moment, but land sakes that was enough, wasn't it?

The way he'd figured her, Miss Sanders should be as undone as the pretty blonde crying on the rocks over there. And he had seen tears come up behind her eyes—

despite doing his best to ignore them. So how was it she was trotting across the clearing with her hands on her hips, all teacher in command? Where'd a woman so quiet and tiny get such a core of steel?

His eyebrow shot up as Miss Sanders began to clap softly as she walked toward the children. She stopped about six yards out, speaking just soft enough to be heard. "Clap once if you can hear me."

He thought the tactic crazy until one little girl's eyes widened and looked up. Miss Sanders repeated herself, still clapping. "That's right, clap once if you can hear me." Startled out of her crying fit, the little girl clapped. A second girl next to her also looked up, sniffled, and clapped. Mason scratched his head, amazed.

"There you go. Now come over here and clap twice if you can hear me." By now all three of the little girls were clapping and moving toward Holly. Even a few of the adults looked up from tending to Miss Sterling, their attention drawn by the change in the children.

"Clap three times if you can hear me," Holly went on, garnering the attention of the two youngest boys. "Now four." Miss Sanders's voice steadied with every call, so that now she sounded as if this had been an ordinary school day. "Now five." The whole clearing was looking at her as the children quietly gathered around her and she kneeled down to their level. Mason realized his mouth was open, and shut it promptly, his own hands on his hips. He'd never seen anything so oddly effective in all his days.

"It's time to be calm and quiet. We're safe, and things will be all right from here. Everyone have all their fingers and toes?" The voice was sensible and cheerful, as if it didn't belong to the same woman who'd just stood over Arlington's body. The smallest girl—a tot of four or five from the looks of it—actually bent down to inspect her shoes, no doubt wiggling her toes inside.

"*Da*," the little girl said, dark braids bobbing. One of the older boys laughed, and a sliver of tension left the small sets of shoulders. Mason shook his head, befuddled.

"We're going to walk over here," Miss Sanders instructed, pointing to a spot that would shield the children from both Miss Sterling and the shrouded body of Mr. Arlington. "We'll sit down by age. Can you do that for me?" She pointed to the second largest boy, placing him in charge of the task. "And you," she said, pointing to the largest, "will go into the railcar and get everyone's bags so we can make sure everyone has what they need. My town is just over that hill and you'll all get to visit tonight. You'll get some supper, too. But we've lots to do to make that happen so I'll need everyone's help."

As Mason stood watching this small woman accomplish this very large feat, the train conductor came up with an equally stunned look on his face.

"Who is that?" he asked Mason as both men stared.

"That," Mason said, not bothering to hide the respect in his voice, "is Holly Sanders."

Chapter Three

Holly had walked the four miles from the railroad track to town hundreds of times, but none so tiresome as the trek felt today. As the slanted afternoon sun spread heat across the scrubby spring landscape, home and safety felt far away. She couldn't tell if she was too shaken to feel the long walk, or too numb to feel anything but her feet inside her tight, pinching boots.

The many small feet making the journey beside her surely lengthened the miles. Some of the children wore their trauma outright, crying and clutching to Miss Sterling and herself. Others, like Liam, were so silent Holly couldn't help but worry. Bucky and the other townsmen had taken the wounded bandits back to the Evans Grove jail while Mason laid Mr. Arlington's body over his own horse after seeing the train back on its route. None of that changed the awful truth that no child should have to witness men gunned down.

Certainly not orphans. *Why add this to the burden of their lives, Lord?* Holly understood the charitable sentiment of the Orphan Salvation Society. Better lives awaited these children out here than the parentless squalor they knew in eastern cities. Still, to be hauled out of the place one knew, plunked onto a train and displayed before prospective families in town after town for placement—how could that be anything but traumatic? Even if many of them found spots in loving homes, her heart ached for the grueling process, the rejection of being "passed over." Some of them were so heartbreakingly small and the train had made so many stops already.

"I'm glad you're staying," Holly offered to Miss Sterling. The woman had said next to nothing as she carried Galina, one of the smaller orphan girls, against her hip while holding the hand of a shy girl named Heidi. Miss Sterling had introduced each of the children on the train, and Holly was struggling against her fatigue to remember all their names. The three other boys—Tom, Patrick and some other German-sounding name she couldn't recall at the moment—had been boisterous and quiet by turns, unsure how to handle the experience. Who could blame them? Holly herself was anxious one minute, exhausted the next. Heidi, the very quiet girl who had sat next to Miss Sterling on the train, hadn't said a word since the shooting. Even though she mostly hid in the agent's skirts, Holly had spied gruesome scars on the girl's face. How cruel for a girl to have known so much pain so young. "I think the children couldn't go on, and, Miss Sterling, nor should you."

"Please call me Rebecca. We'll have to stay. I'll need to make…arrangements." Her voice caught on the word. "I've no idea how to proceed under the circumstances. I've…" Her voice fell off in a wobbly sigh.

"Call me Holly. Try not to think about that. I'll help you send some wires when we get into town. We'll sort it all out in the morning."

"You were awful brave, ma'am," Liam offered to Rebecca. "You, too, Miss Sanders." It was the first time Liam had spoken of his own accord, only piping up to answer questions before this.

His attempt at morale boosting warmed Holly's heart. "As were you. I'd have been afraid to sneak off to where those robbers hid their horses, but Sheriff Wright says you were a right clever deputy today."

"Me, a deputy." The thought brought the first smile to Liam's face since the incident.

"How long 'til that man gets here?" whined young Lizzie in Holly's arms, fussing with her shirt collar.

Tom, a thin, sickly-looking lad, coughed and wiped his forehead. "Why didn't *we* get to ride the horses? Those robbers should'a been the ones that had to walk!"

"Sheriff Wright will be back with the wagons soon," Holly replied. "The robbers can't walk because we hurt them."

"Bobbins isn't hurt, but I am," Lizzie offered, nodding toward the raggedy bunny doll in one hand while holding up her other hand to Holly. "I gots an ow right here."

Holly dutifully offered a medicinal kiss to the pudgy pink thumb. "Which is exactly why I'm carrying both of you." She caught Rebecca's tight, drawn face out of the corner of her eye. *All of us hurt today.*

Liam stepped up to walk beside Heidi, taking her hand from Rebecca's. He pointed toward town with his other hand. "One wagon will go back to the train and get our things. And the banker, and the safe, too. The other wagon's comin' to fetch us. We won't have to walk much farther. I been there and back already, remember?"

As if on cue, two wagons pulled into view half a minute later. Ned Minor was driving the wagon from Gavin's General Store while Mason Wright brought up one with crates lined up as seats along either side.

"If you're the sheriff, why aren't you with the robbers?" the boy named Patrick called as Ned's wagon went on by toward the rail line, and Sheriff Wright pulled up to the weary band of travelers.

"Doc Simpson's tending to their wounds while Bucky keeps watch. Besides, with wounds in their legs and their arms tied up, they're not much trouble to anyone at the moment. I'm more worried about your lot than those sorry souls, anyhow." He climbed down off the driver's bench and motioned toward the wagon's payload. "Nothing fancy, but it sure beats walking the rest of the way into town."

"By a mile," Tom wheezed, climbing in. He called out to Miss Sterling. "Here, ma'am, this corner seat oughta be for you."

Holly frowned. "Surely Miss Sterling ought to sit up front."

"In truth," sighed Rebecca, "I think back here with all the children would be best." As Sheriff Wright helped Rebecca into the wagon bed, Holly found she couldn't argue the request, even knowing the ride was far bumpier in back. Having been through what they all witnessed, wouldn't she want to surround herself with the hugs of children? As she handed little Lizzie and Bobbins up into the wagon, Holly's thoughts cast back to so many of her own students. Fright made one crave the familiar.

Cargo in place, the sheriff swung into the driver's seat and extended a hand to help Holly step up beside him. "My." Her own sigh was almost as large as Rebecca's. "What a blessing it is to be able to sit down and ride. I feel as if these boots have grown teeth."

Sheriff Wright picked up the reins and gave them a snap. As the cart lurched into motion, he glanced down at Holly's feet. "Fancy footwear there."

Fancy? By Evans Grove standards, perhaps, but not compared to what she'd seen in Newfield. "I had hoped to make a fine impression on the bank." She had, until she'd seen how her homespun look measured up to all those frocked ladies and brocade waistcoated bankers. Holly felt the top of her head, unsurprised to find her best hat gone. "I wasn't planning on braving a gunfight in my Sunday best." Holly's "Sunday best" compared poorly to Rebecca's finely cut traveling clothes. Why, even the children seemed in better clothes than she— though she knew that orphans on such trains were deliberately well-dressed in order to impress prospective families. Holly was neat and tidy, but certainly no sight to catch any eye.

Surely not Mason Wright's eye, although a surprising smile did cross his serious face. "You did right fine, considering." The smile quickly evaporated. "Although I'm never one for changing plans at the last minute like that. Too much risk."

She'd wondered how long it would take his initial concern for her safety to yield to his annoyance that she'd been allowed to go at all. "And just how do you suppose I could refuse Mr. Brooks's offer to get the funds so quickly? I *did* wire back word this morning. As I see it, arranging a stop in Evans Grove seemed far safer than going all the way to Greenville and taking the stage back."

He gave her what Holly had come to call his "book look." "That's all fine," he nearly muttered, "*...in theory.*" Truly, the only time Mason Wright ever seemed to give her any attention was to exercise his obvious opinion that "book learning" didn't do one a whole heap of good in the real world. "Only that wire never came and I was saddling up to ride off toward Greenville." Some days it felt like he viewed her as a dull, dry textbook best ignored. "Five more minutes and I'd have been gone when Liam came into town." His brows furrowed. "I'd have been miles out of town with no way to help you all if..."

Today of all days she wasn't going to let him get away with it. "*If,*" she finished for him, "I hadn't found a clever way to send Liam off for help." She stared at him until he lifted his gaze from the reins and returned her stare. "You did say I saved the day, did you not?"

That was a fool thing to say, for a look of regret washed across his features. She should have known he didn't really mean it. "Perhaps I ought to deputize *you.*"

It was the first time he'd ever paid enough attention to her to tease her, and she felt that unwelcome girlish fluster return. "Don't talk such nonsense." Still, a tiny new spark of confidence refused to be extinguished. She had been brave, even though she felt more fear than she could ever remember. She'd made a difference today, hadn't she? A real difference. "I prayed as hard as I ever have and, well, I had some very clever help."

He tipped his hat. "Nice to be appreciated."

"And what if I was talking about Liam?" She'd teased him right back. She'd never done that, never even had enough of a conversation to have the chance. All these clever words didn't change the fact that she knew—*deep down knew*—Sheriff Wright had walked into the line of fire for her life. There were a million serious words to be said about that, but she could find none of them in this moment. Still, she couldn't leave it at a joke, a levity over something so solemn as a life—*lives*—saved. Finding that same pool of courage that had shown itself on the train, Holly extended her hand to touch the sheriff's arm for the briefest of moments. With all the solemnity she could muster, she said, "Thank you."

They'd never touched before today. Not even to shake hands. Today, when he'd grabbed her at the railroad clearing and hauled her away from Mr. Arlington's dying body, she'd felt his grasp for the first time. She'd noticed how he steered clear of her at church picnics and town meetings and such. He spoke to her only when necessary or when she sought him out. He'd never paid her much mind.

And she just touched him. Every sensible bone in her body told her to regret it, but she found she couldn't.

To her delight—or her horror, she truthfully couldn't say which—Sheriff Wright held her eyes for a long moment before guiding the horse around a turn. "I was doing my job." He'd closed up the moment so neatly and completely, Holly wasn't even sure it had happened at all.

But today has happened, her frayed spirit wanted to yell. *We can't go back from it.* "Mr. Arlington was just doing his job, and now he's…gone." The memory of his blood seeping into the ground produced a shiver. *We can't go back.*

"Best not to dwell on that." He cocked his head toward the back of the wagon. "Not with all those little ones about." After a short pause, he asked, "I think it was smart not to send them on, but have you got any ideas how we're going to manage it?"

She did. The plan fell solid into her head as if God had sent it by telegraph. "I asked Ned to get Miss Ward to round up the ladies' society and see to supper. When I get in, I can ask Reverend Turner to meet with them while they eat. He'll know how to ease their minds and such. While he does that, Charlotte Miller and I can make up pallets so we can sleep them all in the schoolhouse. I'd let Miss Sterling have my bed in the house next door and offer to sleep with the children, but I don't think she'd accept." Holly cast a glance back to see Rebecca's cheek resting on the head of a little girl. "I imagine it's hit her hardest of all, poor soul."

"And you?"

She was startled he asked. Such surprise did little to dismiss the black knot of fear that hadn't left her stomach since her first glimpse of the bandit's eyes. Like peering right into evil, it was. "I'll be fine."

Sheriff Wright shook his head. "Your hands are still shaking." Holly tucked her hands into the folds of her skirt. "See to yourself is all I'm saying." His voice sounded uncomfortable with the words, as though letting them out by force rather than concern. He straightened his hat and shifted in his seat. "You've been through just as much as they have. Sleeping with a gaggle of fussy youngsters doesn't sound too sensible to me."

Sensible? There were days when Holly felt like hearing that word once more would drown her in dullness. Nothing about today—nothing about how she currently felt, or who was in the back of this wagon, or what body would be lying in the back of Doc Simpson's office—felt sensible.

And as for sleep, Holly didn't think sleep would visit her tonight. Not when the clamoring silence of Mr. Arlington's lifeless body echoed every time she closed her eyes.

When the wagon pulled up on Second Street and the church steeple came into view, Mason finally let down his guard. He'd barely been able to speak after she'd said "Thank you" with all that frailty in her eyes, and the spot where she touched him fairly burned from the memory. The impulse to grab her up and pull her from harm's way had been a primal reaction, one his body hadn't yet released. Holly Sanders always made him jittery ten ways 'til Sunday, and today hadn't helped.

"Oh, thank You, Jesus!" Her sigh echoed far too close to his shoulder. "I don't know when I've ever been so glad to be home." Mason was sure he could hear her big blue eyes flutter.

There were good reasons he sat far away from those eyes during church services—on the rare occasions he even darkened the church door. It wasn't disinterest that kept Mason away from Holly Sanders's endless classroom projects. He resisted the pull of that woman with every protective bone in his body, knowing her book-and-fairy-tale world had no room for someone with the dark tale his life told. He wasn't blind to her admiration—he'd caught too many of her stares not to see she fancied him—but that was only because Holly Sanders didn't know the full story. If he told her, it'd put an end to her admiration, surely. Only, some part of him liked that regard as much as the other part of him resisted it.

Seeing her in danger today had jumbled up his insides too much to think clearly. "I'm glad to have everyone safe back in town," he admitted, meaning far more than the words conveyed on their polite surface.

Evans Grove was a small town, laid out in a tidy little grid around the town square they were just passing. As the wagon rumbled past Victory Street where the church was, he saw Miss Sanders's nose wrinkle up in thought. "Speaking of safe," she asked, "what will you do with *the* safe? Doesn't it belong to the railroad?"

"I've been thinking on that." He had. That safe contained more gold than Evans Grove had seen in a good long while, and while *he* knew from Curtis Brooks that there weren't other railroad passengers' funds or valuables in there, others did not. "It's not the kind of thing we can leave unprotected. As for the rail line, I filed a report with the conductor, but with that kind of damage, I doubt they'll want it back. It'll spend the night with me in the sheriff's office and then we'll get Charlie Miller to open it in the morning." Mason felt sure the village smithy—husband of the same Charlotte Miss Sanders just spoke of recruiting to help with the children—would be able to work that damaged door off its hinges.

"And then what?"

He allowed himself the luxury of watching her face's peculiar vitality when working out a problem. All scrunched up and amusing, it was. It must be what made her the type to be a good teacher. Not him. Mason would rather deal with bandits than herd youngsters any day. The whining from the back of the wagon this afternoon had just about done him in, even though it didn't seem to faze her one bit.

"The 'then what' is best kept between just a few, if you don't mind." He did not care to venture into a detailed discussion about anything with her, and keeping that gold hidden and secure was his top priority. Far too much depended on it.

"I'm sure you and Mr. Brooks will work something out." She turned, looking behind her down the street for the other wagon.

"They'll be another hour, I expect."

"Are you sure they're safe?"

He'd already gone over the tactic twice with Curtis Brooks. "I wouldn't be here if they weren't. You just worry about—"

"Look at that!" came a small voice from behind them on the wagon as they drove past Gavin's General Store, which happened to have an unfortunate display of hard candies out in the window. "I'm hungry!"

"Me, too," came another, followed by two more. Mason's own stomach grumbled in sympathy.

"Goodness." Miss Sanders's hand went to her stomach. "I don't think I've eaten since breakfast. I do hope Beatrice got to the ladies' society."

"You know Beatrice," Mason chuckled. "She gets to *everybody*."

As the town square came into view, Mason pointed to the collection of tables now set in the grove of Hackberry trees that gave the town its name. A gaggle of women chattered and scurried around Beatrice Ward, dashing here and there under the spinster's barked commands. Flowers, tablecloths and other frills made the last-minute meal seem as if it had been planned for weeks.

"What a welcome for those tired folk!" Miss Sand-

ers placed her hands on her chest. "God bless Beatrice
Ward and the ladies' society."

Now there's a thought I'd never have, Mason pondered as he pulled the wagon onto Liberty Street and
headed for the town hall.

It was a matter of minutes before the wagon was surrounded by the good people of Evans Grove, and Miss
Ward was giving a long, too-formal welcome speech.
Impromptu as it was, the cobbled-together spread and
Miss Ward's grandiose gestures could make a person
think they had stumbled into the annual town picnic.
Had Miss Sterling taken note of the many buildings
that were still in bad shape? Would Mr. Brooks realize
how many lives had been washed away a month ago?
Hope was wearing mighty thin in Evans Grove, but at
least it was still alive.

"Come, Rebecca, sit down and have a glass of water.
I'll tend to the children." Mason watched Holly Sanders
guide Miss Sterling to a seat. How did the teacher manage such a cheerful and upbeat tone like that? He felt as
if he'd lived a month in the last five hours. She must feel
as bad, if not worse. He got his answer when he saw her
put her hand to her forehead and straighten up far too
slowly from helping that tiniest of girls. He wasn't the
only one hiding wounds today in Evans Grove.

Mason told himself to look away, but when her gaze
met his, he found he could not. A shadow crossed her
pale blue eyes; he could see it even from this distance
across the shady clearing. His mind pulled up the unwelcome memory of the desperate grip she'd given him
over Mr. Arlington's dead body. He recalled the hesitant
touch she'd given him in the wagon. The day had done

something to her, to be sure. Taken something from her, although he couldn't say what just yet.

Then again he wasn't sure just what the day had stripped from him, either. He only knew something under his ribs was out of place, and it wasn't the sort of thing Doc Simpson could put right.

He needed to get out of here, away from the jumble her eyes made of his thoughts. He forced her touch out of his mind, tamping it down the way he tamped down all those sorts of things anymore. He had a foursome of criminals, a broken safe full of gold and a body to tend to. He had no time for picnics. Ignoring the look Beatrice Ward gave him when he snatched a pair of rolls from the buffet table, Mason turned back toward the wagon and the duties still awaiting him.

Life wasn't going to allow him such an easy out, for Holly Sanders caught up with him just as he was about to swing up into the seat. "You should eat." Her tone of voice was...what? Complicated was the only word that came to mind—half request, half scolding, and weighted with the combined gains and losses of the day.

He held up the pair of rolls as his answer, unsure of what words to use given the set of her eyes.

"More than that." Her hands parked on her hips while her voice wove a combination of lecture and teasing. Did she realize what that half-playful tone did to him, or was that just a cruel trick of circumstance?

"Too much yet to do." He shrugged. "I've got... things...to attend to that can't wait for supper." He saw her shoulders sag and knew he hadn't hidden the weight of his tasks behind an innocent word like "things." She'd tried to re-pin her hair during the ride, but wayward strands of her chestnut-colored locks still eluded that tight bun she always wore. The lace on one of her sleeves had torn, and he realized the brown smear on the hem of her pretty skirt was blood.

It bothered him that her gaze followed his, that she knew what his eyes registered. She worried her hands together, delicate fingers rubbing each other as if it would erase the taint of the day. "Where is…he?" He knew she was speaking of Arlington's body, but her eyes looked up from her skirt to fix on Liam. The boy sat quietly on a bench running his fingers around the rim of a glass of lemonade. All the children were a heartbreaking mix of fidgety, tired and afraid.

"He's at Doc Simpson's, I suppose. He's got no kin here to lay him out."

Her sigh pressed against the hollow spot opening in his chest. "He has a wife…*had* a wife. And a daughter, according to Miss Sterling. We should wire—"

"No point until the morning, really. It's kinder that way, anyhow." Mason tried not to think of the story she should never know, the story of his own worst night. He'd barely survived the endless, excruciating hours after coming home to the body of his wife. To the loss of the child who in two months' time would have come into the world as his firstborn. *No*, he thought, *bad news is best saved for daylight.*

She straightened her shoulders—almost by sheer will this time, not hiding her wince. It was the worst kind of torture that she'd shown a new side of herself to him today. He hadn't counted on Holly Sanders's gumption, thinking she had smarts enough but no strength. Her bravery at the rail line had shown that a lie. A man with his history could recognize a glossed-over wound a mile off. "Miss Sanders, you all right?" The words tumbled out of him, odd and over-fussy.

"Why yes, of course I am," she replied too quickly, her voice pitched too high for calm.

"Surely that can't have been the first time you've seen a man dead?" It was a fool thing to ask. Evans Grove had lost so many in the flood, nearly everyone had kin or friends now gone, and this was the last kind of conversation he should be having with Holly Sanders.

"No." She looked him in the eye, her expression fierce and kind and hurt all at once with a dozen other things besides. "But it is the first time a man's been killed right in front of me." Her hands fisted against that pretty skirt. "And I hate the way it feels. When I think of what it must feel like for Rebecca or any of those sweet children, I..." She bit off the end of her thought, jaw working to hold her composure steady. "I'd better go tend to the beds. We'd best get those exhausted children washed and trundled off right after supper."

How well Mason knew that impulse, that "stay busy or it'll swamp up over me" drive. It had been his constant companion in the months after Phoebe's death. Phoebe's *murder*.

"You should eat." Without thinking, he offered one of his rolls with her own earlier command. It was a pointless gesture—the woman was perfectly capable of fixing herself a plate—but he found himself unwilling to go so far as to voice the "take care of yourself, too" he was thinking.

The message got through, anyway, for she managed to open her hand and take the roll. With a half a smile, she took a reluctantly obedient bite, straightened her shoulders one last time, and turned toward the school-house.

Mason was still pondering the image of that half smile when he fell asleep at his desk in the sheriff's office three hours later.

Chapter Four

It took longer than Holly guessed for her and Charlotte Miller to get things in order. The simple task of gathering up bedding and getting the nine pallets laid out on the schoolroom floor felt endless. Still, she reminded herself all of Evans Grove was pitching in to help. Pauline Evans and Beatrice Ward had consented to partner up to get Mr. Brooks settled at the Creekside Hotel, although Holly wasn't sure Mr. Brooks would survive that team. His importance surely ensured a warm welcome and attentive hosting, but none of that would change the wounds of the day. Even friendly, attentive strangers were still strangers.

"Goodness, I think that's the last of them," said Charlotte as she folded the facecloth of the last washed child. "Why don't you take Miss Sterling across the yard to your house to wash up," Charlotte suggested, making Holly think she and Rebecca now looked as bedraggled as she felt. "I'll mind the little ones until you get back." A few years older than Holly but with just as much energy, Charlotte rubbed her neck but smiled at the row of clean faces peeking out from under blankets and afghans. "The ones who aren't asleep already won't stay awake for long."

When Rebecca hesitated, Holly took her by the arm. "I'm sure Charlotte will send for us if any of the children need you. You need rest, and tomorrow's tasks will come soon enough." She was sorry to have mentioned tomorrow's sad tasks, for she saw Rebecca's eyes well up. The poor woman had been holding back tears all day. Holly felt like crying herself, still feeling the pull of nerves wound tight.

Rebecca looked back at the schoolhouse twice during the walk across the yard, but allowed Holly to bring her into the tidy frame teacherage that sat across the school yard from the classroom. Home had never felt more wonderful. Holly loved her home, took comfort in the familiarity of her things. She'd always felt the house's contents gave her a measure of strength and stability after venturing out into the prairie to help meet the need for frontier teachers. The teapot and the pretty china cups that had been her grandmother's, the rows of precious books, all these things seemed to offer a welcome embrace as she pulled the door shut. The house was warm and cozy, for she had remembered to duck in and start the stove—not to mention start some water warming—just after supper on the square. "I think some tea and a wash up will do wonders, don't you?"

Rebecca gave a silent nod. She clutched a handkerchief in a white-knuckled fist, rosy lips set thin and tight. Hanging on by the thinnest of threads, she was. Holly couldn't blame her one bit—out here in the middle of nowhere, alone to face such a daunting task. Holly's big trip to Newfield had felt so large and important yesterday; now it felt small and inconsequential. She laid her hand over the woman's delicate fist. "It will be all right."

"How?" It was more a hopeless groan than a question. Rebecca's eyes overflowed, and tears slid silently down each of her flawless cheeks. Holly felt the lump in her own throat grow larger and thought about how the horrible gray morning after the flood had seemed to snatch away every good thing in Evans Grove. She'd stood that morning and watched the sun fail to rise over Fourth Street, fail to part the gray that cloaked the battered homes. Houses of folks she knew and loved looked like piles of strewn kindling. Soaked and bone tired, Holly had asked the same question of Reverend Turner.

Holly now gave Rebecca the same answer the Reverend had given her. "That's not ours to know tonight. Let's hand it over to the Almighty for a while so we can sleep."

Rebecca shook her head. "Lord only knows what will happen to those children." She dabbed her eyes. "I've lain awake praying that God would find them homes even before Newfield. Nothing's come of it. These children have been passed over stop after stop. I've been delighted to see so many of the children we set out with find spots in good homes, but I never expected these last ones to pull on my heart so much. The whole point of the Orphan Salvation Society is to take these boys and girls out of the grime of the city and give them a hopeful future. I know a foster family isn't the same as an adoption, but it's close. Only we haven't come close for these children at all. Greenville is our last stop. If they're not placed, I'll have to take them back to New York unplaced…" She clenched her jaw to stop a sob. The desperation in her voice told Holly that whatever waited in New York wasn't good.

"Shush now. All of that can wait for daylight." Holly pulled up one of her mama's favorite sayings from memory. "God hasn't closed his eyes, but you ought to." She checked the kettle. "Evans Grove is full of good people who'll help you get over this rough patch, you wait and see." Her mind cast back to the ragtag handful of children. They were neither strong nor pretty; surely not the kind to be caught up by families at first sight. Still, the teacher in her could already see bits of character and personality that made them special—even if they didn't know it themselves. All God's children were worthwhile, were deserving of love and security. "God's watched over them today, hasn't He?"

Rebecca voiced the thought that came immediately to Holly's mind. "And how has God watched over Stuart Arlington today? I can't see the point in something so senseless. Those men had no reason to shoot Mr. Arlington. None at all." She began to cry harder. "So much has been lost."

Holly put an arm around the poor woman. "Now don't go thinking such things. We just can't know the Lord's hand in something like this. He's mightier than those horrid men, even if it's hard to see at the moment." She was talking to herself as much as Miss Sterling. "Sheriff Wright will see that justice is done. He saw to our safety, even risked his own life to do so. Why, he even got back your bag and jewelry, didn't he?" It seemed a poor consolation, but Holly was grasping for any silver lining.

"Baubles," Rebecca said bitterly. "Trinkets."

The kettle whistled, and Holly turned to tend to tea, taking comfort from the warm scent of the brew as it filled the home. "A good meal and a cup of tea. Some of the best medicine for a heavy heart I know, short of prayer."

Rebecca laid her chin in her hand. "I fear I'm plum prayed out."

Holly set a cup in front of each of them and sat down. "Of course you are. I'm down to just groaning toward heaven now. Still, God hears every groan. I like to think He hears the groans especially. Sugar?"

"Thank you, yes." The woman's elegant fingers traced the china handle. "They are lovely teacups."

There, for just a moment, was the refined lady Holly had admired on the train. "They belonged to my Grannie Hollyn. I'm named after her. She loved pretty things like this."

Rebecca's blue eyes looked straight into Holly's. "You are so kind."

Holly's conscience pinched at the way she'd envied Rebecca on the train. *I'm not proud of that. Forgive my unkind spirit, Lord. I was so very wrong.* "They're dear children, the lot of them. They deserve a happy ending, and we'll just have to find one in all this. Now finish your tea and let's get you cleaned up. I expect you'll fall asleep as fast as the rest of them."

Rebecca smiled and drank her tea, but Holly knew it was more likely that neither of them would sleep soundly. Tired as she was, too many things piled into her memory every time she closed her eyes. It would be hard for sleep to befriend her tonight.

An hour later, Grandpa's clock on Holly's mantel chimed ten as Holly slipped under the familiar coverlet and felt her body sink into the mattress. Every inch felt tied in knots; every joint seemed to groan. Dickens, her shy calico who'd stayed hidden under the bed during Rebecca's visit as he always did on the rare occasion Holly had company, jumped up to curl against her side. "What a day, hmm, Dickens? Mama was right; one should never pray for excitement."

Dickens offered only a low purr in reply. Holly stroked the black and brown patches that covered his back, seeking solace in his large yellow eyes. "I'm safe," she said to the both of them, aloud so she'd believe it. "I'm safe, thank heaven."

You're safe. Those had been the words Mason Wright had said to her as he led her away from the spot where Stuart Arlington's body lay bleeding into the Nebraska soil. She didn't feel it yet—she mostly felt alone and lifeless. *Help me, Lord*, she prayed as she stroked the cat and waited for sleep to wipe the day from her bones. *I want to trust You, but it's hard to see how You'd want any of this. Rebecca and Mr. Arlington were trying to do right by those children. Those men were only out for greed. I know you still brought our funds to Evans Grove, and You brought them more quickly than we'd dared to hope, but this? Why such pain when we've already known so much loss?*

Her eyes grew heavy enough so that even the specter of Mr. Arlington's lifeless eyes could not fight off their closing. "Now I lay me down to sleep," she recited the childhood prayer, somehow needing the peace of her youth, "I pray the Lord my soul to keep."

She left off the final couplet. The Lord had taken enough souls today.

"You're serious." Reverend Turner looked shocked— but not unpleasantly so—when Holly knocked on his door far too early the next morning. She was unable to wait one minute longer to tell him of her idea.

Holly pulled her shawl closer against the morning drizzle. "I shot up out of bed wide awake sometime near four. The whole thing came to me just that quick. Just that strong."

Poor Reverend. Holly had been dressed before dawn, had bolted out of the schoolhouse the minute Charlotte and Amelia Hicks had come to tend to the children's breakfast. She'd barely been able to keep her idea from Rebecca, knowing Reverend Turner was the first person she must tell. Still, the children's waking faces sealed her determination, as if the idea was doubling in size and strength every moment she delayed. She'd practically run through the fine morning rain to the Reverend's house to knock down his door with her plan.

Holly grabbed his arm. "Reverend Turner, I don't see how that could be anything other than the work of the Spirit, don't you?"

He stifled a yawn. "It very well could be."

Holly reined in her exasperation. "Of course it can, Reverend. It must. These children could so easily stay here, find homes here among our families."

"It's possible."

Reverend Turner's wife, Mary, called from behind him. "For goodness' sake, James, don't make Holly stand in the doorway like some kind of stranger." Mary affectionately nudged her husband out of the way to pull Holly into the warm room. "How are you, dear? Such a horrid episode. Curdles the blood to think what you all went through and those poor, poor children."

"Holly has had an idea about those young ones." Reverend Turner shut the door and adjusted the suspenders he'd thrown on in a hurry. "She thinks they ought to stay."

"So I couldn't help but hear." Mary's eyes narrowed as she turned the thought over in her mind. After what seemed like a decade, the minister's wife looked up at her husband. "Why not?"

"Well," Reverend Turner said, tucking his hands in the suspenders he'd just adjusted, "there might be very complicated reasons why not. I've no idea how these things with such agencies work."

Holly knew better. The minute the idea pulled her head up from the pillow, she knew it was the right thing. Knew like she'd never known anything else. A truth even harder than fact, if such a thing were possible. "It won't be complicated," she asserted without any such facts to back it up whatsoever. "It's the simplest thing, I'm sure of it. Miss Sterling said she's been praying these children find a home, and Greenville was their last chance. They won't need a last chance in Greenville if we give them homes here. Can't you see? *We're* the answer to those prayers." Holly had to stop herself from grabbing the Reverend's arm again and shaking it.

Mary came up beside her husband. "James, didn't you tell me just last night Evans Grove needed something to spark hope back into it?" The love of Mary's twelve grandchildren—most of whom lived in Denver and Iowa now and only came in for holidays—played across the woman's face. "What's more hopeful than children?"

"I've said prayers over far too many graves this past month," the Reverend admitted as he turned from them to pace his front room floor with pastoral seriousness. Mrs. Turner laid an encouraging hand on Holly's arm and smiled her agreement. Still, the Reverend pondered Holly's proposition for what seemed like a century. Finally, he turned back to the women. "Well…" he said, eyes narrowed and face so unreadable it made Holly want to burst.

"Well what?" Holly nearly yelled. She'd left her patience and good manners back in the teacherage. The moment she knocked on the Reverend's door, some bit of her heart resolved she would not leave without his consent. This was to be and it was hers to make it so.

"Well, I think I ought to thank God for answering my prayer through you. I don't know if it can be arranged, but if God wills it, I think these children should find homes in Evans Grove."

"He does!" Holly proclaimed, grabbing the Reverend's arm.

"So quick to presume the Lord's perfect intent, are you?" His words were scolding, but his eyes twinkled in amusement.

"I believe He does," Holly corrected. "Truly. I tell you I've never been more sure of anything in my life." All the strain and sorrow of yesterday had evaporated in the brilliant light of this idea. It seemed no surprise at all that the sun was peeking out through the gray clouds as she pulled open the Reverend's door. "I'll go tell Rebecca—Miss Sterling—right away. Surely she knows what needs to happen in order for the children to stay here."

"I'll tell you what," Reverend Turner said. "I'll go talk to Mayor Evans and Miss Ward. They'll need to be in on this if it's to be successful. Why don't you talk further with Miss Sterling and we'll meet back at eleven? We'll see how it goes from there."

Holly stepped out into the brightening morning and dashed down the block to the schoolhouse. She didn't bother to step around puddles or even care about whether her wrap stayed straight.

She didn't bother to look around at all. This was why she went to Newfield. This was why yesterday's horrors could be laid at God's feet. This was why Stuart Arlington could rest in peace. Holly didn't have to see "how it would go from here." She already knew.

Mason was just stepping off the green onto Second Street when Holly Sanders slammed into him. "Whoa, there!" Short as she was, it surprised him she could muster enough force to knock him off balance. Had he not looked up the moment he did, they both would have found themselves smack in a mud puddle. As it was, he had to grab her and hang on for dear life to keep the pair of them upright.

"Oh, my!" She was nearly giddy, and he found he couldn't quite summon the impulse to release her tiny waist. "I'd have surely fallen. Oh, my." Her fluster amused him too much to be sour at the jolt. "Good morning!" She looked up at him with doe eyes.

"Morning," he managed, still a bit stunned. He'd had a terrible night, filled with dark dreams when he wasn't kept awake by the incessant complaining of his wounded prisoners. There wasn't enough coffee in the world to make his eyes as wide and glowing as hers currently were. Here the sun was just barely creeping into the sky, and Holly Sanders looked as if someone had just handed her a birthday cake. "What's gotten into you?" He didn't mean it to sound gruff, but he wasn't in the habit of recovering from such early morning assaults—not the ones that wore bonnets and smelled like vanilla, anyway. He instructed his hands to let go of her.

She got a determined look on her face, one of those "anyway" looks he saw on her during tiring town meetings. A pouting set of her chin that said "I will do this or that anyway, no matter how you object or complain." He waited for her hands to plant on her hips in exasperation—what she usually did in meetings—but they flew to her chest.

"The most wonderful, perfect idea. That's what's gotten into me."

Now he was even more curious. "And what is that?"

"I believe God wants the orphans to stay here."

She said it like fact. An indisputable truth like *Tuesday follows Monday* or *two plus two equals four.*

"God wants the orphans to stay here." Mason repeated slowly, thinking it sounded more like *two plus two equals seventeen.*

"Yes, I truly believe that." She straightened her shawl. "They need us, and we need them."

Mason scratched his chin. Now he really needed more coffee. "Not too many folks around here would argue for more mouths to feed. Some folks don't even have a roof over their head to host their own kin, much less take in an orphan."

"And some folks have lost far too much and have buried too many of their own kin. Before yesterday, all I could see when I looked at my class was the empty seats. They weren't even my own blood, but their loss…" Her voice caught on the word. He'd never realized how much care she had for her students. "Well, it was all I could see. All the loss, everywhere." She gestured to the town square behind him. "Didn't you see what happened last night? How people behaved? The way they acted like…like the world was starting to turn the right way again?" She started walking toward the schoolhouse with swift, purposeful steps. For a tiny thing, that woman could move fast. "They're *supposed* to be here. They're God's gift to us."

Chapter Five

"I hardly think these urchins are a gift from God."
Beatrice Ward's scowl had started with Miss Sanders's
first word and hadn't let up for the entire meeting.
"They're a burden." The old woman mopped her brow
with a handkerchief as if the eight children made her
physically ill. "Evans Grove has borne enough burdens
already; why on earth would we add more?"

"God calls us to bear each other's burdens, Miss
Ward," said Reverend Turner. Mason had wondered how
long it would take before the pastor regretted including
Beatrice. Still, Mason recognized what the Reverend
already surrendered to; The only thing worse than Beatrice Ward *in* a meeting was her vengeance for being
left *out* of one.

"I must say I agree with Holly." Pauline Evans steepled her hands as they sat around the reverend's dining
table. "I can't ignore how this town looked and acted
last night. We pulled together."

"We've been pulling together for weeks. Some of us
don't even have a roof over our head." Beatrice mopped
her brow again. That bitter old biddy never, ever missed

a chance to point out that her home had been damaged
beyond occupancy. It wouldn't surprise Mason if Beatrice didn't think her loss was as bad or worse than
Pauline's, who had lost the love of her life to the flood's
raging waters.

He'd had enough of her raining all over Miss Sanders's optimism and couldn't keep quiet any longer.
"Mayor Evans is right. Things felt like the old Evans
Grove last night. Considering the day we'd just had,
that ought to count for something."

"What I'm counting," Beatrice said as she tucked
her handkerchief back into her pocket and narrowed
her eyes at Mason, "is how many criminals we have
housed in our jail at the moment."

Oh, no you don't. Mason went right on as if he hadn't
heard her, addressing his point to the Reverend and
mayor, instead. "If Miss Sterling is agreeable to it—"

"And she is," cut in Holly. "She most definitely is.
She said all we need is a selection committee to place
the orphans with families, and I'm sure I can get folks
to serve on that."

A committee. He knew enough to steer clear of com-
mittees. He'd see Miss Sanders's idea safely launched
and keep out of the way. She needed something to do,
to heal, and this seemed like a good fit that thankfully
wouldn't include him. "Then I can't see what harm
would come of asking the good people of Evans Grove
if they've a mind to take these youngsters in. Miss Sterling and I are wiring New York about the late Mr. Arlington as soon as I'm done here."

"Oh, that's just so sad," Pauline Evans said quietly.
"I'll say a prayer for his poor wife."

"In that same wire, Miss Sterling can inform her

organization that they won't be going on to Greenville for the moment, and hopefully won't go to Greenville at all. It might take a day or two to get a response, so we've got time to see what people think."

"I know what they'll think," Holly declared.

"I know what *I* think," Beatrice snapped.

Mason refused to swallow his sour grin. "Never been any question of that."

"I believe we are in agreement." Pauline stood, hoping to cut off Beatrice's reply. "I don't see why we can't hold the Selection Committee meeting at two-thirty and announce a town placement meeting tomorrow at noon." Mason made a mental list of places he needed to be this afternoon in case anyone had the fool notion of asking him to be on any committee.

"I don't see the point in rushing this," Beatrice grumbled as she stood.

The mayor met Miss Ward's scowl. "I see every reason for urgency. It's a kindness. These poor children have been through enough. The sooner they're surrounded by caring families, the better." Pauline ignored Beatrice's derisive sniff and turned directly to Mason. "I trust all here will serve on the committee?"

He immediately put up his hand. "I don't think I'm your man."

"I couldn't disagree more," Mayor Evans said.

"Nor I," added Miss Sanders with an enthusiasm that burrowed under his skin.

Even Miss Ward joined the campaign. "I have to insist you serve, Sheriff. We have no idea what kind of element we may be bringing into this town with these children."

Did she think he could spot a future bank robber in

a ten-year-old boy? Glory, he hated how she was itching to see the worst in everyone. "I highly doubt there's any danger."

Miss Sanders gave him a look that told him she'd need an ally to hold off Beatrice, and she was dearly hoping it was him. Hang her, she somehow yanked the words out of him before he could stop the mistake. "All right."

"Thank you." Her smile made him regret it already.

"I do appreciate it, Sheriff," Mayor Evans said with an equal smile before turning toward Miss Sanders. "Before you go, Holly, could you stop by town hall with me a moment?"

As Miss Sanders and Mayor Evans headed toward the door, Mason turned toward the Reverend. "Have you got a minute to talk with me about Arlington before I take Miss Sterling over to the wire office?" In truth, he had no reason to discuss the agent with Turner at all, but he surely didn't want to have one more word of discussion with Beatrice Ward. Ill-acquainted with God as Mason was, even the Reverend was better company than a Beatrice who hadn't gotten her way.

Or had she?

As she walked out with Pauline into the bright noonday sun, Holly saw the town in a new light. Yes, buildings were still stained and damaged from the flood. Everything still had the gray-brown tinge of mud crusted in its corners, but it felt as if April had finally poked its head through the trials of March. Evans Grove had turned a corner; she could feel it. The funds were here to help pay for repairs and now eight children would call Evans Grove their new home. *Funds.* Here it was noon and she hadn't even thought to ask a vital question: "Pauline, were Sheriff Wright and Mr. Brooks able to get the safe open this morning?"

"It took a bit of doing, but Charlie Miller came over with some tools and they were able to pry the safe door off its hinges. According to Mr. Brooks, everything is bumped up a bit, but intact. We transferred all the gold coins to the town hall safe so all is in its proper place." Pauline adjusted her wrap. "Which brings me to my point. How does Mr. Brooks strike you?"

At first Holly was going to retort that she hardly knew the man, but they had been through a great deal together, so it was a sensible question for Pauline to ask. She thought for a moment before replying, "He seems genuinely interested in helping the town. Of course, he's very refined, but not in a bad way. How he kept so calm with those bandits threatening him is beyond me." She paused when she noticed Pauline's troubled expression. "And of course, he sent the money more quickly than any of us hoped. Why do you ask?"

Pauline crossed her arms over her chest. "It's exactly that. He sent the funds so quickly and came here personally." She gestured around the square. "I have trouble seeing why we merit such interest from a big Newfield bank. Naturally, I'm glad…but a tad suspicious. I was hoping you'd have a solid impression of him one way or another."

"Mr. Brooks hasn't done anything that would make me doubt him or his motives." She thought of his fine brocade vest that had torn during the robbery, and the monogrammed handkerchief he'd handed little Lizzie without hesitation when she'd gotten a bloody nose. "I'd argue Evans Grove is a bit…rustic for his tastes, but if you're asking my opinion, I find him trustworthy."

Pauline stopped and turned to face Holly directly. "Do you think he trusts us? I can't help but think he insisted on coming with you because he's concerned the money won't be handled well."

This was why Pauline made such a good mayor. Holly would have never considered such a thing. "I don't know," she confessed.

Pauline sighed looking up and down the numbered streets than ran north-south through town. Evans Grove had a total of eight streets, but Pauline was proud of them all. "I don't, either."

"He seemed to be thinking of a long stay, if his bags were any indication. It looked like he brought at least a week's worth of clothes."

They reached the front steps of town hall. "That sounds to me like a man ready to scrutinize."

She sounded as if she were personally under scrutiny. Holly put her hand on Pauline's arm. "You've done such a fine job under such dreadful circumstances. Even if he is here to watch over things, all he's going to watch over is how well you handle that money. Let him look all he wants. He'll only find out what a wonderful place this is."

Pauline's eyes widened. "That's a perfectly brilliant idea, Holly."

"What is?"

"Let him look all he wants. Let's ask Mr. Brooks if he will serve on the Selection Committee. We can tell him he's a needed objective viewpoint. He'll meet everyone and see how well we handle challenges."

Holly gave Pauline's arm an encouraging grasp.

"You do make a fine, fine mayor. I think it's an ideal plan, but I won't take one bit of credit for it. I think you, Mayor Evans, should extend a formal invitation to our new friend Mr. Brooks as soon as possible."

Pauline turned and went back down the town hall steps. "No time like the present. I think I'll head over to the hotel right now. Are you headed back to the schoolhouse, then?"

Holly peered down across the square to where she could see Rebecca coming out of the wire office with Sheriff Wright. She looked upset. Who wouldn't be after having to wire such tragic news? "Charlotte and Amelia are tending to the children this morning. I think I'd best see to Miss Sterling. I'll need to find out how the placement meetings are run, and she looks as if it's been hard to send that wire."

Pauline's expression tightened. "Of course it's hard. She'll need a friend." She turned to Holly. "Good thing she found one on the train."

Holly smiled. "She did, didn't she? Maybe some good can come out of this yet."

"If you ask me, it already has."

Rebecca dabbed her eyes as she and Holly walked toward the schoolhouse. "I knew that wire would be difficult to send, but I'd hoped to handle it better."

"You've been through a tremendous shock. And you're far from home. No one faults you for grieving Mr. Arlington's loss. It's the worst kind of news to have to wire home." Holly took hold of both of Rebecca's hands. "And now you'll have the best kind of news."

The OSS agent shook her head. "I still can't believe they agreed."

"How could they not? The Selection Committee will be formed this afternoon. Of course, you'll need to be there to help us set up all the specifics." She gave Rebecca's hands a stronger squeeze. "Tomorrow at noon, your children will find their new homes right here in Evans Grove."

"I don't know what to say. I feel as if my insides have been untangled and re-tangled a dozen times over. To think two days ago I was packing them up to leave Newfield thinking we were nearly done. Or *done for.* Really, I was so worried that this lot would never be placed." She put a gloved hand to her forehead. "We've so much to do. I don't even know if they all have clean clothes."

Holly swept a hand around the muddy grime that still permeated far too much of Evans Grove's buildings and streets. "We're quite used to looking at patches of mud in these parts. A washed face, some combed hair and an eager smile should do just fine. Should you go tell them now?"

"I want you to come, too. It was your idea after all."

"Oh," said Holly, fingering her cross necklace. Mama had given it to her for her sixteenth birthday, and she'd not taken it off since, loving it even more when Mama passed three years ago. "I don't think it was my idea. Given to me, maybe, but not mine."

"A good idea is only as good as the person who sees it through."

"Well, then," Holly said as she pushed open the schoolroom door, "what do you say we see this through together?"

"I couldn't be more—" Rebecca's consent was cut short by a high shriek and a flying stuffed rabbit that landed square onto her shoulder.

"Give that back!" came a girl's voice.

"Make me!" came a deeper reply.

The sound of a squabble—and something large falling over—filled Holly's ears as tiny Lizzie plowed straight into Rebecca and bawled into her skirts.

"Charlotte?" called Holly at the same moment Rebecca shouted, "Children!" She scooped up Lizzie and handed her the toy rabbit. The child buried her face into the poppet and continued crying frantic sobs.

Heidi, the young girl with the burn scars, walked up with eyes narrowed in disgust. "Patrick's mean."

Stepping into the schoolroom, Holly found poor Charlotte outnumbered and overwhelmed. Two of the desks were turned over, half the books were out of their shelves, and what meager belongings the children had were strewn everywhere. "What's happened in here?"

"Amelia took sick and had to go lie down. They were doing fine until—"

"Patrick t-t-took Bobbins!" Lizzie howled.

"Did not!" countered Patrick as Rebecca put Lizzie down and stalked toward the dark-haired boy. "I found him, that's what I did."

"And then you kept him away from Lizzie," Liam chimed in. "Just to be mean."

"I thought he was g-g-gone." Hugging Bobbins fiercely against her chest, Lizzie wiped a runny nose on her sleeve. "All gone and gone and gone."

"Well, now, I can plainly see he's not gone at all," Holly offered in a cheerier tone, pulling Lizzie toward the bookcases. "Do you think he can help you and me and Heidi put these books back on the shelves?"

"You will all help set this room to rights," Rebecca

commanded, "most especially Patrick who will also sweep the room…"

A collection of groans and even a "nyah-nyah" filled the schoolhouse.

"And you will do so in fifteen minutes or less because I have a very important announcement, which I will not share until all is done." To punctuate her point, Miss Sterling pulled out a filigree pendant watch and peered dramatically at its face.

"I'll go get Mr. Patrick his broom," Charlotte said, giving the boy a sour glare. "And Tom should be right behind him with the dustbin, since the two of them partnered up against poor Lizzie."

Tom, as if it might improve his case, began a spontaneous coughing fit and sat down in one of the desk chairs.

"Thomas White," Rebecca scolded, "I'd thought better of you. You'll indeed be right behind Patrick with that dustbin and I expect Miss Sanders to find her floor the cleanest it's been in years. Friedrich, line those desks back up where they belong. Liam, take Galina and Sasha out to the pump and wash whatever that is off their hands and come straight back."

"I'll take care of those hands," Charlotte offered. "Liam can get the broom and dustbin from the closet in back and help the boys sweep."

Liam bolted upright at the injustice. "What'd I do?"

"Did you do anything to stop this when it happened?" Holly asked.

Liam rolled his eyes. "Who can stop those two when they get somethin' into their thick heads?"

"Qui tacet consentire videtur," Holly quoted, point-

ing to the small narrow cupboard at the back of the schoolroom.

"Huh?" Liam's mouth hung open.

"It's Latin for 'he who is silent seems to consent.' A quote from Sir Thomas Moore." Holly gathered up a stack of slates and handed them to Heidi. "These go up in that red box over there."

"I didn't con or sent to nothin' those two did." Liam yanked the cupboard door open and nearly speared Patrick with the broom. "I been trying to keep the peace all morning," he muttered as he handed the dustbin to Tom. "But with nothin' to do, it's been mighty hard."

Fourteen minutes of grumbling labor later, Holly and Rebecca sat the children at the lines of desks in the now tidied room.

"Thank you for showing Miss Sanders how you can respect her hospitality," Rebecca began, her hands folded neatly in front of her as she stood before the children. "Yesterday was very difficult for all of us, and I know we're all very sad about Mr. Arlington. We must all be brave and try to make the best of things."

"I'm bored," said Patrick as if boredom were akin to bravery.

"I'm thirsty," said Tom, managing another cough for emphasis.

"It's cold in here," Galina whispered quietly to Holly.

Rebecca held up a silencing hand. "Enough! You'll have other things to think about if you all will just listen to what I'm trying to tell you. Actually, to what Miss Sanders has to tell you." She gestured toward Holly.

"The truth of the matter is that everyone in Evans Grove is glad we were able to help you yesterday. As you can probably guess, we've had some rough patches of our own since a big storm, and it feels good to do something nice for someone else, doesn't it?"

Lizzie nodded in agreement, but for the most part the other children didn't respond.

Holly rubbed her hands together, suddenly failing for the words to convey the right welcome. "Everyone is sad about yesterday, but we do have to make the best of things, and we…we think the best thing may just be for all of you to stay here."

Tom slumped in his chair. "Who wants to live in a schoolhouse?"

Holly pursed her lips. Why was it suddenly so hard to say what she could barely refrain from shouting to Reverend Turner and the others? "When I say 'stay here,' I mean more than in the schoolhouse. I mean really stay. In homes, with families, as a part of Evans Grove. Everyone thinks you should live here and be part of us."

Liam's eyes held a tightly checked wonder, as if he wasn't quite ready to believe what he thought he'd just heard. "You mean live here? For good?"

There was something in his tone, a tender disbelief, that clutched at Holly's chest. "Yes, Liam, that's exactly what I mean."

"What Miss Sanders is saying," Rebecca added, "is that you all are invited to a placement meeting here, rather than in Greenville, so that families right here can take you in. You wouldn't have to go any farther."

Galina ran her hand along the desk. Holly had seen her do the same thing to the bookshelves in what passed for a library along the classroom's west wall. She guessed the little girl would have her nose forever in a book once she mastered reading, and the craving to help her do so was like a physical itch Holly could already feel. The girl's huge dark eyes lit with a cautious excitement. "It's nice here."

Patrick crossed his arms over his chest. "It's kinda small. What if Greenville's better?"

"What if it's worse?" Tom moaned.

Lizzie sat up straight in her chair and raised her hand, making Holly wonder where a girl in her circumstances learned such classroom behavior. "Yes, Lizzie," Holly called on her, nearly laughing at the tot's seriousness.

"Bobbins wants to stay."

The smile Holly felt spread across her face seemed to radiate up from a glowing patch under her ribs. She couldn't remember when anything had felt so right, when she'd ever been so sure of how God had put her world in order. Which was odd, considering everything that had happened. This surely was the "peace that passes all understanding" the Bible spoke of, for she ought to be worried about a thousand details, but wasn't. "We want Bobbins to stay. You are all welcome to stay if we can find enough families to take you in. I'd be very happy if you all were placed right here in Evans Grove and came to school."

"Now," Rebecca said as she planted her hands on her hips, "you all know how this works. I'll meet with the Selection Committee this afternoon. Tomorrow will be the placement meeting where you'll meet with families. Miss Sanders, Mrs. Miller and some other nice people will come in this afternoon to help you get washed and dressed and ready to look your best." She caught Holly's glance out of the corner of her eye. "By God's grace, this terrible event has brought you to your new home, and I hope you'll all show our gratitude."

There was a moment of stunned silence, as if the children still weren't sure it was all happening. Then Lizzie parked her elbows on the desk with an enormous pout. "I want to wear my blue dress but it's dirty."

Patrick, scratching as if the soap had already found him, moaned. "Am I gonna have to take a bath?"

And so it began. Holly walked across the school yard to start the first of many pots of hot water as the schoolhouse behind her seemed to buzz from the flurry of activity inside. Her smile was steadfast and satisfied; this was how it was supposed to be. This was God's plan for these children and for Evans Grove. His plan for her.

Chapter Six

Holly wasn't half surprised when a knock came on her door while tending to the fourth pot of hot water. She pulled open the door to Charlotte Miller's wide, hopeful eyes. "Is it true? Are we really going to place the children here?"

Holly had seen how the woman had fixed on Sasha Petrov, the little Russian tot with black braids and enormous blue eyes. "Don't you think Sasha could find a good home somewhere in Evans Grove? Surely you must have some idea of a family that would welcome her." She placed a hand on Charlotte's arm and smiled. "I know *I* have a very good idea where Sasha would be happiest." When the woman only smiled broadly in admission, Holly asked, "Have you asked Charles?"

"He's agreeable, if a little worried. Children can be a handful."

"Nonsense. I've seen the way you look at her, and how she takes to you. Sasha coming into your home was my first thought when I realized the children ought to stay here."

Charlotte hugged the pile of linens she was holding

as if hugging the child. "I know this is a foster placement, not an adoption—at least not yet—but she's found
her way into my heart already. How is that possible?"

With God, all things were possible. "Children can
do that." She ushered Charlotte in, motioning for her to
add the towels to the pile collected on her table.

"How does it work?' Charlotte asked as she put down
the linens.

"I'm not sure of the details, but Charlotte, I don't
think there's a soul in Evans Grove who would stand
in the way of you and Charles taking in Sasha. God
couldn't choose better folks to watch over that little
sweetheart." Holly tested the water and then added another log to her stove. In ten minutes they'd have enough
for yet another bath. "She's taken to you, too."

Charlotte's sweet smile lit a stronger glow in Holly's
heart. "She has, hasn't she?"

"Sasha will be the first child placed if I have my
say. With you and Charles." Holly pulled a towel and
facecloth from the pile on the counter and set it on the
stool next to the tub that sat in the middle of her floor.
The girls were washing up here while Reverend. Turner
had taken the boys into his home to clean up. "Sheriff
Wright asked me to come talk to him for a moment.
Would you like to give Sasha her bath here? She's next
in line."

Holly told herself to remember the sparkle in Charlotte's eyes if Miss Ward gave anyone trouble—and she
surely would—in this afternoon's Selection Committee
meeting. No doubt about it—whether for now as foster
placements or forever as adoptees—these children belonged in Evans Grove.

* * *

"Mercy," Mason heard Miss Sanders exclaim as she peered into the office fronting the two small cells that served as Evans Grove's jail, "is there room?" Small as the space was with four bandits, Bucky Wyler and Doc Simpson packed inside, the walls felt as if they would burst out any second.

"You quit your hollering now," Bucky was shouting at one of the louder criminals over Mason's shoulder. "What Doc Simpson's got for you is bound to be better than what might be waiting for you tomorrow in Greenville."

Miss Sanders caught Mason's eye with a bit of a start. "Perhaps I ought to come back."

"No," he replied, trying not to grin. "I think your timing's just right." He grabbed his hat off the hook by the door. "It's too tight in here and Bucky's got things well in hand. I could use the air." He was glad to see her looking a little bit like her old self again.

She clasped her hands in front of her while they walked. She often did that, closing in on herself as if she was reluctant to take up too much space in the world. "What's going to happen to those men?"

"There'll be a trial in Greenville, but I've no doubt the judge will sentence them for robbery and the leader for murder." He paused for a moment before adding, "I expect the leader will hang." Beatrice Ward would have greeted such news with a righteous vengeance, but Miss Sanders's expression was somber.

"They've done a terrible thing, surely, but I still can't quite stomach the idea that more death makes anything better."

His mind shot back to the image of Pheobe's two

killers swinging from the gallows back in Colorado. The sight of their deaths hadn't brought him any peace, only closure. "Justice isn't healing. It's just order and balance."

She looked at him, and Mason suddenly found his statement philosophical and wordy. A smart woman like her probably laughed at sentiments like that coming from someone like him. Rather than frown, he could see her ponder the words, taking them in with a seriousness he hadn't expected. "That's very true." She wrapped her shawl tighter as if the harshness of the world had just blown in like a cold breeze.

"We got word from New York for us to send back Mr. Arlington's body on the train east this afternoon. We're sending him on home to his family."

"That's so sad." Her shoulders gave a little shudder. She wasn't any more over yesterday's trauma than he expected she would be, which was why he had to ask what he was about to ask.

"I spoke with Miss Sterling earlier, and she doesn't want to accompany Mr. Arlington's body back to the train today." When Holly raised her eyebrows in surprise, he continued, "She says she wants to remember him alive. She thought if her last glimpse was of him being loaded onto a train in a box, that'd be hard to do."

"I imagine that's so. Last looks hang on a long time, don't they?"

"That they do, which is why I think you should come with me when we take Arlington back."

She stopped in her tracks. "Me? Whatever for?"

Mason turned to her. "Same reason, actually. You need to see that platform calm and safe, not the scene of some horrible crime."

"So I'm to replace my visions of robbery and murder with the sight of an innocent man's coffin being loaded onto a train? How can that possibly help?"

"Order and balance, like I said."

Fear iced the corners of her blue eyes. "I don't like the idea at all."

"I knew you wouldn't." He crossed his arms over his chest, letting her know he wasn't going to let her get off so easily. "Can you accept that I might just know a bit more about this than your book learning tells you?"

"I believe in God's sovereignty and in Heaven's justice. I don't need some pilgrimage to the train tracks to get me over what happened yesterday."

Mason looked down at her hands. They were clasped so tightly her knuckles were white. "If your hands didn't still shake when we talked about it, I'd say that'd be true."

She unclasped her hands and put them behind her, like a child hiding a stolen cookie. It would have made him laugh had it not been so sad.

"Look, Miss Sanders, I been through this enough times to know this is one of those things where you need to get back on the horse that threw you. You need to go back there, and the sooner the better."

She rolled her eyes, pretending at calm dismissal. "It's a fool notion."

"So humor a fool. Think of it as doing Miss Sterling a favor, if that helps." He'd already decided he'd stand here until next Thursday if that's what it took to haul her back to that clearing. She wasn't going to admit what yesterday had done to her, and he couldn't stand the thought of it festering in her. If she thought him brusque and controlling, well, it might make it easier to keep his distance from her on that confounded committee.

He must have put on a determined face, for she softened her expression. "You really think I ought to? So soon? I have the Selection Committee meeting and so do you."

He nodded. "We'll go after the meeting. It'll help. Miss Sterling, well, she's a bit down the road from ready, seeing as she knew Arlington well and all. You'll be fine once you get past the jitters."

She deliberately put her hands back in front, probably to prove him wrong, but her fingers still wound around each other. "I'm not jittery."

Mason knew jittery when he saw it. The outside kind one could easily see, and the inside kind that hid behind the eyes. He simply arched a doubtful eyebrow at her.

"Well, perhaps just a touch," she admitted. "Any decent person would be. What I really need is for these children to be placed—all of them—tomorrow afternoon. That's the best tonic I could have, knowing such good came out of all that loss."

"Order and balance, just like I said." He pulled out his pocket watch. "The Selection Committee meets in an hour, right?"

Miss Sanders couldn't quite hold back a chuckle. "I think Mayor Evans was right not to give Beatrice any time to work up a head of steam. She's also smart to put Mr. Brooks on the committee as well, so he can see how well Evans Grove steps up to a challenge."

Mason settled his hat down farther on his head. "Brooks, hmm? That is a good idea. She's done Robert proud, don't you think?"

Miss Sanders's sigh was heavy. "I do, indeed." She

fingered the cross she always wore around her neck. "It'll feel good to do something happy for a change tomorrow." She cocked her head to one side. "Who do you think will take in Liam?"

Mason recalled Liam's scraggly red hair and wisecracking grin. "Beats me, but Lord have mercy on whoever does."

"We owe him." She parked one hand on her hip. "Running off like that took a great deal of nerve."

"Thinking of sending him took a great deal of nerve, too." He really needed to nip that impulse to compliment her. He was still so amazed at how she'd handled herself that he'd been too encouraging already. They *did* owe her; that's why he was forcing her to come to the railroad tracks today. Evans Grove owed Miss Sanders the chance to settle herself and move on.

Over her shoulder, Mason saw Beatrice Ward marching down Liberty Street in the direction of Town Hall. "Not that you're asking, but I figure the Selection Committee meeting this afternoon is going to take even more nerve than any gunfight."

"Oh, no." She dismissed his notion with a wave of her hand—the first easy pose he'd seen out of those hands since yesterday. "I'm sure it will be fine. What could go wrong?"

"What *else* could go wrong?" Holly was near to boiling as she stalked out of the church parlor and climbed into the wagon Sheriff Wright had waiting. Beatrice Ward had so cornered her after the Selection Committee meeting that the sheriff had time to go fetch the wagon, load Mr. Arlington's casket, and pull up before that old hen had finished her speech. "Here Miss Sterling is trying not to cry for all that's gone on and how grateful she is, and that woman can only list every reason why Evans Grove is…" she allowed herself just the slightest imitation of Miss Ward's clipped speech, "…'coming undone.'" The spinster must have used the judgmental phrase a dozen times in the last hour alone. "Pull out before I say something I regret!"

Sheriff Wright held up a gloved hand, his eyes on the church doorway. "Not just yet." Holly followed his gaze beyond the frowning Miss Ward to the heartbreaking figure of Rebecca Sterling standing in the doorway.

The lovely blonde stood pale and still, staring at the wagon's mournful payload. It never ceased to astound Holly how a man's remains, or a friend's body, or a wife's grief could contain itself to a simple pine box. Death belonged in a bottomless black well, not the neat confines of simple carpentry. Then again, death had no confines at all for those who believed in Jesus, did it? "The presence of that sure hope," Reverend Turner had said in one of the far-too-many funerals held in Evans Grove since March, "can only balance out hurt, not erase it." It was the very reason Beatrice's nit-picking bothered Holly so; here God had handed them hope, a balance for their hurt, and the spinster couldn't see it for her hunt of fault and error.

This was a side of the businesslike sheriff Holly had not seen before. How had he known to hold the wagon still, to disregard all of Rebecca's declarations that she had no desire to see the casket off? Without words or gestures, he seemed to read Rebecca's eyes even from this distance and let her say this momentary goodbye to her colleague. Holly felt a tear slide down her cheek to see the fragile way Rebecca's hand gripped the church doorway, to see the way her body caved slightly toward Reverend Turner when he took her elbow. It was clear Mr. Arlington had been important to her—maybe even a father figure, for Holly had found him to be such a kindly older gentleman—and she looked so very, desperately alone.

Rebecca gave the slightest nod to Sheriff Wright, who gave a slow nod back before edging the horse gently forward. Even Beatrice fell mercifully silent. The silence continued, heavy as a blanket despite the tug of a spring breeze as they rolled down Victory Street and made a careful turn to head south down Second Street toward the path that led to the railroad. Mr. Arlington was making his final journey home.

Holly turned once to look at the sheriff, but he was somewhere else. Hat pulled far down, spine rigid, hands tight on the reins, it wasn't hard to see that Mason Wright had closed off the world for the moment.

She let him be for a long while before finally asking, "How do you know so much?"

He seemed startled out of his thoughts, yanked back to the present by her question. "So much? About what?"

She couldn't think of another way to put it. "About death. About killing and grief." The words seemed ugly said aloud, and she had to look away, fingering a smudge on her skirt instead of braving the look she thought she might find in his eyes.

When he didn't answer for a while, she regretted her question. "I'm sorry. I suppose I ought not to pry. It's just that…" Again, the right words seem to fail her. Mason Wright seemed so brave and strong—now more than ever—and she'd always found him handsome enough to unsettle the mousy girl who lived inside the book-learned schoolmarm. "You seemed to know just what ought to be done."

He gave a low chuckle, but it was too dark to be called a laugh. "Do I, now?"

"It seems so." Holly felt foolish, treading where she had no right. And yet, he'd never paid so much as a lick of attention to her before all this happened, and she couldn't help but be curious about the parts of him she could see now.

He turned to look at her, and Holly felt as if she could see a dozen sad stories in his eyes. "I know too much for my liking." He shifted the reins in his hands. "I've buried kin, if that's what you're asking."

It wasn't, really, because Holly could see his acquaintance with death went deeper than that. "You've buried *dear* kin, haven't you? Is that how you knew Rebecca needed to say goodbye when she said she didn't? Or why you think I need to come today?" She couldn't say what made her so bold, only that his pain seemed so plain to her that she couldn't help herself. *Please, Lord*, she prayed as her questions hung in the air between them, *let this be the Spirit pressing me on, and not my own foolishness.*

"I buried my wife." The words were thick and heavy, as if he dredged them up out of a place that never saw daylight.

Chapter Seven

Sheriff Wright had been married.

Moreover, he'd been widowed. No wonder he defended Pauline Evans so fiercely and had taken such care with how they wired Mr. Arlington's poor wife. "I'm so sorry," Holly whispered.

He might not say more—and she had no right to ask for details—so Holly kept quiet, sending up a prayer for the poor woman's soul.

"It was out in Colorado territory," the sheriff said after a long pause. "We had a little ranch. Not much, but enough to…make a start. Phoebe was smart and brave. She always saw everything as a grand adventure. Loved being far out in the wilderness like that, fancied herself building up a whole estate like some kind of founding family. Saw the open space as something she could fill."

He paused for a minute before continuing. "Me, I liked the space but worried about how far out we'd gone. I was away too much, said she needed neighbors to turn to for help in a rough patch, especially with a baby on the way. Phoebe laughed at that. Said I saw danger where there wasn't any and worried too much."

Phoebe. Her name had been Phoebe. The way he spoke her name made Holly wonder how many years had gone by since he'd said it aloud.

"I was away, out driving cattle, when…" He swallowed, hard, and scuffed his boot against the rail of the wagon. "When the attack came. I was gone. Nobody was there to help, and I wasn't there to protect her. I wasn't there when it mattered most." Something fierce overtook him, as if he'd thought he could talk about it but found he couldn't. "How could a woman in her condition do anything to defend herself?" he accused himself. "She was lying facedown in the doorway when I rode up." His jaw worked, clenching at the memory that stiffened his spine as if someone had hit him from behind. When he turned his eyes on her, they were so dark and tormented that Holly felt as if she'd stumbled into a cave holding a pack of wolves. "A pregnant woman, facedown, curled up over her belly as if that could do any good."

Holly's hand went to her chest, the picture all too real. She flinched from the pain-sharp edges of his words.

"I left the bloodstain on the threshold. To remind me. As if I ever had any chance of forgetting. I could have ripped the whole house up plank by plank and still never gotten it out of my head. Not even after I found the men responsible and made sure they could never hurt anyone again. It won't go away and it never should. Ever."

"I'm sorry." Holly could only whisper inadequate words. How does a soul live with that kind of weight? So desperate a darkness? She remembered him saying bad news could wait for morning, and her heart twisted at how she'd dismissed the remark as polite compassion.

"So yes," he nearly hissed the word, "I know a lot about killing. I have killed. Never forget that about me. I am not an honorable man."

Holly didn't know how to respond. The pain in his tone prickled between them, and she knew she ought to be afraid. The invisible wall he kept around him—the one that had come down a moment earlier—held this wounded beast inside. Still, she knew that beast wasn't all there was to Mason Wright. It was something that had wrapped itself around the man, but it wasn't the entirety of the man himself.

But to reach any part of him, Holly would have to get past that wall—and it wouldn't be easy. Now that he'd spoken his piece, his defenses were up again. Holly looked down at her lap and prayed for some kind response, some word stronger than that looming wall. "I've never seen you act with anything but honor. You ran out into those bullets to pull me to safety. Isn't that honor?"

"Duty isn't honor." Mason barked the words at her, regretting the mistake this ride had become. Why did he keep doing this, going near her when he ought to stay away? He hadn't spoken aloud of Phoebe to anyone in nearly four years. Was some part of him thinking the awful memories would pull up enough pain to squelch what he was starting to feel toward this woman he couldn't hope to deserve? He knew he welcomed the sting of so harshly forcing Holly Sanders to face her fears. He wanted Holly to finally realize he was dangerous and to stay away. But no, she wasn't staying away. The pity in her eyes made him want to hit something. Phoebe deserved pity. Him? On his darkest days, Mason could easily argue that he deserved the pine box currently occupying the back of his wagon. He certainly deserved far worse than the compassionate look the teacher was giving him. Her regard made him angry. "You've only seen me doing my job."

He wanted to shout and growl *Stop coming near me*. To tell this foolish, innocent woman what it was like to dig his family's grave and rip the pretty, hopeful curtains off the windows because he couldn't bear the sight of them. He wanted to thrust his hands in her face, tell her about how he didn't wash Phoebe's blood off them for two days, certain the stain ought to stay forever and repulsively believing it would be the last part of her living body he'd ever touch.

Why not? Why not scare her half to death with who he really was? Tell her what he did and thought and craved in the black blotch of time after he let Phoebe die—the thousand awful things no one else knew. She'd be so much better off if she ran away.

Instead, he said nothing. He would take her back to the clearing and make her face her trauma. It would help her…and she would hate him for it. That was as it should be.

They rode the whole rest of the trip in silence, broken only by the whistle that announced the coming train. Miss Sanders gulped audibly as they pulled into the clearing. He kept his gaze off her eyes, but could see the whites of her knuckles where she gripped the wagon bench.

"I don't want to go down there." Her voice was raw with fear, not the controlled schoolmarm's voice she'd used with the children.

Her panic got to him more than he planned. Somehow the harsh tone he needed here became harder and harder to muster. "You need to."

"No, I don't. Not today I don't."

Her hand rose in his direction. Mason hated how he edged himself out of her reach, sure if she touched him he wouldn't be able to hold the distance he needed. She did need this, and while he ought to have been kinder about it, he couldn't be. "Yes, today. Now." Instead of saying *I'll help*, he said, "Waiting won't help." Before she said anything that could change his mind, Mason set the wagon to moving toward the long black line of the train snaking its way around the bend.

"You can just let me off and I'll watch from here."

Life had handed him the perfect chance to push Holly Sanders away for good, and he was going to take it. This was what she needed to heal in the long run, and if she blamed him for the way it hurt right now then all the better. He urged the horse a bit faster. "You're going down there."

"Let me off."

He braved a look at her, regretting instantly how the fear in her eyes doubled the pain under his ribs. "No."

"I've changed my mind and I don't wish to go down there."

For a split second Mason was tempted to back off. To be kind, to go slow, even to hold her shoulders steady while she edged into the clearing. Only he couldn't afford to be even the least bit kind. Not to her, not with the cannon-fire of feelings going off in his chest. So, even though it felt plain awful, Mason pronounced "Too late," and sped the wagon up a bit more.

The only time he dared to touch her was to reach up and help her down out of the wagon, and even that was torture. The tremble in her hands made it nearly impossible to drop her grasp and look away. Mason busied himself with the somber task of loading Arlington's casket onto the train, stopping only once when he heard a small, meek sound. He looked up to see Miss Sanders standing stiff and straight, arms wrapped tightly around herself, forcing in deep breaths he could nearly feel from his careful distance. She would make it. She would earn the order and balance he knew would allow her to put this behind her.

He didn't go near her, didn't look at her or talk to her, only watched from across the clearing until the set of her shoulders told him she'd found strength she probably hadn't known she even had. Then, still keeping his distance, Mason walked to the wagon and swung himself back into the driver's bench. Only then did he allow himself one indulgence: he leaned over and extended a hand to help her into the wagon.

She didn't take it. Instead, Miss Sanders hoisted herself up and settled rod-straight onto the bench next to him.

He should have been glad she said nothing, did not take his offered hand, didn't even look at him. Only he wasn't. As he drove them back to Evans Grove in dry, tight silence, Mason found himself more miserable than ever.

Hours later, Holly looked up as Rebecca came into her house. The last of the daylight spilled into the darkened room from the doorway behind her. "Holly?"

It hadn't even occurred to Holly that the room had gone dark. She'd been so lost in her thoughts.

"Holly?" Rebecca called again, coming to stand in front of her. "Holly, are you all right?"

She was so tired of being asked that question, mostly because she no longer knew the answer. "No, not really."

"Are you ill?" Rebecca didn't look much better, bless her. Her face wore the same drawn pallor it had in the church doorway earlier this afternoon.

Tucking her handkerchief back in her pocket, Holly dragged her thoughts out of the fog that had engulfed her since the long, dreadful ride back from the train tracks. "No, I'm not ill."

"Well, you're surely upset, from the looks of you. Was it awful, taking…" Rebecca still avoided saying the words. "Was it awful going where you did?"

Mason was right. Rebecca hadn't been ready.

Holly startled herself with the thought of calling him Mason. She'd never called him that to his face, of course, but when had he become Mason in her thoughts? *Today*, she answered herself, *when I peered in at the wolf in the cave*. "It was difficult." How could she explain this afternoon when she barely understood it herself? All she currently knew for sure was that she felt as if she'd been wrung through Beatrice Ward's newfangled washing machine. "The conductor was very kind."

Mason was not. He'd made her stand in that clearing until her hand stopped shaking and the dark memories of the afternoon had cleared. There had been some part of her that thought he would stand beside her, supportive—it had been his idea, after all—but he stood away from her. Watchful but distant, he left her alone to find her own way out of whatever still made her hands shake.

No, he hadn't been kind. But he had been right. With

time, her peace returned, and she'd known this was the right thing to do. Still, she could not bring herself to thank Mason. Too much else had transpired between them on that ride. Holly had simply climbed into the wagon when she knew the inner storm had settled, and they'd ridden home to Evans Grove in silence.

Rebecca pulled a second chair out to face Holly. "I'd like to think we've become friends."

"We have." Holly leaned her elbow on the table, weary of all the tumult. "I'm glad you're here, glad the children may get the chance to stay here."

"Then while the Turners are seeing to the children's evening chores, why don't you and I take a walk." Rebecca extended her hand to Holly. "It's a lovely night, and I need to take our list of suggested questions for tomorrow's meeting over to Miss Ward at the hotel."

Holly let Rebecca pull her from the chair. "Is Beatrice asking to see the list of questions again? We went over them at the meeting. Twice."

"Miss Ward insists we add three questions about the children's 'spiritual upbringing.'" She gave the last two words the exact righteous intonation Miss Ward would give.

"Sasha is four years old. How is anyone going to ask her three questions about her spiritual upbringing?"

Rebecca shrugged as she opened the door. "She knows Jesus loves her."

"That won't be enough for Miss Ward. I expect she'll want an exact verse—or take points off for lack of one." Holly breathed in the calm, crisp air and looked at Rebecca. "This is a matter for the heart, not a quiz. Don't you think the Holy Spirit can guide the right parent to each child, and help each child reach out to the right parent?"

"I'd like to think that's how it works. I certainly pray for every child and the home they'll eventually find." They began to walk south down First Street. Holly realized how good it felt to be pulled out of a sullen mood by a trustworthy friend. Rebecca was turning into a good friend, the kind Holly wished would choose to stay in Evans Grove even after the children were placed. That seemed impossible, but then again, what of the past days would have seemed possible even a week ago? *Give her a home here, Lord. She'd be happy here, perhaps. Somewhere, under all that finery, she seems hungry for good people who simply care about her. Evans Grove can give her that.* "I believe God brought these children to Evans Grove, you know that. It could be that way for you, too. I've so enjoyed having you to talk to, someone else who pours their lives into children's futures."

"'That's a lovely way to put it. It was my father who put me onto this train with these children, and quite frankly, I didn't want to go. I'd had…a bad experience and even thought of this position as some kind of punishment, or maybe it's kinder to say 'medicine.'" The wind jostled the budding tree branches overhead and swished their skirts. Holly could see there was much more to Rebecca's story than those vague words, but chose not to push the woman into saying more. She only nodded and offered a small smile.

"I'm loath to admit it, but my father was right," Rebecca continued with a sigh. "Helping these children has been good for me. I care about them very much. I suppose I do pour my life into their futures. You have a way with words, Holly." When they turned to walk west down Victory Street, the sunset's rays made Rebecca's golden tresses dance in the breeze. What a stunning beauty the woman was—she was the farthest thing from "mousy." Rebecca carried herself like a queen, with an enviable air of culture and refinement. Was it wrong to think a woman like that could find a life in somewhere as rough-hewn as Evans Grove?

"I do want these children—all of them—to find good futures." Rebecca's words lacked confidence, and worry furrowed her brow.

"Rebecca," Holly began, "what happens to them if they aren't placed?" She hesitated before adding in a quieter tone, "The stories aren't true, are they?"

"Some of the orphanages do a wonderful job, but it's never the same thing as a stable home. Greenville is the last hope for these children. We had a whole car full of youngsters when we started out." The woman hugged her chest and gave a sigh. "It's been heartbreaking to watch them passed over at stop after stop."

"You really do care about them a great deal."

Rebecca's response was only another sigh. "I'll be praying hard tonight, that's certain." She gave Holly's arm a quick squeeze. "With God's help and your help, things could turn out splendidly." After a moment she added, "And since we're friends, you and I, do you want to talk about today? Something is bothering you—and not just the placement meeting."

Suddenly, Holly's broken heart didn't seem like much of a burden to bear. She was useful, respected even if not loved, and never, ever had to feel as if no one in the world wanted her. She'd not just lost a colleague to a terrible crime. She wasn't alone, healing from some "bad experience," facing an enormous challenge in a strange place. Her pain over one man's disregard seemed self-indulgent right now, even if it did hurt mightily. "It's nothing. It was just…much harder than I thought it would be." That much was true. "I believe I'll be better now that I've forced myself to go back there." That wasn't quite true. Mason had forced her, but she didn't want to get into that with Rebecca. She wiped stray hairs out of her eyes, feeling mussed next to Rebecca's windswept beauty. "I'm just very weary."

They passed the general store, and Mrs. Gavin waved at them from the lighted window. "Back in New York, when I was very, very tired, I would go buy a new hat."

Holly laughed. "We've no haberdashery here, I assure you."

Rebecca gave a wink, "So then why don't we ask Mrs. Gavin to let us in for a new hair ribbon? I'm certain Miss Ward can wait another fifteen minutes."

Holly hadn't bought a hair ribbon in years. She hadn't even bought anything new for her important trip into Newfield. Perhaps there were things Rebecca could teach her that no one would find in any book. Holly knew a man like Mason couldn't be turned with a simple hair ribbon, but how long had it been since she'd felt pretty? Since she'd even tried? She managed a playful smile as Rebecca knocked on the front door of Gavin's General Store. "Maybe even thirty minutes."

"It's the eyes that get me," Mason told Bucky the next afternoon as they stood in the back of the church hall and watched the children line up for the selection meeting. "There's something sad about them."

Bucky squinted to see whatever it was that Mason

saw, but merely shook his head. "What? I just see shiny smiles."

That was it, in a manner of speaking. Those smiles were too shiny. "Don't you think no tot ought to grin like that when they're up for auction? Seems plain wrong. Unnatural."

Bucky stared at him. "Wait a minute…I thought you were *for* this whole thing."

"I am. I was. I mean I still am, but seeing it now, seeing them lined up like something to be bid on…"

"Nobody's buying nothing here, Mason. It's sweet what Miss Sanders is doing. Good Christian charity for some poor youngsters." Bucky furrowed his eyebrows. "What's gotten into you? You're never a sack of sunshine, but today—"

Mason cut him off. "I know, I know." He'd been prickly ever since dropping Holly Sanders off yesterday. He'd gotten what he wanted, so he should feel better, only he didn't. He felt worse, and somehow the pleading look in these orphans' eyes sent his mood darker. "Young ones ought to have mas and pas, that's all." He nodded over to little Galina, twirling about in her frilly dress. "Not have to parade for them."

Bucky, forever a candy-coated optimist since his recent marriage to Cynthia Levermore last Valentine's Day, only sighed. "You'll die waiting for a perfect world, Sheriff. Nothing short of Heaven'll ever be perfect." Bucky's eye twinkled. "But my Cindy, she comes mighty close."

"Perfect enough to be thinking about adding to that new household?" It hadn't even occurred to Mason until this moment that Bucky and Cindy might be one of the families to take in one of the orphans. He'd been hard-pressed to see Bucky so smitten as a husband, much less consider him as a father. Still, Bucky was a good man.

Bucky came as close to flustering as the big man got. "We might, but—"

"Hey, I was just fooling with you. I—"

"No." Bucky interrupted his interruption. "It's just that…well…"

There was something oddly startled behind Bucky's glare. A slightly frantic, slightly smitten grin Mason had put down to newlywed foolhardiness—only this was more. Mason turned to face his friend. "Wyler, what is it?"

The man turned red and scratched his sandy hair. "It's just that, well, Cindy…she thinks…" Bucky leaned in and whispered, "She thinks we may already have a young'un on the way." He shrugged, the grin on his face turning positively goofy.

Mason's heart twisted in two—one half in painful recollection of the elated whoops he'd howled to the treetops when Phoebe told him he was going to be a father, the other half in joy for his friend's new happiness. "Congratulations!" The words felt thick and bitter on his tongue.

"Shhhh." Bucky looked away and adopted a falsely casual stance. "Cindy doesn't want anyone to know 'til she's sure."

"Would all the eligible families please come to the front of the room," Reverend Turner called out. "I think it is only appropriate to begin such a momentous meeting with prayer."

Mason listened to the words but felt nothing. It was as if he were standing on the outside of a house on a cold night, looking in at the warmth inside but locked outside. He'd had Bucky's gleeful enthusiasm once, had believed God created love and families. He didn't have the right to another try at happiness for himself—not after the way he'd let Phoebe and their baby down— but these kids...if anyone deserved a chance, they did.

Miss Sterling stood in front of the children. "Please talk with each of the children. Ask them about what they do well, their likes, all those things. Think about your needs and your household as you talk, and then give your requests to Miss Sanders at the end of thirty minutes." Miss Sanders had come up with this format instead of the usual "select a child out of the line" model Mason knew the Society used. He had to agree it seemed kinder and wiser given the circumstances.

An hour later, Mason folded his hands again as Reverend Turner said a prayer over the Selection Committee's approved placements: Tiny Sasha, the youngest tot in long, dark braids, would go to Charlotte and Charlie Miller. Helen and Theodore Regan would have Galina join them out on their farm, and little Lizzie—and her stuffed rabbit Bobbins, Holly Sanders had pointed out with a smile—would make their home with the Hutchinsons.

"What do you think?" Curtis Brooks came up to Mason after the meeting, eyebrows raised in an invitation of Mason's opinion.

Mason found himself shrugging, at a loss to put a definite endorsement on the process. "Three little girls found homes tonight. Hard to argue with that." It had been heartwarming to watch Miss Sanders and Miss Sterling bundle off the girls to supper and their first night in new homes. Still, Mason found he couldn't ignore the four boys and quiet girl who trudged off to another night in the schoolhouse with obvious disappointment. "Scrawny as they are, I'd have thought the boys would go first, given all the work that needs doing around here. But I reckon the girls are less trouble to get settled."

Brooks let out a chuckle. "Those boys are a handful, I have to admit. Strong, but feisty." The banker tucked his hands in his pockets. "Young Liam there is a clever lad. All that energy needs a good place to go or…"

"Or it will go bad twelve ways to Sunday." Mason swallowed a smirk of nostalgia at his mama's favorite saying for when his own boyhood behavior left something to be desired. "Boys with empty time always fill it with trouble."

"That's been my experience," Brooks sighed.

"Are you a father, then?" Mason had realized earlier that other than his bank affiliation, no one in Evans Grove knew anything about the man. He'd shown a fair amount of wisdom on the Selection Committee, but Mayor Evans had put him on there to observe, not necessarily to contribute.

"Me? Gracious no. I've got a passel of nephews, but no family myself." He rocked back on his heels. "The right match hasn't come my way yet, and business keeps me busy."

But not too busy to be here, Mason thought. Mr. Brooks still hadn't explained his presence beyond "wanting to help," and hadn't made any declaration about how long he was planning to stay.

"How about yourself?"

Brooks had no idea the weight of that question. People never did. Mason gave the answer he always gave. "I prefer my solitude."

Mason was glad the banker only nodded. Holly Sanders would have asked eleven questions of him. She'd been efficient and quiet around him today, and he was glad of it.

"Miss Sanders spoke in glowing terms of your little town and its ability to rebuild. Looking around, the place has taken a far bigger hit than I expected."

Sometimes that teacher's capacity for optimism made Mason shake his head. "Times have been hard—no doubt about it—but Evans Grove has good people."

Brooks tucked a hand into the pocket of his fine-cut trousers. "Lost a lot of good people, too."

"Too many." Far too many. The morning of the town's Easter service Mason thought there wasn't a dry eye from here to Newfield. He'd gone to church that morning out of respect for all the grieving. And maybe, if he was honest, on the hope of finding a little solace of his own. Reverend Turner talked in passionate tones about how "death had lost its sting," but Mason couldn't agree. He clung to the belief that Phoebe and her baby were in a better place, but knew he had no passage there himself.

"It's been my experience that times like that bring out the best in some but the worst in others." He turned to look directly at Mason, clearly looking for information. "If there's 'worst,' you'd be the one seeing it. How would you say the town is faring, Wright?"

Mason cataloged his life as sheriff since the flood. "A few drink more than they ought to. Some punches get thrown between men balled up with worry over their homes or their lost kin."

"Any theft? Missing goods or…"

Mason saw where this was heading. "Or gold?" he

cut in perhaps more sharply than he ought to. "Mr. Brooks, your money is secure and will be put to good use. What you saw on the train has nothing to do with how Evans Grove shoulders its troubles. The only bandits in this town are locked up in my office."

"I didn't mean to imply…"

"Didn't you? Miss Sanders didn't tell tales—she's right that this here is a fine town. That spread the whole town put on for you and the youngsters ought to have told you that. There's nothing but good people here, people who ought to have every chance to rebuild and get on with their lives. In answer to your question, it's done nothing but bring out the best in folks."

"Three children placed!" Mayor Evans fairly beamed as she walked up to them. "I don't know when I've been prouder of our little town. Miss Sanders has more insight than the whole of us put together, seeing how a blessing could come out of such a tragic turn of events." She turned to gaze upon the bustling room with an air of proud affection. "It's a sight to see, isn't it, Mr. Brooks?"

To his credit, the banker looked genuinely impressed. "A fine thing, indeed."

"I'd like to think you know now how the good folk of Evans Grove rise to a challenge. I believe your objectivity has had value to our committee. Robert always said that sometimes a fresh eye is the sharpest of all."

"He was a fine man and a good mayor," Mason added, catching the slight waver in the widow's voice. No, sir, death still seemed to have plenty of sting left to go around.

"That he was." She gave a small sigh. "He would have been the first to back Miss Sanders's idea. Robert cared a great deal about helping people in need."

She turned to look at Brooks. "His father founded this town. Did you know that, Mr. Brooks? Evans Grove was grown from the belief that good people do good business. And we do. Your bank's funds are in capable hands."

"Oh, I don't doubt it, but I do like to keep a close eye on things. That's good business, too. Even your late husband would understand that."

"Robert believed in people. He trusted what could be accomplished with strong faith and hard work. Those aren't always assets that show up on ledgers, but they mattered dearly to Robert."

"Sounds like an admirable man. I'm truly sorry for your loss."

Mayor Evans swallowed hard. "He is greatly missed. But you should know, I share Robert's values. We can accomplish mighty things here."

"I look forward to watching mighty things accomplished."

Her look showed that she, like Mason, had noticed the telling emphasis Brooks gave to the word "watching." She gave a leery smile. "All I want is for hardworking people to get the fresh start they deserve." She glanced over her shoulder as Ned Minor called her name from the front of the room. "And I'd say these sweet little girls got just that. If you'll excuse me, Mr. Brooks, Sheriff?"

The banker tipped his hat. "Good evening, ma'am."

Mason tipped his as well, watching her walk toward the young hotel clerk. Minor had lost his mother in the flood, and she'd extended so many kindnesses to the young man as they both grieved their losses. "She's a strong woman, she is. I don't know that anyone would have thought she had so much steel in her before the flood took Robert. Stepping into his shoes took no small amount of nerve."

Brooks looked after the woman as she talked with the lanky clerk. "Mayor Evans is certainly an astonishment, I'll grant you that."

Chapter Eight

Holly turned the corner the next morning to be greeted by an unwelcome sight: Mason Wright. She wasn't ready for this, didn't want the discomfort of admitting he'd been right about going back to the clearing. Her hands had stopped shaking, and she no longer saw bandits and guns when she closed her eyes.

Mason's piercing dark glare? Well, that was another story. That had stuck with her.

Facing the problem head-on, Holly made herself walk over to the sheriff. "Good morning." She forced her voice bright as sunshine, pasting a smile on her face.

His expression remained unreadable. Was he annoyed or pleased at her effort to be cordial?

"Morning." He hid under his hat brim.

"I want to…I ought to…well, thank you for yesterday." She didn't want to thank him at all. She'd spent over an hour in prayer asking God where to go from here, and hadn't liked God's request for gratitude at all. Obedience didn't stop the words from feeling dry and hollow in her throat.

Mason hadn't expected thanks, that was clear. "For what?"

Holly chose words that were furthest from his idea of what happened yesterday. "For being kind enough to force me to do what was best."

He nearly flinched at her use of the word "kind," as she knew he would. She felt it a stretch of the truth herself—she still felt her gulping breaths at the railroad track as if they'd been physical blows. "I'd not call it kind," he said. "Necessary, maybe."

At least he'd looked at her. Granted, it was a narrow-eyed, "what are you up to?" kind of glare, but Holly pressed on, changing the subject. "I thought the selection meeting yesterday didn't go too badly."

Mason kicked a small rock out of the dirt with the toe of his boot. It struck her how much he occasionally reminded Holly of a hurt child—all prickly defiance and awkward silence. "But not as well as you'd hoped."

Holly had thought she'd hid her disappointment better than that. "What do you mean?"

That brought a near smile from him. "You wanted to see every one of those youngsters placed the first time out. It bothered you that the boys and Heidi didn't get picked up."

Holly started to protest, but he held up a silencing hand. "That's okay. It bothered me, too. Hated to see them shuffle back to the schoolhouse like that when the younger girls were skipping off to new homes."

It had been difficult in the schoolhouse last night, that was certain. When the boys weren't acting out to show how much they "didn't care about some stupid home in this tiny town" as Patrick so bluntly put it, they were quiet and sullen. Heidi hadn't said two words the whole night. Holly straightened her skirt and looked square at Mason. "The boys need something physical to do. They need to work off their anxiety. I was on my way to ask Charlie Miller but I wonder if you have any ideas." Holly had indeed been on her way to check up on Sasha and ask Charlie, when God had seen fit to throw Mason in her path.

"Me?" He looked as if it were the most absurd thing in the world to be asking him. "I hardly think I should be occupying a squirmy herd like that in the sheriff's office. Even if I thought it was a good idea to let those boys near the robbers after what they've been through, I expect we'd hear from Miss Ward within the hour."

It was the most words she'd heard Mason say to her since the railroad tracks. Besides which, he was right. "You have a point there." She hesitated, then chose to ask the question that had nagged her since the placement meeting. "You do think they'll be placed, don't you? We won't have to send them on to Greenville? I can't bear the thought of a fine boy like Liam being passed over in one more town."

Mason actually managed a small smile at that idea. "He's got backbone, I'll give him that, but I can't say most folks would think of him as a fine boy." He looked at her, a long, appraising look. "You do see it, don't you? Why they've come this far without being placed?"

His tone of gentle condescension—the sort of tone she might use to explain spelling to a toddler—irked her. Did he think her some sort of fool who didn't know how the world worked? She planted her hands on her hips and looked straight up at him. "Why don't you explain to me how good Christian men and women could fail to see the potential in those young boys?"

He broadened his stance. "Folks are looking for stronger stock."

"There is more to life than brute force, Sheriff." It was an amusing assertion for a tiny woman to make to a large brute of a man like Mason Wright. Why was he always making her wish she was twice her size? There were times when she wanted to stand on the church steps just to be able to look down on him and give him the good scolding he deserved.

He swept his hand toward the crop fields. "Maybe not here, not now."

"We can honor qualities other than strength here in Evans Grove. We are not barbarians." She couldn't stop herself from adding, "No matter how some of us occasionally behave."

The grin that stole across his face shocked her. "Leave Miss Ward out of this."

A good Christian woman would not have laughed. She would have scolded Mason for his terrible tongue. Still, Holly found she couldn't. Beatrice had been such an awful old biddy at last night's placement meeting, she might have called her a barbarian if the word had come to mind. "Mason!"

The familiarity jumped out of her mouth, improper and unbidden. His eyes widened and Holly's hand flew to her open mouth. She deserved every bit of the red her face must be turning. She knew nothing good could ever come of her thinking of him in such familiar terms. "Sheriff Wright," she corrected far too late to be of any good, "I'll thank you to mind your tongue." It was exactly the wrong thing to say, for shouldn't she have minded her own tongue far better than she just had?

A dreadful gap of awkward silence stretched between them. Holly couldn't think of what to say, and the sheriff couldn't seem to find a safe place to look. While the distance between them had always frustrated Holly, now its loss seemed to open the way for a disconcerting friction. He knew she thought of him as "Mason." Oh, how that made her feel small and foolish. She felt a child's urge to turn and run, hating how she'd lost control of the situation—if she'd ever had it to start.

Mason coughed and settled his hat farther down, hiding deeper under the brim. Holly wanted desperately to be able to judge his reaction to her slip, but he'd stepped and turned slightly, as if to dodge the whole thing. Why must there be so much pretense between them?

Holly smoothed her skirt, which was no less a blatant avoidance than his hat, now nearly meeting his eyelids. She forced a formal tone into her voice, but it came out more of a squeak. "I remain confident the boys will find homes here."

"Sure." Holly's only consolation came from the fact that Mason was even worse at hiding his discomfort than she. Which raised the question: was he charmed by the admission, or repulsed by it? He hadn't turned tail and run, but Mason Wright didn't seem the sort to back down to anyone, much less a ridiculous tiny church mouse like Holly.

An uncomfortable pause hung between them. "Any news regarding the robbers?" They'd already discussed this, but she was willing to revisit the subject as a change of conversation.

Mason leaped upon the topic. "Nothing you haven't heard." He straightened and fingered the lapel on his vest that bore the tin star of his office. "Things mostly depend on how fast I can send them on."

"To Greenville?" Holly practically exhaled at the safer topic—and how awful that the topic of murderous bandits was safer territory than her telling slip.

Mason pivoted back to face her, his shoulders relaxing just a bit. He cast his eyes back down the street toward the jail. "I want them out of here. Our jail is not really built to hold four men, and I want the leader to stand before the county judge for murder. If I have my way, those thieves will be on tomorrow's train for Greenville."

A murder trial? She'd tried not to think of that. Holly still had a hard time swallowing the fact that she'd watched a murder take place. Even worse, poor little orphans like Sasha and Galina had been witness to such a cold-blooded crime. The realization brought a chilling thought she'd forgotten to ask him earlier. "Will Rebecca or I need to go before the judge? Give a statement or some such thing?"

"No. No need for anything like that here." There was a flash of warmth in his eyes, a startling counterpoint to the edge she usually found there. "I'd never put you through that."

Holly didn't know what to say other than a meek "Thank you." She hadn't realized how much she'd dreaded the prospect of testifying until Mason removed it from her shoulders. More astounding, he'd given thought to protecting her. He'd worried about keeping her from further distress. She was right in her persistent belief that his harshness wasn't all there was to the man; he *was* capable of caring. He'd cared deeply about his late wife. Did she dare to think that could mean he could care again? If he healed? She knew she wore her heart on her sleeve, but his was hidden behind a lifetime of scars.

Mason coughed. "What I mean is…I have plenty of witnesses to call on before I'd put you or Miss Sterling through anything like that."

"Yes," she sputtered, still flustered, no longer capable of dismissing the glimpse of Mason's true spirit she'd seen. "I'd just as soon put all that behind me."

Holly suddenly understood his impulses even better that she had before. He was throwing up every wall he could think of in order to keep her out—only she'd already seen what was on the other side.

Knowing that, Holly found she could actually look him in the eye. They were too much alike, each covering admissions neither planned to make. "I'll pray for justice to be done."

He wasn't dismissive of her Godly comment, but he didn't embrace it, either. "Well now, you go ahead and do that."

She could count on one hand the number of times she'd seen Mason in church—and most of those had been funerals. He'd made it clear yesterday that he thought himself beyond redemption.

"I will, indeed. Do you believe in God's mercy, Sheriff? Even for weak boys and barbarian spinsters?" *And for men who can't bring themselves to ask for the forgiveness they deserve*, she added silently.

"I know Miss Ward believes she has no call for mercy, as she's certain God admires her very much indeed. Except I do find myself hoping He doesn't take a shine to my roof the way he did to Beatrice's."

How cleverly he avoided her question. "He seems to have let your roof be. But what about you? A man who runs headlong into gunfire must give thought to his soul now and then."

Her question drew his eyebrows together in an irked scowl. "Have you been scheming with Reverend Turner behind my back?"

"Why?" Was something indeed pricking the soul of the good sheriff?

"He asked me much the same question."

She'd thought God's insistence that she reach out to Mason today to be just for benefit of her conscience— a command to clear the air. Maybe there was more to it. "What answer did you give him?"

He examined a scar on his thumb, still scowling. "I told him I kept to my business and let the Good Lord get on with His."

Holly smiled, rather sure of the answer Reverend Turner would give to a dodge like that. "And I suspect the Reverend told you each of us *is* God's business?"

Rolling his eyes, Mason tipped his hat back. She was glad to see him come out from under the shadow of his hat brim. "As a matter of fact, that's pretty much it word for word. Do you all rehearse?"

"Not at all." Holly folded her hands calmly in front of her, the jitters of their earlier exchange replaced by strong certainty that this was a talk she and the sheriff had needed to have. If it took a bit of embarrassment to get to this conversation, then so be it. "But we do all read the same book." She turned toward Charlie Miller's smithy shop. "God bless you, Sheriff Mason Wright. You and your roof."

"My leg's on fire," the lead bandit moaned for the fourth time.

"I called Doc Simpson and he'll tend to you when

he can." Mason looked up from the wanted list the county sent over earlier this week. The man's face, while sweaty with fever, matched the crude drawing. It hadn't taken long to confirm Mason's suspicion that at least two of these rascals—if not all four—were wanted men. Mr. Arlington hadn't been their first murder. If the one wouldn't hang for Arlington's murder alone, it seemed more than one of them would be swinging for the collection of crimes he saw on the county list. No mercy for these evil men.

Mercy. The word brought Holly Sanders's face to mind. For a handful of seconds, he allowed himself the indulgence of the teacher's own slip: *Holly.* How much richer and easier it rolled around his mind than the formal "Miss Sanders." Holly. He'd always felt like "Miss Sanders" had too many s's anyway.

She'd called him Mason. Worse yet, she'd called him Mason in an unguarded moment, which meant she *thought* of him as Mason. That took his thoughts to all kinds of dangerous places. She was always careful to call him "Sheriff Wright" or just Sheriff—and he knew why. It was the exact reason he forced himself to think of her and address her as Miss Sanders, even when not in her presence. He needed that distance, relied on that formality.

It was gone now. She'd pulled that formality out from underneath him like a rug. *Mason.* He could hear how it played across her lips even now, that shock of surprise that popped her eyes wide and turned her cheeks bright pink. He'd known he was in for trouble when she crossed the street resolutely toward him. Why wouldn't that woman keep her distance? Hadn't he given her enough reasons to stay away from him? Her stubborn streak must run a mile wide.

Mason found himself smiling, and wiped his hands down his face in frustration. Clever as she was, couldn't she see that no good would come of caring for him? He'd lost the right to love or be loved, and no amount of her stubborn optimism could change that. The light in her eyes could never outweigh the dark in his past. He couldn't afford to ever let Holly Sanders—*Miss Sanders*, he corrected himself with a befuddled shake of his head—near enough to tangle his brain.

"Sheriff!"

If Mason needed the perfect—or most relentless—distraction, it just walked though his door. Beatrice Ward stalked up to his desk and planted a fussy yellow basket full of eggs down on his desk. He peered inside with raised eyebrows. "Easter was last month, ma'am."

Before he'd met Beatrice Ward, Mason didn't think a woman could *hrumph* like that. She made that noise with more spite than even his grandpa could ever muster. "They're not for you. These are for baking projects at the church this afternoon. I simply found my cause could not wait, so I came right here."

The old biddy had never met a cause that *could* wait, near as Mason could tell. Everything was an urgent matter to Beatrice Ward. Bucky Wyler once joked he thought Miss Ward ate panic for breakfast, and it looked as if she'd downed a whole heaping plate of it. "What seems to be the trouble, Miss Ward?"

"Those urchin boys cannot be controlled. Ruffians, the lot of them. I have grave concerns about what might happen if they're not properly supervised."

"Miss Sanders starts classes back up next week, and

I expect they'll have plenty to do when that happens." He stacked the county notices and slid them in a desk drawer.

This took the woman aback. "We're educating those vagrants? I hadn't even considered that." This clearly wasn't a pleasant prospect in her eyes.

"I always took you to be in favor of book learning. You said Miss Sanders was the best educated mind in Evans Grove, and that's why she ought to be the one to go to Newfield." Mason longed to add, "and we all saw how that fared, didn't we?" but knew better than to poke an angry bear like Beatrice on one of her streaks.

She sniffed, her nose high in the air. "An education is wasted on someone unwilling to better themselves."

Here Holly was so ready to see good in those children, and Beatrice Ward could see nothing but faults. It made Mason wonder just who ought to be heading up the Ladies' Benevolent Society in town. Near as he could tell, Miss Ward didn't have a benevolent bone in her body. "They seem eager to me." It was true. When they weren't trying to act like they didn't care, the boys were near desperate to have someone see them as worthy of placement. It's what made yesterday's meeting so painful to watch. "That Liam fellow struck me as right smart."

The mention of the scrappy redheaded boy made Miss Ward's eyes narrow in disgust. "He's the worst of them, Sheriff. He has crime in his eyes—you of all people should be able to see it. He's no good. They're all no good. Last night only proved that, don't you think?"

"Last night only proved that cute, sweet little girls are easier to place than a squirmy herd of boys. And then there's the quiet girl—Heidi's her name, isn't it?

Surely a woman of your Christian charity could see her potential?" It bothered Mason that he'd used the same words Holly had just proclaimed to him.

Miss Ward leaned in and tapped her temple. "I don't think she's all together, personally. We've no place for feeble-minded waifs here."

Feeble minded waifs? Mason nearly rolled his eyes. "What is it you'd have me do, ma'am?"

"Confine them to the schoolhouse."

Mason thought of the two cells behind him—there wouldn't be much difference. "They're children, Miss Ward. Locking them up in the schoolhouse will only cause more trouble. Little ones need to get out and play, to be occupied." Again, it irked him that Holly Sanders's words kept coming out of his mouth.

"We can't have them running around town." She plucked her basket up off the desk, signaling that she'd said her piece and would now expect him to do something about it.

"Miss Sanders just told me she was on her way to ask Charlie Miller if he could use one or two of them as helpers. Give them chores and such."

She sniffed again, making Mason wonder if the only reason she'd joined the Selection Committee was her sheer insistence at being involved in everything. "It's not an ideal solution."

"Ideal went out with the dam. We're all just doing the best we can."

"My leg's still killin' me, Sheriff! I'm dyin' here. I swear I'm expirin' this very moment!" Evidently, the bandit thought an audience might better his case.

Beatrice Ward nearly flinched at the reminder that

she was in the same room with murderous thieves. She clutched her basket of eggs close. "I'll be going."

"If you see Doc Simpson," Mason called to her as she made quickly for the door, "let him know he's got an impatient patient over here."

The look Miss Ward gave him in return let Mason know she'd just assume the man's leg fester and fall off for his sins.

Mercy? No, sir, life didn't have much mercy, no matter what Holly and her kind chose to believe.

Chapter Nine

"That's that." Mason pulled the cell door shut and tucked the keys back into his pocket. An hour ago he'd loaded the four handcuffed criminals—still moaning and complaining—into the back of a wagon and put them on the train to Greenville to stand before the circuit judge. They could have a lengthy wait; judges traveled from town to town. He'd have to travel to Greenville when the time for their proceedings came, but that was a welcome price to pay to have those bandits out of Evans Grove. Not only were they unpleasant company, but he just plain didn't like the thought of them anywhere near Holly, Miss Sterling, or the children.

Holly. Hang it all, he couldn't stop himself from thinking of her as Holly now that he knew she thought of him as Mason. In the restored silence of his office, she seemed to push into his every thought.

He was almost grateful—almost—for the knock on his door. "Hello there, Reverend." He tried not to be annoyed that he'd had more conversations with Reverend Turner in the past week than in the past two years.

"Good afternoon, Mason. Those bandits off to justice?" He nodded to the now-empty cells.

"That's my hope. What can I do for you?" Mason motioned to the chair in front of his desk.

The Reverend sat down, resting his hat on one knee. "Well, I suppose the bandits are tied in to why I'm here. Some of the children—mostly the boys—are asking what will happen. I'll be honest. I don't care to see a grown man say they want to 'watch 'em swing,' but it disturbs me to hear it out of an eleven-year-old boy's mouth."

"They're just frightened boys mouthing off, Reverend. I don't know that you need to worry much."

"I've talked with Miss Sanders, and she feels the best thing we can do is give them the facts. Tell them what's going to happen—in a way that's fit for their ages, of course—so their imaginations don't run wild off their high-strung emotions."

Mason pursed his lips. "That sounds like something Miss Sanders would say. That woman can turn anything into a lesson." He pulled open a drawer where his copies of the county records were kept. "I'll write her up some facts and she can tell them whatever you all think they can handle." He gave Turner a long look. "But the men'll hang, Reverend. Some, if not all. Not many ways to pretty that up into a happy tale fit for tots."

The pastor folded his hands in a way that made Mason nervous. A quiet, careful, you're-not-going-to-like-what-I-say-next kind of gesture. "No one's expecting you to tell them fairy tales."

It took Mason a handful of seconds to register Turner's words. When he did, he cocked his head in stunned disbelief. "Me?"

"You are the sheriff. To them, you are the law, and this is about crimes and punishments."

"I hardly think…"

"Don't forget, Mason, they saw you shoot a gun, too. They need to understand the difference between what you did and what those bandits did. What little structure they had has been turned upside down and they need to know it'll be set to rights."

Mason crossed his arms over his chest. "I'm not your man. Not on this one." Bad enough that Holly seemed to think he was an honorable man, one to admire. He couldn't stomach the thought of standing up in front of a bunch of youngsters and pretending to be someone who always knew the right thing to do.

"Miss Sanders thinks you are, and I agree." It was then that the good Reverend wielded his best leverage. "Miss Sterling thinks it's a fine idea, and so does Miss Ward."

Now he was sunk. Once Beatrice Ward got it into her head that something ought to be done, she was like a swarm of hornets. Turner knew it. Holly did, too, hang her. There was only one way out, and it pleased him about as much as hugging a hornet's nest. "Then we'll all meet with the children. That way Miss Sanders, Miss Sterling and you can fix any missteps I'm bound to make when I explain how a bad man hangs for what he's done." He gave the final words a sufficiently dark emphasis, hoping his reluctance to be this week's justice lesson came through loud and clear.

"Miss Sanders told me to tell you she'll have the children gathered tomorrow at ten."

Did she, now? "Mighty presumptuous of our good schoolmarm to assume I'd agree to this." He raised an eyebrow at Turner, swallowing a "you were in on this, too" accusation. The reverend's resulting smirk set Mason's teeth on edge.

"Well, you know Beatrice."

Oh, he knew Beatrice Ward all right. And so did Holly, who Mason was certain had dropped this particular bug in the old meddler's ear. Mason had to admit he'd just been soundly outfoxed. There was a good reason Turner waited until today's train for Greenville had left. Mason had a mind to saddle up his horse and invent a need to turn in court paperwork this minute. There had to be something to do, some way to appease the children—and maybe even to keep Holly from thinking she'd won this round. He found himself thinking of clever Liam. What would Liam ask of Holly if she put him to a task he dreaded? "Well, in that case, I'll need cookies."

That stopped the reverend midrise as he stood to take his leave. "Cookies?"

The thought of Holly Sanders, hands on her hips, directing an amused scowl at Liam—or was it at him?—made Mason grin just a bit. "You don't expect me to tell stories to children without them getting cookies to take their minds off the big, bad wolf, do you?"

Holly couldn't decide if she should scowl or smile as she opened the teacherage door the next morning to Sheriff Wright. "What kind of sheriff requires cookies for something like this?"

He tucked his hands in his pockets, his expression softening just a bit. "One who never wanted to do it in the first place?" The way reluctance played across his face, Holly couldn't help but think the man looked entirely too much like Liam.

"Well, I certainly can't argue with the power of cookies to soothe the childhood mind." Holly nodded toward the basket behind her that Charlotte had brought over the hour before. "I know they work with me. Why don't you come in. We ought to talk before you give your lesson."

Her use of the word "lesson" returned the sour look to his face. He clearly didn't want to be here, but at least he had cleaned himself up for the occasion. The fresh shirt and shave seemed almost out of place on the usually mussed sheriff. For a split second, her heart wondered if the effort was for her, or for the children, but the look in his eyes told Holly she might not be his favorite person right now.

"I shouldn't be giving lessons on anything," he nearly muttered.

"Yes, you should." She held up the basket. "You knew enough to ask for snacks. You're a natural."

"You don't play fair, bringin' in Miss Ward like you did." He took his hat off to reveal combed hair. Holly thought about making a comment, but kept silent. He was here against his will, but he was here, and that ought to count for something.

"Beatrice simply recognized a good idea when she saw one."

"You mean when you *handed* her one."

This was going to be hard for everyone, but it truly needed to be done. Best to get on with it. "We really should prepare and the boys are in the schoolhouse, so here will have to do." She watched how he kept his elbows close to his sides as if one wrong turn would knock something over. Knowing what she did about his sparse office and his curt personality, it was likely he found her house full and fussy. *A mouse house,* the old familiar, critical voice in her head whispered. She cringed, wondering why she felt compelled to defend her house to a man who'd seen it before. Everything had too many meanings with him—she never knew what to think or how to act anymore around this man.

"It's nice." His tone was tight and obligatory.

Holly motioned to the table and took one seat while Mason settled himself gingerly in the other. "I'd offer you some tea, but I don't think we have time."

"I'm not much for tea," he said with a forced smile. He did manage to eye the cookies, raising one mischievous eyebrow in a request she was helpless to refuse. How could a man so dark show such glimmers of amusement?

"One." Holly found herself using her teacher voice.

Mason managed a slip of a genuine smile as he took two. Dickens surprised her by coming out of hiding to inspect him. Mason's smile faded a bit at the yellow-eyed appraisal, but he didn't mention the cat so neither did she.

"I've asked all the schoolchildren to come, not just the orphans."

He didn't look happy about a larger audience. "Why?"

"What happened at the railroad tracks has ended up affecting our entire community. We should deal with it as an entire community." Holly reached down to give the cat a soft stroke down his smooth back. "Plus, it gives a way for the orphans to meet Evans Grove's other children before Monday's classes."

He put the cookies down, interest lost. "I'm not sure I'm eager to be an entire school's civics lesson."

"It's all of us. You, me, the reverend and Miss Sterling. Why don't you think of it more as a conversation than a lecture? The children will have lots of questions."

Mason ran a hand down his face. "That's what I'm afraid of." He eyed her. "I can't be the one to give them lessons on right and wrong. I'm not...that kind of man."

The way his jaw tightened, Holly realized just how far Mason saw himself from righteousness. And yet he upheld the law with a fierce determination. No wonder the man always looked as if there were a war going on behind his eyes. "You're *exactly* that kind of man. You're the sheriff."

He rolled his eyes the way he did every time she offered him any kind of affirmation. "Aren't we just inviting them to spend too much time thinking of something best forgotten?"

She leaned in. "Are *you* likely to forget it anytime soon?"

He leaned back and gave a reluctant sort of growl.

Holly eyed the clock on her mantel and smoothed out her skirts. "Ready?"

"No."

"No matter, that." She reached to catch his elbow, but stopped herself. "It will be fine, you know, and it's the right thing to do."

Mason walked into the schoolhouse feeling like an outnumbered man heading into battle. Holly had rearranged the seats so that all of the children sat in a big circle, with some of the parents standing behind them. The setup made him feel less like he was on stage, but the sea of upturned faces—not to mention Beatrice Ward's beady eyes—still set his nerves on edge.

Holly introduced each adult to the children in the room. Beatrice produced an irritated cough until Holly introduced her as well, making sure to declare her title as Chairman of the Evans Grove Ladies' Society. "Bad things happen sometimes," Holly began once the introductions were completed, "but good people—clever people—can often find ways to make good things happen out of bad ones. The Bible tells us all things work together for good for those who know God, and that's exactly what's happened here in Evans Grove."

"That doesn't mean," Reverend Turner went on, "that the bad things always go away. Some bad things, like Mr. Arlington being shot, can't be changed. It's all right to be sad about that, because Mr. Arlington was a nice man doing good work."

"The children and I will miss him very much," Miss Sterling added with a bit of a wobble in her voice.

"He *was* nice," Friedrich added, stubbing the floor with his foot. "Those men were bad."

Holly looked up at Mason, cuing him to take that opening. "It's never right to take a man's life like that," he began, fighting the awkward feeling in his chest. "What those men did was wrong in a lot of ways. They were trying to take what wasn't theirs and they had no reason at all to do what they did to Mr. Arlington."

"They were robbers and killers, that's what they were," Patrick pronounced, his eyes narrow and angry. "Robbers and killers *hang*." He put so much emphasis on the word that Heidi flinched and Lizzie clutched her rabbit tighter. Mason could just imagine the scenarios boys like that were describing amongst themselves. Holly's idea was starting to make sense.

"Robbers and killers are brought to justice, and that's what happened." Mason directed his answer straight to Patrick. "The men who hurt Mr. Arlington hurt other men and robbed other people. And men who do things like that over and over—especially those who kill—do get sentenced to hang." It seemed somehow less savage to say they were *sentenced to hang*. But was there any point in trying to make little minds understand that the execution of justice was different than vengeance killing?

And why should he, of all men, be making this point? He had killed—fiercely, gladly—when he found one of the men who'd killed Phoebe. They were robbers as well, even though he and Phoebe had had little of value. Certainly nothing worthy of murder, which made them all the more despicable in Mason's eyes. He'd have killed them all if given the chance. Oh, he knew Holly would call it something safe like grace, but it was only dumb luck that another lawman had caught the others before Mason had. He'd stood outside their jail cells the night before their hanging, gun in hand, craving to be the very vengeance he'd just told these children was wrong. Justice hadn't even come into his mind back then. He'd lost the ability to be "just" the night he'd failed in protecting his family. Now, Mason could only pretend at justice, and it clawed at the deepest part of his guilt to be sitting here, in front of Holly Sanders, in front of the children, claiming to know right from wrong.

"Bad people must be punished to protect good people." Mason grasped at the proper words, inadequacy licking at his heels. "My job as sheriff is to make sure the bad people get caught so they can be punished and good people can be safe."

"That's why you tried to kill that robber," Tom said.

"I shot him," Mason quickly corrected as the question struck too close to home, "because he was going to hurt Miss Sanders if I didn't. I tried to *wound* him so we could stop him. I *wasn't* trying to kill him."

"Why not?" Liam asked. "He'd just killed Mr. Arlington. I think he ought to die for what he did."

It stung deep to hear that coming out of the mouth of an eleven-year-old boy. Mason knew what rage was— but a young boy? Even a hard-luck kid like Liam? Maybe the only grace he could ever hope to reach would be the chance to set these youngsters straight. "We can't think of it like that," he said, looking right at Liam. "More killing won't make anything better. That's why we have laws and judges and such."

"But Mr. Arlington's gone," Galina said with sad eyes. Helen Regan placed a tender hand on her new little foster daughter's shoulder.

"He is, honey," Holly consoled, "and that's wrong and sad. Those men will pay for what they took from us and from Mr. Arlington's family. We can't change that. But you also have Mr. and Mrs. Regan to take care of you now because you needed to stop here in Evans Grove. So now you have good things to help you feel better about the bad things."

"You are safe here," Miss Sterling cut in. "It's Sheriff Wright's job to see to that. The men who robbed the train—who *tried* to rob the train," she corrected herself, "will pay for what they've done in whatever way the judge and the law think best."

"Our job now," Holly continued, "is to be the best people we can be right here. You all," she said as she motioned to the town children, "need to welcome new friends to our school." She nodded toward the orphans. "You have new homes, new classmates and a new community to help you start lives right here. Reverend Turner, Miss Sterling, Sheriff Wright and I are going to do our very best to help with that. So if you have any questions or worries, I want you to come straight to one of us."

Mason had the sinking feeling he'd just been drafted onto a team not of his own choosing. Coddling children was not something he had any plans to do. He wasn't even sure he liked children—they were loud, insistent, irritating and unreasonable.

Come to think of it, except for the "loud," he'd just described how he currently felt about Holly Sanders. The sweet smile she gave him at the end of her speech did nothing to squelch the annoyance rumbling in his gut. No, it didn't matter at all that she was pretty and clever and tender, or that she had a soul too kind for this broken world. She was pushing him into places he didn't want to go, into thoughts and feelings he couldn't have ever again. Believing in her brand of endless grace would be his undoing if he wasn't careful. His only choice was to keep his distance, focus on her irritating flaws, and remember she'd done nothing but send trouble his way.

It was time to put an end to such nonsense. Cookies or no cookies, the second this meeting was over he was going to put every inch of space he could between himself and Holly Sanders, and keep it that way.

Chapter Ten

Rebecca put the last of the desk chairs back in its place. "How long?"

Holly took a quick count of the children—town and orphan—playing together in the school yard and surveyed the rows of desks to be sure her newly expanded classroom had the right amount of seats. "How long what?"

Rebecca came up beside her. At first Holly thought her smile was for the happy combination of old and new students, but Rebecca wasn't looking out the window. "How long have you been sweet on Sheriff Wright?"

Holly sucked in a shocked gulp of air, feeling the blood rush to her face. How embarrassing to be so bold with her feelings that a stranger could guess them easily! She let her breath out in a sigh and clasped her hands together. "Forever."

Rebecca turned from the window and leaned against the sill. No judgment twisted the corners of her smile; instead, the agent's expression was warm and understanding. "He's handsome, I'll grant you that, but awfully prickly. You must surely see some other side of him I don't."

"Oh, he keeps folks at a distance, that's true. He likes to make himself out as prickly," she said, using Rebecca's too-true adjective, "but that's not him. I'm sure he wasn't always that way."

Rebecca shifted to peer out the window in the direction of Mason's office. "Did something happen to him?"

Holly craned her head to follow Rebecca's gaze, knowing she wouldn't see the lawman walking down the street. He'd looked as if the "civics lesson," as he called it, couldn't end quickly enough. For a man who had insisted on cookies, he'd bolted out of the classroom empty-handed. Mason kept people at a distance because of his self-enforced exile. It was as if he felt he didn't deserve the love and support of good people, and she was just beginning to learn why. Phoebe's death was part of it, but not the whole of it. Holly could see glimpses of Mason's true nature, even if no one else could. He wasn't prickly, he was desperately lonesome.

Still, she wasn't the kind of person to tell other people's secrets, and while he'd never said as much, she knew Mason hadn't told anyone else about the pain he carried. "He's had a great loss." It didn't feel right to say more than that. She shrugged. "He's not so much mean as he is sad, really. He lives with so much unnecessary pain."

Rebecca crossed her arms over her chest. "You surely sound like a woman who has lost her heart." She raised a blond eyebrow. "Does he know?"

Holly turned from the window to sink down onto one of the desk chairs. "Some days I'm sure he knows. As you can see, I'm not as clever as some at hiding my feelings. The other day he shocked me and I called him 'Mason' to his face!" She put a hand to her cheek, feeling the mortification rise up all over again. Oh, the look he had given her after that gaffe. It made her want to crawl inside a barrel and swoon at the same time.

"Mason. It's a strong name. And he seems a very brave man."

"I could tell you a dozen stories—small acts of kindness he does when he thinks no one is watching, or riding off in the middle of storms to find someone who's missing or hurt. He has always been brave. But when the flood hit…when it looked as if the dam wouldn't hold and the water kept rising…it was as if he knew what had to be done and never feared what it might cost him to do it." She cast her gaze away from Rebecca as the image of a soaked, bleeding Mason struggling up out of the creek with Josiah Norman's young boy returned to her memory. "More than once I watched him walk into harm's way to keep someone safe. And when he ran into the clearing to pull me away from that horrid man…" She didn't want to speak any further than that. After all, those were terrible moments for Rebecca.

"And what does the sheriff feel for you? Do you know?"

"Quite honestly, I'm not even sure he knew I existed before the robbery. He'd never speak to me unless I asked him a question. And yet, every once in a while, I'd catch him looking at me. In a… certain way that would make my heart stop." She rubbed the spot where he'd held her arm at the train tracks. "He'd look away right after, of course, but there was always this moment where…" Holly shut her eyes for a moment.

"Where I suppose I was imagining things that might not be there."

Rebecca perched on the chair next to Holly. "Men are puzzles, that much is surely true. I've found they rarely say what they mean when it comes to women, and hardly ever act according to their true feelings. Men pay attention to women they don't care for if they feel it might advance their position, and they'll ignore a woman who catches their eye just because they can't think what to do."

Holly looked up at the regal woman, looking elegant even in an undersized school chair. Rebecca seemed so well versed in society. Surely she'd entertained dozens of suitors with her looks and charms. It felt silly to talk about Mason to her here, like this, as if he were some schoolgirl infatuation. What she felt for Mason was so big and complicated—not childish at all. Still, she was aching to talk over her confusing emotions with someone. "I can't say Mason—" she surprised herself by using his given name out loud "—is at a loss for what to do. He seems quite sure of himself. There are days I think he goes out of his way to avoid me, where he says things he knows will hurt me. It's clear he doesn't want me to like him. I don't think he wants much of anyone to like him."

"A broken heart can build a very tall wall around a person. Some hearts bear such wounds that they'll shut out even good things rather than chance pain again."

Holly turned to face Rebecca, caught by the pain reflected in the woman's words. Miss Sterling had a broken heart, that much was clear. Only she was starting to heal; the children had seen to that. Healing was exactly what she wanted to give to Mason. "That's just it. He's wounded. I can see so clearly why he's behaving the way he is, why he thinks he has to be alone." Holly found her speaking the words as much to Rebecca as to Mason. "He's wrong. No one has to be alone. No hurt is so deep it can't be healed. Surely," she added, feeling as though she might have ventured too far, "as people of faith, we understand that."

"The sheriff has no faith?"

"I think he does. Or did. But now he sees himself as so unworthy of love—anyone's, even God's—that he doesn't think it possible that God or anyone else could care for him." Holly stood up and shook her head, walking to the bookshelf where a copy of *King Arthur* sat tilted to one side. "He's so brave, so honorable, it seems like such a waste to have a man like that exile himself. It's like he's built a great, deep moat of guilt around himself. He pretends as if I've no hope with him, and then he does something kind and my heart…" She swallowed the rest of that thought as she righted the book.

Rebecca tucked a loose tendril behind her delicate ear. "One could always build a drawbridge over that moat."

Someone like Rebecca Sterling could, yes. "Not me. I've not that kind of boldness."

Miss Sterling rose, tall and grand. "Nonsense. You're as brave as he. I've watched you at the meetings. You know how to stand your ground. You won't let Miss Ward get away with unkindnesses toward others. So why do you stand by and let Mason Wright be cruel to himself?"

"I've never thought of it that way, that he believes he must be cruel to himself." The way he spoke to her on the return trip to the train tracks, the way he'd cast himself as the worst kind of man, it made even more sense now.

"You said he saved your life."

"He saved all our lives, Rebecca."

The smile that crossed her face surely caught a thousand men's hearts back in New York. "So go save his."

She made it sound so effortless. "How? With what?"

"With whatever it is God knows he needs."

Holly blinked. In all her lamenting over Mason Wright, had she ever asked God to show her how to serve him? How to point his wounded soul toward the healing of salvation? Not once, and that had to change.

An hour after his fiasco in the schoolhouse, Mason looked up from repairing his office door to see Liam watching him from across the street. He'd been there yesterday, too, until Beatrice Ward had shooed him away for no good reason—as if he had less right to walk down the street than one of Evans Grove's more permanent citizens. Just to show Beatrice, Mason had called the boy over and sent him on an errand for more nails from Gavin's General Store. The extra nickel he'd given the lad for a piece of licorice, well, that was just to show Liam that not everyone in town found him a nuisance.

Liam was back again today. Evidently, Mason was growing a little redheaded shadow. No sense in not putting him to work. For a stretch of time the boy had swept off the office steps, beaten dust out of the jail cell cots, and generally kept Mason's company. He was a nuisance, but hang it all if that smirk of his didn't pull a smile out of Mason every once in a while.

Or a groan. Liam was still in the office later that afternoon when Beatrice showed up again. "It's my opinion that the entire Selection Committee ought to be present during services tomorrow. If we're to officially welcome these…" she paused, casting a look at Liam that Mason would never describe as churchlike "…unfortunate souls into our congregation, then the committee should be there."

It wasn't to his credit that Mason gave the same reluctant moan that escaped Liam's mouth. "I'm not much of a churchgoing man, Miss Ward."

"Nor I," Liam said too quickly, and Mason shot the boy a look.

"I'm entirely aware of that, Sheriff." Miss Ward looked straight at Mason, her words fairly dripping with disapproval. "Nevertheless," she said as she turned to include the boy as if it were an act of charity to bestow her judgment on both of them equally, "I'll expect to see you—both of you—in church. Front pew."

Mason felt such sympathy for the lad—who looked as if he dreaded the long, fussy service as much as Mason himself did—that he bought a pair of sandwiches at the hotel for them to share back at the office.

"School? Do I have to?" Liam moaned with a mouth full of ham.

"Yes, you do. You can't hang around with me all day, and we know better than to leave you to your own devices."

The boy licked a smear of mustard from his lip. "I'm not much for book learnin'. Besides, I like it here with you."

"Quieter than the schoolhouse?"

"I'll say. Even with the three girls gone." It wasn't hard to catch the hitch in the boy's voice at being passed over for placement. All the boys had been doubly squir-

relly since that meeting, and Mason couldn't blame
them. "Patrick's broken a desk already and Tom coughs
all night so's none of us can sleep a wink." He patted his
stomach as if he'd just finished a feast, then produced
a loud yawn as further evidence. Without so much as a
"by your leave," the boy then walked over and launched
himself onto one of the cell cots with a bounce hard
enough to squeak the springs. "I could catch a Sunday
nap right here on this cot, I could."

Mason yawned himself—he hadn't been sleeping
well lately and he had an invitation to supper at the
Wylers' house tonight. "What's stopping you?"

"You might lock me up when I wasn't looking, that's
what."

Mason swiveled in his chair. "That's what you take
me for? A man who fattens children with ham sandwiches and then locks them up while they sleep?"

Liam settled back in against the wall, sliding his
ever-present newsboy cap down over his eyes. "Not
good children, not *town* children, but some 'guttersnipe'
of an orphan? Why wouldn't you? Plenty'a folks in this
town probably think a jail cell's just 'zactly where I belong."

Mason cleared away the remains of the meal. "Not
everybody thinks like that."

Liam scrunched down a bit farther in the cot, wiggling himself into a comfortable position. "Don't have
to be everybody, does it? If that Miss Ward keeps up,
us boys'll be on our way before you know it. Greenville
won't be no different, neither. New York'll be worse.
Trust me, there ain't nothin' good at the end of this line
for someone like me."

Standing up and coming to the cell doorway, Mason

stared. The boy spoke entirely too casually. Did he realize what he was saying?

"Miss Ward's only one person. Other folks want you to stay. I'll tell you, when Miss Sanders gets it in her mind to help someone, not even bossy old Beatrice Ward can get in her way." He knew firsthand how stubborn Holly Sanders could be, didn't he? The woman's will was as fierce as her heart was kind—he knew that best of all. "You'll find a family here, just you wait and see."

Liam gave an incredulous "Yeah," before rolling onto his back. "Only a matter of time before someone scoops up a prize like me."

Mason hated the jaded edge in Liam's words. "I know for a fact that Miss Sanders thinks you're smart."

"Well, she thinks you're noble or something, so we all know how misguided she can be." The boy pushed his cap down over his eyes and sighed.

Mason was ready to take him to task over his smart mouth but stopped, his curiosity overriding his annoyance. "And how do you know that?"

"Oh, she's always going on and on about you. 'Sheriff Wright this' and 'Sheriff Wright that' and 'we should all be grateful for how he saved our lives and all.'" He crossed one foot jauntily over the other, making the cot springs squeak again. "You're her hero."

It was more than a little disconcerting to have such facts cataloged by an eleven-year-old. "No such thing."

Liam pushed his cap back to stare at Mason. "Not according to her. Not when it comes to you. And she won't let nobody tell her different, so if you ain't figured out she's sweet on you, you're nowhere near as smart as I thought you were. I bet even Lizzie knows, and she's all of five."

The boy was right, but that didn't make it okay for him to be spouting off like that. "You're in way over your head there, mister." Just because it needed saying, he added, "Miss Sanders is a fine lady who's got better places to put her affections than the likes of me. And you'd best keep your opinions to yourself."

"I got an eye for such things. Take Miss Sterling, for example. She's had her heart broken bad. She never talks about it, sure, but I can see it just the same." He tapped his temple with the air of an expert, smirking under the brim of his cap. "My ma was the neighborhood matchmaker, she was. It's in the McLoughlin blood."

Mason was tempted to make good on his threat to close the cell door. "It could be tanned on the McLoughlin hide if you keep up talk like that. You wouldn't be the first boy I paddled for telling tales. I expect Miss Sanders has a few choice punishments for smartmouthed lads, too."

"Yep," Liam sighed, not a bit rattled, "Ma always said it was the truth that got denied loudest. She likes you. But it's more than that. You like her, too."

"She's a nice lady and a good teacher. We're friends."

Liam raised an eyebrow. "That ain't what I said."

"I know exactly what you said. And I've had about enough of that." Mason rattled the cell keys at Liam. "Hush up."

"'Course, she's not as pretty as Miss Sterling, but she's kind, and really smart. I sorta figured you for the kind to go for the lookers, though, seeing as—"

"Liam!" Mason slammed the keys on his desk and

sat down, trying to decide if it was more dangerous to keep the boy here or send him back to the schoolhouse to have a similar conversation with Holly. Evidently, he was smart enough to know when to quit, for Liam silently held up his hands in surrender and kicked back for a nap.

By rights Mason ought to be angry at the boy for his bald-faced nerve. The youngster was beyond irksome. Still, one clear truth held Mason's annoyance in check: Liam's conversational dodge—clever as it was—had simply shown how frightened he was of never being placed. The lad would do anything to keep from hoping a family would actually want him. Like him, Liam had learned the hard truth that life hurts less when lived alone.

But, Mason thought as his chest pinched at the freckled chin jutting defiantly out from underneath that newsboy cap, *did it really*? Did it have to, especially at that age? Especially if there was something Mason could do about it? Was that the real reason he'd said "yes" to the Placement Committee?

Lord, deliver me from this boy.

Almost ten seconds went by before Mason realized he'd just said his first prayer in years.

Holly pulled the box from under her bed and foraged through the piles of books until she found the volume she sought: *Illustrated Psalms*. It was a small burgundy volume, and the gilded letters on the front and side had lost nearly all their shine. The red ribbon marker was thin and faded with age, though it hadn't seen much use. The book had been a prize for perfect memorization of scriptures when she was younger. Lovely as it was, Holly always preferred her own Bible—the one with her name in Mama's lovely handwriting and with all her favorite passages underlined—to the slim volume of psalms.

Bringing the lamp to the center of her table, Holly sat down with the book and looked through the texts. David was such a valiant, imperfect figure in scripture. Her fingers found the 25th Psalm almost immediately:

Remember, O Lord, Your tender mercies and Your loving kindnesses,

For they are from of old.

Do not remember the sins of my youth, nor my transgressions;

According to Your mercy remember me,

For Your goodness' sake, O Lord.

She couldn't imagine any better way to show God's word to a man like Mason. He might chafe at the gift of a full, thick Bible, but somehow this little volume felt almost like a book of poems. They were poems, after all; deeply human, deeply emotional poems penned by a man whose life had taken as many turns and stumbles as Mason's.

Holly read the passage from Psalm 32 that Reverend Turner had preached the Sunday after the dam had broken:

For this cause everyone who is godly shall pray to You

In a time when You may be found; Surely in a flood of great waters

They shall not come near him.

You are my hiding place;

You shall preserve me from trouble;

You shall surround me with songs of deliverance.

She believed these words with all her heart—and she wanted to share them with Mason in the hopes of healing his. For Mason's sake and for her own, too, since she knew his heart had to heal before she could ever hope he might give it to her. Rebecca had spoken such truth: though she longed for Mason's love, she'd never been bold enough to clearly show her feelings. That had felt brazen. But speaking the truth, speaking mercy to a man who beat himself up while ignoring how others admired him—how could that be anything but good?

Holly held the volume in both hands and tilted it slowly forward, nearly laughing to herself at the "drawbridge" imitation. God's word was the strongest bridge she knew.

Holly thought for a long moment before reaching for her pen and inscribing the book. When she blew the words dry and tied the book shut with the new ribbon Rebecca had bought her, she felt…beautiful. Lovely in the eyes of God.

She would give him the volume. *As soon as you grant me the opportunity, Lord. But be quick, or my courage might fail.*

Chapter Eleven

Mason walked down First Street, trying to decide if he was delighted or annoyed. Supper at Bucky and Cindy Wyler's home had been a baffling mix of good home cooking—a treat for any bachelor—and aching affection. Cindy fairly glowed with the secret of her impending motherhood, and if Bucky didn't stop grinning like a fool, folks would certainly begin to guess. They were like any and every newlywed he'd ever met—full of hope and dumbstruck with love. Not that he begrudged either of them such enormous happiness, but it stuck in his craw the way all such domestic bliss did. His mind cast back to the orphans passing the candy in Gavin's store window—suddenly aware of how hungry they were. Being alone was tolerable when he could put companionship out of his mind, but hard to bear when it was displayed in front of him.

I've had that, he tried to remind himself. He'd been that way those first months with Phoebe, grinning as widely as Bucky did now. Folks were lucky to get a love like that once in their lifetimes, if at all. He'd let his one chance at love fall to ruin, and nothing could change those odds. The whole "'tis better to have loved and lost" opinion? Well, he never could quite agree with that, even if Holly would surely quote it to him if given the chance.

Holly. How many times had she come to mind tonight? She'd settled in his mind like a wisp of smoke, hiding in corners, unseen yet everywhere. How many times had he told himself that Holly Sanders was too delicate to share his life? Unless he kept away from her, he was bound to hurt her, fail her as surely as he'd failed Phoebe. Trouble was, Holly wasn't weak. She might be delicate, but glory if that woman hadn't shown herself to be strong.

And what had he done in response? He'd been downright mean on their return to the train tracks. He'd meant to drive off any tenderness on her part toward him…but all he'd done was prove to himself how fine she was, how courageous and determined—not to mention how quick she was to forgive and seek peace between them, no matter what he did. He should have gone down a block, should have gone out of his way so that he didn't have to see the light on in Holly's window. Instead, he found himself at the corner, standing, staring. *Like a kid in a candy store window,* he chided himself, but still did not move. Her home was like her—tidy, orderly, filled with fine things that were smooth and soft. His rough edges and broken pieces would never fit into her world, so why did she persist in looking at him the way she did?

Mason's heart slammed up against his chest when he saw Holly's curtains move aside and he recognized her silhouette in the window. He ought to duck away, only he couldn't make his feet move. He let out a breath when she left the window, only to nearly gulp it back in again when her door opened to cast a wedge of golden light out into the night.

"Mason?"

Did she have to use his name right now? *Don't, don't, don't.* But his cautions fell useless at his boots as he found himself walking toward her. Even cast in shadow, he could see the surprise in her eyes.

"Mason, that is you, isn't it?" She looked around, recognizing what he already knew: no one else was out and about. Her voice was hushed and startled, as if they'd not seen each other in a dozen years. As if he were some sort of delightful surprise. The helpless pull he felt around her, the sensation that was like thirst or hunger only different, surged up worse than ever. She was so small and tender, hang her, it wasn't fair. The deep night and the sapphire sky seemed too eager to coax him on.

"It's me." His voice was gruff, words choppy to match his near-stumbling steps. It felt like sliding down a mountainside, tumbling momentum pulling his balance out from underneath him.

"I'm so glad." The way her face changed when he stepped into the wedge of light was just about the most tempting thing he'd ever seen. "I was just thinking about you."

Now that was downright cruel. How on earth was he supposed to resist a notion like that?

"Oh, look at all those stars." She tilted her head up to the sky, stunning as it was tonight, then reached behind her to shut the door. It was a practical thing—one could always see the stars better from the dark—but it felt far too intimate to be standing here in the dark near her. "I love the April sky." She pointed up, naming some constellation he didn't hear. He was too busy staring at the perfect curve of her cheek.

It took him a moment to realize she was holding a book tied up in a ribbon and she was visibly nervous. He made her nervous—how did that somehow make it all the more unbearable to feel his own heart thumping like it was? He'd meant to make her scared of him, hadn't he? So why did that hint of anxiety make him want to comfort her? "What's that?" He blurted it out just to force more conversation between them.

She blushed, her thick brown lashes flicking down as she ran one hand over the too-pink ribbon. "It's a book," she whispered with a tiny breath of delight he felt in every corner of his chest. "It's a gift, actually." Mason was certain the world tilted around the moon when she added, "And, well, it's for you."

She held it out to him. She was trying to be bold and confident about it, but he could see through that in a heartbeat. Her eyes held an uncertain, wobbly daring he'd never associate with her in a million years. Mason took the book from her hands, and the one place where his finger touched the back of her palm sent such a jolt through him that he wasn't sure he didn't audibly gasp. The way she sucked in her breath, he knew a similar sensation had gone through her at the contact, too. He was losing control of the situation—he knew that—and couldn't bring himself to care.

Illustrated Psalms of David, the title said. The silver of the embossing glinted in the moonlight, giving the book a starlit quality. Psalms? Bible verses? He couldn't help but ask, "Whatever made you want to give me these?"

It seemed to be just the wrong question, for her face flushed even more. It was a curious thing; time seemed to slow down, stretching itself out to let him discover every detail. Mason could read the progression of emotions on Holly's face. She was startled by his question, as if he'd spied a secret she was trying to hide. Then she took a deep breath and decided to answer, chose to go ahead even though he could see clear as day that she was almost shaking. It near terrified him to see so much of her feelings, to know things he was sure he ought not to know.

"You." Her voice was high-pitched and unsteady, but she pulled in another breath and started again, stronger. "You need these. You think you don't, but you do. Read what I've written inside. That'll tell you best of all." She reached out and moved his hand to the tail of the pink ribbon.

The power of the flood's tide itself couldn't have stopped him from pulling on that ribbon. She'd inscribed a book to him. She, who loved books more than anything, was gifting him with one of hers. No one had ever done such a thing. Mason wasn't even sure he still owned a book, anywhere. Some part of him came loose with the bow; he could feel it.

"To Mason,
Who believes himself lost, but isn't.
God's eye never wavers,
A forgiven future always waits,
And the true heart knows a true hero.
Holly"

Holly truly thought she might faint. This was far too bold; this was a foolish girl's theatrics rather than any prompting of the Spirit. Holly shut her eyes, mortified, wishing she could even muster the strength to duck back into her house rather than stand here and face his rejection.

Then something rough and warm brushed her cheek. Holly's eyes flew open to find Mason's tentative finger following the curve of her jaw. His face was filled with strain, with a shocked sort of pain. At the same time, she could see easily behind the strain to something far more powerful. She couldn't be sure what it was; only that it was dangerous. When she raised her hand, she honestly didn't know whether it was to draw Mason's hand closer or to shield herself from the storm behind his eyes.

She couldn't breathe. She couldn't move. She'd never been so close to him, and the pull between them was so powerful she couldn't tell if it was seconds or hours before…

…before he kissed her.

Lightly, as careful as if she were glass, the roughness of his jaw brushed against her skin and she felt his lips whisper-light against her cheek. The whole world stopped; Holly's fingers shot straight out as if stunned. It was as if the rush of his breath against her cheek was the only thing keeping her from falling over. Her eyes fell shut and the startled world began to tip and spin in all directions. This was what all the fuss was about. This was why women waited decades for men to come home and why men went to war and why love truly did conquer all.

Holly felt Mason hesitate, and she panicked. There was no thought, no decision, just a powerful need to hang on to him for dear life. She could not bear to feel him shrink back, not now. She'd been given a chance to reach the other side of his somber wall, to peer over to see the man she'd always somehow known was inside. Holly grabbed his hand, determination roaring up from a new place in her ribs that burned so close to him.

He did pull back, but not far, and looked at her with eyes as startled as she felt. Truly, Holly felt as if the flood's wave had broken through a whole different kind of dam and swept them off their foundations. There was a moment, a terribly empty and yet incredibly full moment, when Holly had a clear look at the man inside Mason's battleworn shell. Yes, the man she'd dreamed of was there. Affirmation soared through her. "Mason…" But what was there to say? What words would fit into the huge deluge of this moment?

He opened his mouth to say something, and Holly thought at last she would hear the exquisite sound of him using her name. She knew that would be the only thing more powerful than the fire in his eyes right now. Instead of speaking, Mason lowered his head and kissed her full on the lips.

This was a man kissing a woman. Not the schoolboy joke meant to taunt a mousy girl, but a potent, powerful kiss. *If someone can die of bliss*…she thought as her whole body felt the touch of his lips. As if all of her had been waiting for all of this…and wasn't that true? One hand cupped her cheek where his finger had traced, careful yet insistent. He cared for her. She'd known it all along, no matter what he said. She wasn't a foolish girl seeing affection where it was not. She was a woman who'd been given the gift of understanding a complicated man's huge pain. Mason felt for her what she felt for him.

Just as she thought she might topple over, his hand slid around her waist. He was still holding the book, for she felt its corners press against her back. The thought of him embracing her with her gift in his hands was her undoing, and she slid her hand from his arm to wrap around his neck and pull him close.

It was exhilarating, terrifying…it was everything, *everything* all at once. Holly felt as if the sensation would swallow her whole and she would happily be consumed without a thought for the consequences.

There were consequences, weren't there? She couldn't possibly hold that thought as she felt them lean back together against her doorjamb. His arms were so strong, and she fit so wonderfully inside them. His kisses were fierce and tender at the same time; Holly startled herself by returning the kisses in kind.

He kissed her forever. At least, that's what it felt like. Without opening her eyes, Holly was certain the stars were careening around them, time stilled and speeding at the same time.

But then he stopped, practically growled and pulled— no yanked, for it was a nearly violent move—himself away from her. Holly whimpered from the shock of the withdrawal, bracing herself against the doorjamb. His eyes were wide and confused, darting from side to side as if in danger. There was no need for him to speak, for every inch of him shouted "What have I done?" as if he'd yelled it to her face.

"Mason…" The lack of him, after being so consumed by him, pummeled her.

He nearly flinched at the sound of her voice, taking another step back, running one hand down his face. She felt his next two steps away from her as if they were physical blows, her own hands going to her chest. With horror she realized Mason had the same wounded shock on his face Mr. Arlington had displayed just before he fell to the ground. All-consuming regret. *Regret*.

"I'm…" His voice was broken, filled with a panic she'd never heard from him.

"Mason…" She kept grasping for words that would not come, and yet every time he heard her speak his name, the pain in his eyes doubled.

"No!" he said, putting a hand out when she managed a step toward him. "No, don't."

Don't come near me. Her mind finished the sentence for him, the words scalding. Things had dropped from bliss to disaster in the space of a heartbeat, leaving her with only one word clanging in her head: mistake.

Mason shook his head. "That was wrong." He choked out the words as if they tasted foul. "This can never happen. Ever."

Holly started to ask "Why?" but didn't she have the answer already? He, in concert with every other man of her acquaintance, didn't want her. The moment had gotten out of hand, but once he'd come back to himself, he'd pushed her away immediately. She'd only been fooling herself to think she could have anything more than that—a stolen moment followed by regret.

Mason turned in a slow circle, like a cornered animal. "No," he said twice more under his breath. He couldn't even look at her, and that hurt most of all.

Mason was fighting for air, grasping for control he didn't have. He turned in a circle, trying to put the world back to rights when it had just burst apart in front of him. He looked anywhere but at her, anywhere but into the clear blue eyes that had pulled him under.

To feel so much after being numb for so long…It hurt. It pounded as hard as the years of grief, maybe even harder because it had been his own doing. The force of his yearning shocked him. It came up so fast, unleashed like some huge beast by the sheer tenderness of her inscription. *A forgiven future.* She'd managed to pick the words most able to shred his heart into a thousand wild pieces and he'd lunged at it. Grabbed at the ridiculous notion that such a thing was possible for him, reached for she who held it out to him.

Reached for that sweet, lovely lady as if he had any right to even hope for someone like her in his life. It was a thousand kinds of wrong, a million kinds of cruel and absolute bliss to kiss her that way. She was so perfect, so achingly kind and full of the wonder he'd lost years ago. When she'd reached for him, slipped her hand around his neck, he'd come undone. He found her irresistible. Blindingly intoxicating. He still wasn't sure how he managed to stop, and that frightened him most of all.

What have I done? He tried to pull in enough air to think straight, but nothing helped. He had absolutely no control over the storm raging inside of him. Mason, who always had a plan, who always saw the way out of any situation, was cornered with no escape. He felt too much for Holly Sanders. He could offer her nothing but wounds and scars, and while her tenderness might fool her into thinking she could heal him, he knew better. He was beyond healing. If he could manage one noble thing in this world, it should be to keep Holly Sanders from being sucked into the darkness of his life.

Tonight had shown him one truth: he couldn't be

near her. That boundless mercy of hers would be both their undoing. And that kiss? That achingly sweet kiss? It could never happen again. The forgiven future she offered? That was her misguided dream, not his bleak reality.

He turned, fully aware what an awful thing it was to walk away but unable to do anything else. There was no saving anything here—no point in even talking. He knew her; she'd find something tender to say and he'd be lost. There was nothing but hurt for her if he hesitated even one more minute.

Looking up, Mason spied the one thing capable of shocking his system into clarity. A bucket of ice couldn't have frozen his pounding heart more than the sight of Rebecca Sterling shutting the schoolhouse door.

She'd seen all of it.

Leave it to me, he thought with bile rising in his throat, *to hurt Holly even more.*

Mason twisted back to see if Holly's door was still open, but by some grace she'd already gone inside. Some part of his heart imagined he heard her crying, which wasn't possible from here. More likely she was pacing her sweet little house, as stunned as he, wondering what in the world had just happened. He looked down, almost startled to see the book he still held, the pink ribbon laced between his fingers. Mason cursed his lack of control, cursed the loneliness Bucky and Cindy's happiness had stirred up into a storm that left more ruin in its wake than the broken dam.

Miss Sterling was a friend of Holly's, so Mason doubted she'd spread any talk, but just seeing her reminded him how much worse things could have been. What if it had been Beatrice Ward or one of her cronies out for a stroll? Holly's reputation could have been ruined just because he wasn't strong enough to keep away from her as he should.

Well, his feelings for her, and hers for him, wouldn't be an issue any longer—he'd see to that.

Walking back to his house, Mason clamored for some kind of plan to set things right. He had no other choice than to cut himself off from her completely. The trouble was that there was only one way to do that, and it happened to call for doing the one thing that would make tonight hurt worse: he had to make her hate him. As long as she held him in her stubborn regard, she'd be able to unravel him when his guard was down. Hadn't she just proved that?

He looked at the book in his hand, ran his finger over the soft sheen of the ribbon. He'd read the book tonight—sleep would elude him, anyway—but come tomorrow, he'd give it back in such a way that she'd never forgive him.

It didn't matter that he'd never be able to forgive himself…he was already unforgivable.

Chapter Twelve

Holly sat in church feeling hollow and frail. Normally, Sunday mornings were among her favorite times. Worship was always sweet here. But today she sang the words of the hymn without attention, heard the words of the sermon but didn't listen. She couldn't get over how foolish she'd been. When God had brought her to the idea of sharing her faith with Mason, she'd been so bold, so arrogant that she'd actually thought that bringing Mason closer to God would bring him closer to her, too. She'd believed it might even be the first step in gaining his love.

Didn't she know better by now? Hadn't she learned that she could never be the sort of woman to catch a man's affections so boldly? To catch a man's affections at all? Who was she to think she could—or should—love Mason Wright?

Mason hadn't shown up in church with the rest of the Selection Committee. Mason hardly ever went to church, and she knew that. She'd always known that. Why had she made herself believe she could change him? Perhaps God could change him, and His word was in Mason's hands now, but that proved little comfort. Yes, she'd followed God's leading, and he'd accepted the book. As for her heart…The sting of that rejection was only doubled by the truth that she had only herself to blame. A mistake of her own fool notions, not God's prompting.

A hand on her shoulder pulled her from the dark cloud of her thoughts. Holly looked up to see Charlotte peering at her, Sasha decked out in Sunday best beside her.

"Are you all right, Holly?"

"Of course." Holly pasted a smile on her face and touched the bright yellow ribbon in Sasha's hair. She felt a pang as she wondered if her own hair ribbon was now haplessly in some mud puddle behind Mason's house. "Why do you ask?"

Charlotte raised an eyebrow. "Because you never sit in back and the service ended five minutes ago." She nodded around the empty sanctuary, then sat down beside Holly. "Sasha, see Mrs. Hicks in the doorway there? Why don't you ask her to take you out to your father. He's out by the lemonade, I'm sure." Every Sunday after church the Ladies' Society set out lemonade on the town square, but Holly couldn't bear the thought of being out there today. "What's troubling you?"

"I'm tired. So much has happened this week." That wasn't exactly a falsehood, but it wasn't a complete answer by any stretch. *If only I'd listened to my own good sense*, Holly wanted to say, *then I wouldn't have gotten my hopes tangled up in this miserable mess to start with*.

"Isn't that the truth?" Charlotte sat back, smiling. "It's been a whirlwind. A happy one, though. Sasha is wonderful. I'm so glad you listened when God gave you the idea to keep the children here. Sasha and I thanked God for you last night. Is it all right if she comes with me when I help out in the schoolhouse tomorrow? She's only four, but she loves being there and I don't think she'll be any trouble."

Yet more weight pressed down against Holly's weary shoulders. Her class was about to nearly double in size tomorrow, and she wasn't ready. She'd need a month of Sundays to pull her jumbled thoughts together. If she needed a distraction from thoughts of Mason, there were plenty to choose from—if she could manage to focus. "Of course she's welcome." Charlotte's happy face was a welcome reminder that Holly had managed to do some good. Acting on God's call to her had resulted in new families like Charlotte's. "She looks adorable this morning. And so happy."

"I'd forgotten how exhausting little girls can be." Charlotte paused, cocking her head to one side. "Are you sure you're all right?"

I have no idea. I don't know whether my heart is opening up or breaking in two. "Yes, I'm fine. Just tired and a bit anxious."

Rebecca, resplendent in her Sunday best, came down the church aisle with a frown on her delicate features. "I'm afraid I won't ease your mind. Holly, we have to talk."

Charlotte picked up on Rebecca's serious tone. "I'll leave you two to your business. See you tomorrow, bright and early."

Rebecca huffed as she perched on the pew next to Holly, who began to wonder if she'd leave the sanctuary before supper. "Sunday school isn't going well."

"Mary Turner is usually wonderful with the children."

"I'm sure she is, but Patrick and Liam are giving her fits, and it's only been ten minutes. Ned Minor's gone in there to help, but I think our problems extend beyond Bible classes."

Holly felt a headache blooming behind her eyes. "The days will be a challenge this week, no doubt about it."

Rebecca folded her hands. "Not just the days, I'm afraid."

"What do you mean?"

"I caught Liam coming in late last night. He's been sneaking out."

Holly really had chosen the best orphan to slip out and run for help during the robbery. "Sneaking out? To do what?"

Rebecca looked as if Holly's headache was catching. "He says 'nothing,' but I don't believe him. He had the look of someone who'd just learned a whopping secret. Or been up to serious mischief. When I pressed him, he gave me some clever speech about needing wide-open space, that being cooped up in the schoolhouse was making him 'itchy.'" She offered Holly a sympathetic look. "All the boys are rattled about not being placed, and I'm afraid it's coming out in unfortunate ways. I caught Patrick threatening to dump a cup of lemonade down Friedrich's back just now." She placed her elbow on the pew rail and rested her head in one hand. "And Miss Ward saw the whole thing."

Miss Ward would have volumes to say about that. Something involving hooligans in Sunday school and the criminal tendencies of vagrants, to be sure. "I half expect her to be standing in the back of the schoolhouse tomorrow morning taking notes. And not on vocabulary."

Rebecca managed a sad smile. "Oh, well, Liam showed some very fine vocabulary just now, and I'm sure Miss Ward was taking careful notes. Pastor Turner currently has him standing in one corner. Patrick is in the other."

Holly was almost afraid to ask. "And Friedrich? Tom?"

"Tom's the only one who *hasn't* been trouble. As for Friedrich, I mentioned his fine singing to Mrs. Turner, and won her good graces instantly. He's joining the choir." Rebecca's hands tightened on each other as she added, "If he stays."

Holly put a hand over Rebecca's. "Of course he'll stay. They *all* will." She yearned for the confidence she had yesterday, but it eluded her. Everything felt out of reach this morning…except for God's grace, and the certainty she felt through it that the children belonged in Evans Grove. "We'll place the boys and Heidi, I'm sure of it." She stood up and smoothed her skirts. "I suppose I could give the children such a heap of work they've no time to wander off. Would that help?"

"Honestly, I don't know what tomorrow will bring. For some of them it will be their first day in school."

"Their first day? So late in the year?"

Rebecca nearly grimaced. "Their first day *ever*."

Holly felt as if a giant mountain had just risen up before her. "Well," she said, pushing a stray hair back into place, "I always did say I enjoyed a challenge."

"Very good, Lizzie. That is indeed a fine 'L.' Did you know it's the first letter of your name?" Holly leaned down and wrote "Lizzie" is large capital letters on the top of Lizzie's slate. "Try to copy that."

Lizzie looked up at her. "What about Bobbins?"

Holly had to smile. "Bobbins is a very complicated name, so we'll save that for later."

One of the older town children didn't even bother to raise his hand—a sign the classroom's structure had been skewed out of control today. "Why does she get to bring a toy to school?" The injustice of it pinched the corner of the boy's eyes.

"Michael, we raise our hands in this class."

"Ma'am," he shot back far too sharply, "we don't get to bring toys to school."

She'd had dozens of such exchanges today. It seemed every single student was acting out frustrations, anxieties, or just plain orneriness over the nearly doubled size of the class. The room felt hot and tight despite the fresh spring day. It didn't help that she'd barely slept, and that Beatrice Ward had shown up ten minutes before the morning bell to give Holly her undisputed opinion on the "inborn weaknesses of the poor." Thank goodness Beatrice had left for a luncheon with Miss Sterling. Things were difficult enough as it was without a full day of her "supervision."

"Michael Walworth." She walked over and stood in front of—nearly over—the boy. "When *you* are thousands of miles from the only home you've ever known, when *you* have been witness to a horrible crime and been cooped up in this schoolhouse for days on end and when *you* are in a brand-new home with people who seem nice but you hardly knew before yesterday, then *you* can bring a doll to class, too." Her words were sharper than she would have liked, but Michael Walworth had stomped on every last nerve she had today.

Normally, her school days flew by in a flurry of activity and learning. Today crept along like molasses. When Holly finally stood up and signaled the end of the school day, everyone in the room—and probably even Bobbins—breathed a sigh of relief. The children tumbled out of the schoolhouse and into the yard like a stampede. Even Holly was desperate to get outside under the open sky and sunshine.

Watching the children—for it had been agreed that the last half hour of school would be out of doors for everyone to ease the tension of some children going home and others not—Holly spied Rebecca coming wearily up the street. She didn't envy Miss Sterling her luncheon one bit; Holly would be hard-pressed to say who'd had the more burdensome afternoon.

As they stood together supervising the play yard, Holly tried to offer sympathy between disciplinary commands. "How was luncheon? *Tom, put that stick down!*"

The resulting look on poor Rebecca's face said everything. "Very, very long."

Holly put a hand on her shoulder. "I'm sorry to say I'm not surprised. I got an earful this morning, and Miss Ward told me she was going to corner you for lunch. *Patrick, let the little ones play with that ball.*"

"And here I thought my father was the most opinionated soul on God's green earth. I believe Beatrice could best him." One corner of her mouth turned up. "Or if not, she could surely wear him down." Rebecca scanned the yard. *"Galina, don't go near that puddle!"* She turned back to Holly to ask, "How were the children?"

Holly shielded her eyes from the sun as she guessed how long it would take the "conversation" between Patrick and Michael to descend into an argument. Or worse. Michael had looked ready to throw a punch for the last hour. "Honestly? Awful. I think it will take you, me, Charlotte and maybe even Amelia Hicks to keep the peace tomorrow."

"Goodness. Maybe we should call in the sheriff instead."

Rebecca had meant it in jest. She couldn't know that would be the one thing guaranteed to make tomorrow more awful. "Oh, I don't think it's come to that," she managed, feeling the twist in her chest that had kept her up most of the night. "But I might send a few of them over to be locked up. *Liam, give that back!*"

"Don't tell Miss Ward. She'd march them over there herself. I'm glad the children are already outside. They'd best enjoy themselves while they can."

Holly glanced up at her tall companion. "What do you mean?"

"Simply put, we can't afford another incident. Not if the boys are to stand any chance of getting placed. While I'm not fond of the idea, the children are going to have to stay in the schoolhouse. No wandering, no one outside unless directly supervised." Rebecca glanced over at Liam. "Most especially our little redheaded shadow over there. If Beatrice ever found out he was wandering the streets last night, those boys would be on the next train to Greenville."

"That will be a challenge. They've been complaining about being cooped up as it is. I got an earful when I asked Liam about wandering about." Holly lowered her voice. "I hate to say it, but the way he talked, I don't think last night was the first time. And I don't think it was just Liam."

Rebecca crossed her arms over her chest. "I'm sure you're right. I know they're anxious, and feeling left out with so many of the girls placed, but we can't let it escalate into something that will ruin their chances. I hate to be so strict, but I don't see any other way to keep them controlled. Do you?" She looked understandably dubious. It would surely be a long night trying to occupy those boys and Heidi. "We have to place them— and soon."

Holly sent another prayer heavenward. *Father God, give these boys homes in Evans Grove.* She offered Rebecca the only idea that came to mind. "I have a copy of Jules Verne's *Twenty Thousand Leagues Under the Sea* in my house. The boys probably can't read well enough to tackle it on their own, but it would surely hold their attention if you read it to them."

"It can't hurt."

Holly scanned the school yard. "Most of the town children have gone on their way. Why don't you watch them out here for another half an hour or so while I go take care of a few things. I'll bring the novel back then, and by that time Amelia should be here with supper for you and the children." Holly was exhausted from the strain of the day and her lack of sleep. She needed a cup of tea, a few minutes of quiet, and time to collect her thoughts.

Mason had been in battle once or twice, knew the dread of heading onto a field with the intent of harming his enemy, but even that had been easier than the task before him.

You have to do this. How many times had he repeated that to himself as he walked down the street toward Holly's house? *There isn't another way. She's too misguided and kind. She has to hate you.* Mason looked at the book in his hands. He'd read it last night, trying to glimpse whatever it was in the words she thought would help him. There were familiar emotions in there that surprised him—hate, self-loathing, feeling as if God turned His back. He saw himself in too many pages. It didn't make sense to him that those same pages held such an illogical grace as well. How was it possible for a man to know such turmoil and failure and still trust God? Even praise Him? The words both intrigued and condemned Mason, making him curious for something he was sure he could never reach.

That was Holly's stubborn optimism coloring his thinking again, he knew that. Part of him wanted to pore over the baffling words a second time, but he knew better than to give in to such an indulgence. If he faltered now, he might never do what had to be done. Almost as if he couldn't help himself, Mason opened the book again. Surely it was no accident that his first sight was the jagged edge where he'd ripped out the page she'd inscribed.

Some time in the middle of the night, he'd ripped her inscription from the book. He'd give her back the book, but he couldn't quite bear the thought of giving those words away. Let her think he'd ripped the page out in anger, that he'd burned it. She didn't need to know that he'd been unable to let it go. Besides, it would serve as a reminder why he must never, ever let her that close again.

His chest constricted at the thought of how she'd

react when he showed her. He'd ripped her book. Holly loved her books, and he'd maimed this one—it'd be just as if he'd wounded her. *You have to wound her*, he reminded himself. *You have to hurt her in the worst possible way, or she'll just keep trying.* Steeling himself for the scene, Mason ran his hands down the edge of the ripped page, feeling it like a knife blade. If his words weren't enough to turn her eye from him for good, surely that would seal his fate. To throw her gift back in her face was cruel enough, but to damage it? That was unforgivable. *And that's what you need. You need to be unforgivable.*

Aren't I already?

Mason passed the school yard where Miss Sterling stood with her hands on her hips, frowning. She didn't see him pass—she was watching the children like a hawk. Mason braced himself, and knocked on Holly's door. *Just give me this, Lord; let her be angry.* He wasn't a praying man, and today surely wasn't the day to start, but it'd be so much easier if she was already furious at what he'd done.

Was it any surprise his measly prayer went unanswered? She pulled open the door with a look of stunned pleasure to see him. "Hello."

He started to say, "Hello," but stopped himself. As her gaze flicked down to the book in his hand, he thrust it out. "Take this back."

Her eyes darted back to him, wide with surprise. Time stood still long enough for him to watch the additional rejection take root. "I don't want this," he lied. "Certainly not from you." Her mouth opened, struggling for a response. "Take it." He shook the book again until she put forth one tentative hand, palm up.

Mason tossed the book almost carelessly into her opened palm, and she fumbled to keep it from falling to the ground. *Keep going.* He continued the speech he'd rehearsed the whole walk over. "Don't make such assumptions with me. Your gifts and your attentions aren't welcome. Not now, not ever. I won't have it."

She didn't respond, just slowly clasped the book to her chest as though he'd just sunk a knife there. Now he had to twist that knife.

"I'll not be pushed beyond my..." He was going to say "limits," but that made it sound like the other night had been her fault. Their kiss was no one's fault but his. She'd been nothing but kind, shown him nothing but grace. As he remembered her soft words, his carefully rehearsed speech left him. For one dangerous second he longed to snatch back the book, to take his barbs back and take her in his arms instead. The flash of fantasy was gone as quickly as it came, doused with the ice water of his own weakness. What Holly Sanders had really shown him was how fast and how far he could fall. No good would come to either one of them if he gave in. "Stay away from me." He spit the words out. "I've no place for you anywhere near me."

Her bottom lip began to quiver as tears gathered in her eyes. She usually had a mouthful of words for him, but he'd reduced her to silence. It would have been better somehow if she'd yelled at him, cursed him, thrown that book of hers back in his face or whacked him over the head with it. Instead, she quietly said, "If that's what you want."

He'd been sure he'd realized how much this would hurt, but he'd been so wrong.

What he *wanted*? In that moment, he felt that this

was the furthest thing from what he wanted. But it was for the best. He knew that for certain…didn't he? "It's exactly what I want."

Holly blinked, and one tear ran down her pale cheek. Why was she standing there, letting him berate her so?

"I've no eye for you. Never have. The other night was a slip. A fool move."

Holly swiped the tear with one hand while clutching the book with the other. "Do you really mean that?"

She was going to make him say it loud and clear, wasn't she? "Of course I do. It was a mistake. A weak mistake that meant nothing." He'd hoped to deal her this blow in private, to let her open the book and see his damage after he'd gone, but evidently God saw fit to make him stand and watch. "Open that and see how much I don't mean it."

Mason startled himself with just how hurtful he could be, but it wasn't so hard with his chest exploding in splinters of regret the way it was.

The gasp she made at the torn page nearly made him shut his eyes. It'd stick to him forever. "How could you?"

"Maybe now you'll wake up to just what kind of man I am. Stop your fool notions and leave me alone." He turned, at the limit of his ability to withstand the look on her face, and walked away.

Chapter Thirteen

Holly stood in the doorway, unable to move, barely able to breathe. Mason's disregard had always stung, but his scorn…his utter contempt of her nearly knocked her to the ground. She'd made a terrible, terrible error in giving him that book, in thinking she ever could even come close to bringing him past his pain. Instead, he'd drawn her right into misery with him.

The tears—great, wrenching waves of them—held back just long enough for her to close her front door and stumble into a chair. She opened the book to the ripped page, imagining him tearing it out and flinging it across the room in disgust. She'd put her heart on that page. She'd taken this herculean risk of telling him exactly how she felt and how she believed God loved him, and it had come to worse than nothing; it had come to humiliation. Not the public kind, but the deepest rejection she could fathom.

It hurt so much less when he ignored me, her heart moaned. Holly pushed the book away, lay her head down on the table and sobbed. Unable to hide it, Holly laid her deepest pain before God. She knew that as a child of the Father, she should grieve how she'd managed to push Mason further from faith. That hurt, but there was a deeper wound: there had been a moment Saturday night when Mason stared at her in a way no man had ever done. The longing in his eyes made her believe, for one wondrous moment, that she was beautiful. Not just beautiful, but desirable. She'd always, always felt such things beyond her reach. She'd convinced herself no man would ever look at her like that. And until last night, she'd come to a sad sort of peace with it.

With one breathtaking kiss, Mason had banished that peace and ignited a fierce longing in its place. He'd torn open the hunger to be loved she'd so carefully tamped down. He'd unleashed Holly's soul-deep yearning to be someone's truest affection.

And then he'd crushed it. His words just now made her feel as if she were so worthless he'd do anything to avoid her. It was worse than rejection; it was a condemnation.

When Holly finally raised her head from the table, the small and mousy girl had returned. Holly felt no courage, no peace, no purpose. Every decision seemed beyond her capabilities, and the conviction to place all the children loomed too great a task. It seemed an astonishment that any of them had been placed at all. She was just a plain country teacher trying to do things she should never have tried. Letting pride and vanity lure her into to being someone she wasn't.

The children. Her mind and heart kept going back to the children. They knew what blatant rejection felt like, didn't they? They'd been called worse names than she, had been branded bad seeds for no reason other than for lacking parents. She remembered the way the adults on the train had looked at Heidi's scars, and felt a deep, new affinity for the girl's pain. All the party dresses and trousers and scrubbed faces lined up at the placement meeting—why was there such punishment and humiliation in simply wanting to be loved? Holly looked at the book and felt an urge to yell. To throw her beloved volume across the room. Was it really any surprise that Patrick always looked ready to throw a punch?

There it was. Laid out in her own pain was the reason these children called to her in such powerful ways. They'd been overlooked, rejected not once but many times. She knew that on an intellectual level, but now her heart understood it. She understood them. She saw them, deep into their closed-up, scrubbed-up hearts, and knew a portion of their pain. It was a terrible, ugly thing to be unwanted. It felt like the blackest sin to let a child feel such pain.

There was the foothold she needed to crawl back out of the black hole surrounding her. As long as she could find some sort of use for this pain, she could endure it.

Holly picked up the book and slid it into the back of her dresser drawer. She didn't know what she was going to do whenever she saw Sheriff Wright—she made a resolution never to think of him as "Mason" again—but that was tomorrow's problem. Today she knew who she needed to reach and why.

Holly found Heidi out in back of the schoolhouse, practicing the letters they'd learned this morning. Hearing a sniffle or two as the girl hunched over her small slate, Holly bent down to peer behind Heidi's ever-lowered fringe of bangs. A pair of red, tearful eyes looked up when Holly touched her shoulder.

"What has you so sad?" It seemed silly to ask why

the girl might be sad. She had any number of good reasons to be crying given her situation and all that had happened. One didn't even need a home to be homesick.

"Lots." Heidi wiped her nose on her sleeve, prompting Holly to reach in her pocket for yet another handkerchief. She'd given out eight since Wednesday, and was going to have to clean out the stock at Gavin's tomorrow if this kept up.

Looking for somewhere to start in all that "lots," Holly peered at the slate. Heidi had written the word "Jakob," in an unpracticed hand. "The letter *K* faces the other way, but I like that name spelled that way. Lots of people use a *C* but the *K* stands up nice and tall in the middle like that. Do you want me to show you how to turn it around?"

Heidi didn't speak, but sniffed one more time and handed the slate and chalk to Holly. Settling herself in beside the girl, Holly wiped out the backward letter with her finger and replaced it with one facing the right way. "Who is Jakob?"

Again no reply, but her eyes brimmed up once more, reminding Holly of something Rebecca had mentioned earlier. Holly drew a small flower growing out of the top of Heidi's *J*. "Is Jakob your brother, sweetheart? The one Miss Sterling said was placed in Iowa?"

The girl did not venture a look up, but touched a finger to the flower Holly had drawn as she nodded.

"You must miss him something fierce. I have a brother, too, you know. His name is David and he runs a shipping business with my father in St. Louis. I haven't seen either of them in two years. It hurts something awful to be separated from family like that, doesn't it? Seems a shame the family that took Jakob in couldn't see their way clear to adding a sweet girl like you into their home. I'd stomp on back to Iowa and tell them to keep you close if I could." She put an arm around the girl as a tear left a shiny black splat on the corner of the slate. "Of course, then you'd never have come here, and I'm awfully glad to have met you, so I suppose we'll just have to trust that God knows what He's up to."

"I did it." Heidi whispered it quiet as a secret.

"Did what?"

"Split us up."

Holly tried to look in the girl's face but she turned away. "What do you mean?"

"I made it so they'd take him. I knew that would work, that he'd get placed on his own, but now I miss him something awful."

The realization hit like a rock in the pit of Holly's stomach. "Heidi, sweetheart," she crooned, brushing the child's hair back so she could see her eyes, "are you saying you split yourself up from Jakob on purpose so he would get placed?"

While no words came, the look and accompanying tears were the admission Holly needed. "Why on earth would your brother agree to something like that? Don't you think he misses you, too?"

"I tricked him. I stood far away from him at the station and got some of the other kids to hide me until the train pulled out." Her little lip quivered at the memory. "He didn't want to get placed unless I was taken in, too—he wanted us to stay together so he could look after me, like he always has—but I heard one of the grown-ups talking about how my face…" She touched one of the scars as tears ran down her cheeks. Rejection hurt so very much. Holly wanted to rail at the world for being so cruel to such a tiny, tender heart.

She pulled the girl into a fierce hug. "Oh, Heidi, I'm so very sorry." Holly grasped for words that would make it all better, but everything about that story seemed so desperately wrong. The world was such a broken place today. There weren't words to soothe either of their spirits. Not in all the books on all her shelves.

Some days it made more sense just to go back to bed. Mason had been a mess since his scene with Holly yesterday, his mind unable to focus on work. It wasn't as if he'd never had a bad day. Mason was used to bad days and sour moods. Usually, a ride out to see Bucky lifted his spirits, but now that seemed like the worst of ideas. The absolute last thing he needed was to see Bucky's lovestruck face. Instead, he'd settled on giving Ace a good brushing out in front of the office, hoping the menial task and sunshine would do them both good.

"When you're down, nothing's worse than someone else's happiness, right, Ace?" He stared into the palomino's big, brown eyes, hoping for a little commiseration. Ace simply nickered, stuffing his velvety nose into Mason's neck in the horse version of a hug. "You're always good company, boy." Out of the corner of his eye, Mason caught sight of the last thing he wanted to see. "But look out, here comes bad company."

Beatrice Ward was stalking up the street, headed straight for him with a scowl on her face. Of the half dozen reasons why she could be gunning for him this afternoon, each was worse than the other. He tipped his hat, unable to choke out a greeting.

"I'm ashamed of you, Sheriff Wright. Downright ashamed."

Mason put down the brush, sure this was going to be a very long and painful conversation. "And why might that be?" It was the very last thing he wanted to ask.

"Not only did you fail to attend services this Sunday, but now Reverend Turner informs me you have removed yourself from the Selection Committee." She peered down her nose at him with narrowed eyes. To this day he could never say what color the woman's eyes were because she was always squinting them in judgment.

"That's true." The only thing he had managed to accomplish this morning was to tell the reverend he was resigning.

"You are needed on that committee. You can't just shirk your duties. Especially not *now*."

That didn't bode well. "Now?"

She leaned in. "There have been thefts."

Mason remembered the time Miss Ward left her shawl in church and it slipped under the pew. In the two days it took to find it, she'd accused three separate people of stealing her best Austrian lace. She'd bothered him every day—as if he had nothing better to do than to track down fancy fabrics—until he'd crawled under the church pews himself to find the thing and hush up her groundless accusations. "What kind of thefts, Miss Ward?"

She puffed up and put a traumatized hand to her barrel chest. "My front gate has gone missing."

Now that was most likely a prank. Beatrice's front gate was a huge source of pride for the old woman, a fancy, "been in the family for decades" piece of wrought iron with a swirly "W" on it imported from somewhere back East. Mason had half wondered if one of the reasons the old woman never married was the awful prospect of having to replace it if she gained a new last name. Reverend Turner even once quipped that only God would be mighty enough to mess with the gate, for it had been bent in the storm.

Her face flushed red as she wagged a finger at him. "I know who did it. I do."

Whoever did it was the bravest soul in Evans Grove. Even in his worst moments, he'd not dare incur Beatrice Ward's wrath over that gate. "Who do you think took your gate?" As the words left his mouth, Mason's stomach turned to ice with the realization that *he* was one of the only other people in Evans Grove whose last name began with a "W."

"I should think it's obvious!" Her face was almost crimson now. Today was about to get infinitely worse, and an hour ago he hadn't thought that possible. He waited for her scathing accusation to erupt out of her. Knowing Beatrice, she'd rehearsed this speech the whole way on her walk from the hotel.

"It's those miscreants. Those horrid orphan boys."

Mason didn't know whether to be relieved or annoyed.

She didn't give him a moment to choose. "I tell you, Sheriff," she went on, her temper rising with every word, "you're the only other one capable of seeing those hooligans for the trouble they are. If we don't help that committee see reason, there's no telling what terrible influence those boys will bring to this town. My gate will just be the beginning. You'll see."

It wasn't completely impossible—Miss Ward hadn't hidden her opinion of those boys and if it wasn't just a

prank then meanness was the only possible motive behind a stunt like this—but it wasn't likely. "That gate is
heavy. I doubt those boys could get it far if it was them."

"It *was* them. I suspect it was that hooligan red-
haired boy."

"I don't think Liam is the type to do that." Liam
was a lot of things, but he'd shown himself too smart
to stir up the likes of Beatrice Ward. Mason had spent
enough time with the boy to be able to trust his gut on
that count. Liam was unruly, but he wasn't bad.

"Well, who else would it be?"

Any other day, he'd have left that wide open door
alone, but he was in just foul enough a mood to call
Miss Ward on her accusation. "Who's to say it wasn't
me?" He pointed to the "MW" monogram burned into
the side of his saddle as it sat on the hitching post.

It was the first time he ever saw Beatrice Ward's eyes
open wide. Who knew they were gray? Just as quickly,
they narrowed to irritated little slits. "Sheriff Wright,
you cannot leave that committee."

Being on that committee would mean spending time
with Holly Sanders, and right now there wasn't a worse
idea on God's earth. "As a matter of fact, I'm needed
elsewhere and you all are doing a fine job." He hoisted
the saddle back onto Ace. If nothing else, it was a good
idea to give Miss Ward the impression that he had someplace else to be. "I'll not be missed. Seems to me if
anyone needs to warn Evans Grove about the perils of
placing orphan boys, you—"

She angled herself in front of him. "You simply cannot!"

Mason was sure it never even occurred to the old
biddy that she didn't have any authority to order him on

or off the Selection Committee. "The way I remember it, Mayor Evans did the appointing. Why don't you go talk to her about your concerns?"

She sniffed. "I've already made my views known to the acting mayor."

Clearly Mayor Evans hadn't been able to make her see sense, so that meant that the impossible task came down to him. He finished a buckle on Ace's saddle and turned to the old woman, trying to smile when all he wanted to do was grit his teeth. "Miss Ward, the honest truth is that I have no evidence that those boys have done a single thing wrong since they stepped foot into this town. And with that being the case, I have no opinion where those boys go. I can't possibly say what's best for them or for the families that might take them in, and I have my hands full here. How can I see to law and order if I'm going to meetings about youngsters all the time?"

"Mr. Wright, we are all pressed for time. Ephraim always said, 'there's time enough in every day to do God's will.'"

If Mason were a betting man, he would have wagered his badge that the last thing God wanted was him near Holly Sanders. He was feeling like it'd be better to have two states between himself and that schoolhouse already. Some part of him was in a full-blown panic about what he'd do if he saw her again—*when* he saw her again. "I'll head over to your house later today and see if the thieves left any clues. Maybe I'll find something that will lead us to your missing gate."

"It's not missing, Sheriff, it's *stolen*." She puffed herself up again the way she always did before making some pronouncement. "I'll have you know I have prayed for the souls of lawless thieves who took my gate. The Bible tells us to pray for our persecutors."

Mason was feeling a mite persecuted himself at the moment, but swallowed the "Should I pray for you, then?" remark nipping at the back of his mind. "I'll be sure and tell you if I find anything."

"You be sure and show up this afternoon at our committee meeting, that's what you should be sure and do." She pointed up at him, for he had a good foot over the old woman.

"I wonder if you haven't heard me clearly, Miss Ward. I'm not on the committee any longer. I've already spoken to Mayor Evans."

"So she told me. And I already told her, she cannot excuse you from the committee. It just won't do. I'll expect you at four o'clock." She opened the little pendant watch that hung from a fussy pin on her shawl. She'd accused someone of stealing that once, too. "That should give you more than enough time to gather evidence against those vagrants."

Mason blinked, the incongruity of her demands smacking him like an open palm. She was chiding him to be punctual to a committee designed to place the very boys she'd accused of theft. He'd live ten lifetimes and not figure how that old woman's mind could fit facts together the way it did.

"I'll not be there, ma'am." He words were polite, but he put enough edge in them to make his point. *I'll be in Texas if you keep this up.*

"Nonsense. You'll be there." As if her word commanded the very sun to rise, Beatrice Ward turned and trotted down the street with an air of achievement that sent Mason's head to shaking. For the next five minutes, he kept shaking his head, trying to erase the image of tiny Miss Ward hauling him down Liberty Street by his ear at quarter to four.

Texas was looking better by the minute. Sure, he thought Liam was a fine boy and deserved a chance at a better life. All those kids did. It just couldn't be his task to make it so. Things had gotten too complicated, and while some part of him felt like he was letting Liam and the others down, he knew he couldn't stick it out. Someone else was going to have to stifle Beatrice's continual accusations. After all, the line of people who might take her gate out of sheer meanness could stretch clear around the block.

Chapter Fourteen

"He can't leave the committee." Rebecca gave Holly a concerned look as they packed up the school things. "I think he's the only one holding Miss Ward in check." The daily transformation of schoolroom-to-living quarters had already become tedious. Amelia Hicks and the reverend were outside supervising the children in their precious outdoors time, and Holly reveled in the quiet, remembering that at least she had the chance to go home to her tranquil house afterward, where Miss Sterling could only look forward to another night of keeping the peace. Even her graceful beauty couldn't hide the dark circles Holly could see building under Rebecca's eyes.

Holly began stringing the line that would hold a quilt to serve as a wall between where the boys slept and where Miss Sterling and Heidi made their beds. "Mr. Brooks is a powerful presence. Surely he can keep Miss Ward in balance."

"Not as well as the sheriff can." She stacked slates on the shelves at the side of the room. "I know her type. She'll find a million ways to stall the process until it looks like no one wants the boys. Oh, she'll pretend to be seeing to their welfare, to be 'careful,' but she'll come up with some way to convince everyone else to come to her view. Mr. Brooks will help, but Miss Ward will only think of him as a meddling outsider. I know Mayor Evans wants to help the children, but she has to choose her battles with Miss Ward, and I think she's suspicious of why Mr. Brooks is still here."

Holly had to agree. New to town as she was, Rebecca had sized up the community with startling accuracy. Pauline was so stretched holding the town together that even her usual diplomatic ways hadn't disguised her distrust of the banker. The loan was a wonderful thing—and Holly was sure Pauline would ensure its wise use—but it was becoming clear to everyone that tensions were running high. They certainly couldn't count on Pauline and Curtis Brooks banding together against Beatrice.

Rebecca caught Holly's frown and sat down with a weary sigh. "I'm sorry, I don't mean to be so judgmental. Mercy, I sound just like Miss Ward when I talk like that." She wiped stray locks of golden blond off her forehead. "I'm just so worried."

Holly left the quilt and sat down beside her. "I am, too. It's so hard on the children to feel even the least hint of being unwanted." From the moment she realized her affinity with the orphans' rejection, Holly's resolve to see them find homes in Evans Grove had doubled, galvanizing her with a core of determination and purpose she didn't know she had. She still wasn't sure that was enough to allow her to seek Sheriff Wright's reinstatement onto the committee. Truth was, she was deeply relieved when Reverend Turner told her just now that the sheriff had asked to be excused. The longer she could put off seeing him again, the better. "What about asking Mr. Gavin from the general store to join the committee? Miss Ward respects him." With a wry grin, Holly added, "As much as she respects anyone."

"If I hadn't heard what Reverend Turner just told me, I'd say that might work."

"What did he say?"

Rebecca cast a wary glance toward the schoolhouse door, then lowered her voice. "Miss Ward's gate went missing last night and she believes it was stolen."

"Stolen? Who'd steal Beatrice Ward's gate?"

"If you ask Miss Ward, it could only be Patrick, Friedrich, Tom, or Liam."

Holly felt a scowl bloom across her forehead. "That's absurd. What would those four boys want with a heavy wrought-iron gate? It's bent, besides. It fell over in the storm." She looked around the room. "And really, where on earth would they hide it?"

"I don't know, but I suppose in an hour we'll all hear her theory." Rebecca put her head in her hands. "I can't bear the thought of her undermining everything when the children could be so happy here." Tears threatened at the edge of the woman's words. She needed every ally she could find to fulfill her mission, and she wanted so badly to keep those boys from going on to Greenville. "We only need a few more days to get the boys placed, I'm sure of it. They just need a bit of hope, and Miss Ward seems dead set on squashing it. Reverend Turner said she made some horrible comment about poverty breeding sin. I wouldn't wonder if she's started some awful rumor already."

Holly wrapped an arm around Rebecca. "We're all used to Beatrice's noise. Her bark is much worse than her bite, and somewhere down inside she really believes she's doing what's best." Holly couldn't believe her own words. Had she become so hurt by Mason that she'd defend Beatrice to avoid the pain of seeing him? What kind of selfishness was that?

"I've seen this happen before. It only takes one person to plant suspicions. Getting the children placed is hard enough when there isn't someone undermining it. I don't know how to fight this without Mr. Arlington."

"We'll be fine."

Rebecca let out a sigh of resignation. "I don't think so." She looked at Holly. "Won't you talk to the sheriff? I think he'll listen to you."

I'm the last person he'll listen to, Holly wanted to say. The desperation in Rebecca's eyes pulled the unwanted words out of her mouth. "I'll go talk to him and see if I can't convince him to stay on the committee." It wasn't as if he could hurt her further—he'd done all the damage she was capable of bearing already.

"It will only be a week, maybe less. If we can't place the boys by then…" She sighed again, wiping her eyes with a handkerchief.

"He can manage one more week." With a smile she didn't feel, Holly added, "Sometimes I think his only entertainment is arguing with Beatrice, anyway. And I'm sure it won't even take a full week once people realize what good boys those four can really be."

"For cryin' out loud, I didn't mean to knock you over!" Liam's voice boomed as the schoolroom door burst open to reveal Reverend Turner holding Patrick and Liam by the elbows. Liam sported an angry glare and a bloody nose.

"You did, too!" Patrick yelled, pulling against the reverend's grip.

"You broke my nose, you big lug!"

Holly and Rebecca shot to their feet just as Liam wiped his bloody hand down his last clean shirt.

"Don't be such a—"

"Boys!" Rebecca barked, thrusting her handkerchief at Liam. "Sit. Now. And hush up, the both of you."

Fifteen loud and bloody minutes later, Holly found herself walking toward the sheriff's office with slow, dreadful steps.

Mason stood in the middle of the street and braced himself against the gaping hole opening up in his gut. Of all the things in the world to endure, Holly Sanders coming up the street toward him with that tortured set in her shoulders seemed the most cruel. He couldn't tell if he wanted to yell at her to turn and go back, or just get on Ace now and gallop off. Hang it all if that woman didn't keep poking herself in his life like a wound that wouldn't heal.

"You can't step off the committee." She didn't even meet his eyes. He never dreamed that would bother him as much as it did. "Beatrice Ward is on the warpath about the boys. If she gets her way, they'll be packed off in short order. We…Miss Sterling needs you."

He had to laugh at that. Miss Sterling wouldn't benefit one whit from his opinions or his endorsement. And as for Holly… "You don't. We both know I don't bring anything to the table here. And you know as well as I that Beatrice is all roar and no claw."

"Those boys need families. They need homes, here." She looked up at him then, and the black void in his gut threatened to swallow him whole. "Surely you can stand me for the few days it will take to see them placed."

"It's not what…" Only it was, wasn't it? Just not the way she thought. And the wretched truth was that if he told her the real reason he had to stay away from her, it would make things far worse than they already were. Her cursed persistence was his worst enemy here—if he didn't keep hurting her, she'd never stay away from him. He'd wounded her fiercely the other night, and she was still standing here pleading for him to help save those youngsters. How much pain was this woman willing to take? "It's not that." The words hung weak and false in the air. "You don't need me."

Her glance fell to the ground and she wrung her hands. Mason felt their twisting in his chest. "Miss Sterling has had to get very strict with the children," she admitted. "She's got good reason to think we won't be able to control them much longer. We need the sheriff on our side, can't you see that?" He could have guessed that it was only his badge that kept him on the committee.

He stood there, knowing he'd give in and follow her to the church parlor but trying to dig his heels in and turn around just the same.

She persisted. "It's difficult, I know, but those children deserve our efforts."

Difficult? He deserved every second of torture her eyes gave him. More.

"Don't go. Please."

Without another word, he followed her to the church. While he was sure he already knew his limit, Mason couldn't help thinking he was about to relearn just how much pain he could stand.

* * *

"Change of heart?" Reverend Turner shook Mason's hand as they settled into seats around the table in the church parlor.

"Something like that."

"I told the sheriff we simply could not function without him on this committee," Beatrice pronounced, sure she had persuaded him. It wasn't worth the air in his lungs to try and correct her.

"I'm glad you haven't left us," Pauline Evans said with a genuine smile. "We've no small task ahead of us and we need everyone's help."

"It's no less than our Christian duty," Beatrice said. "Pastor, I do hope you'll open us in prayer?"

Mason bowed his head with the rest of them, sure God was tolerating his sin for the sake of those children more than welcoming any measly contribution he might make. He recognized one or two phrases of the pastor's prayer from the verses in Holly's book. Why must the words "grace" and "forgiveness" punch their way into his life right now? A relentless, unconditional love that sought the best for every soul no matter the circumstances—the more impossible Mason considered these ideas, the more his heart began to crave them. Grace. Forgiveness. Love. With every hearing, the craving—and the pain of their lack in his life—grew stronger.

Curtis Brooks spoke first after the prayer. "Miss Sterling, those boys haven't made the best first impression, but we haven't given them much of a chance." Mason gave the banker points for politely ignoring the way Pauline Evans bristled at the word "we" as if Mr. Brooks himself was part of the town. "How can we change that?"

"I've been thinking about that," Miss Sterling replied. "What we need is for the boys to meet families outside the formal atmosphere of a placement meeting. And frankly, they need to get more physical activity. They're worried and isolated, and it's making them antsy."

"Yes, it is." Holly was eager. "Absolutely."

"Any boy would behave badly under the circumstances they've been forced into." Mr. Brooks looked around the table. "Surely you can see that?"

Mason watched Miss Ward's eyes narrow at the question. She believed those boys naturally bad, but she wouldn't go so far as to utter such an unChristian thought in the church parlor. She hadn't been shy about voicing that opinion in his office earlier, though, and if he knew Beatrice, her scorn would resurface with the first step past the church's door. His inspection of her house had, of course, turned up nothing to indicate foul play regarding her gate.

"I've had just the same thought, Miss Sterling, and I believe I may have a solution." Mayor Evans spread her hands on the table. "What if we formed the boys into a chore crew, and assigned them to help folks with repairs the loans have funded? It's lots of activity, and there are dozens of homes and stores and such that still need work. They could lend a hand for a few hours after school each day."

Holly clearly loved the idea. "They'd feel useful, they'd get to work with people, and they'd have someplace positive to put all that energy."

"Liam's been more than eager to help out at my office," Mason added. "These boys aren't afraid of hard work. That lad shows up and asks for something to do every moment he can get away. I think it would work."

"They'd need constant supervision," Miss Ward warned.

"I'm sure Wyatt Reed and his folks could use a hand on the ranch. Dick and Peggy Carson still haven't replaced their front steps." Reverend Turner sighed. "With Marcus gone, I was hoping they'd come to the placement meeting." Marcus Carson's death had been one of the hardest to stomach. The raging waters had pulled the teen off his feet and bashed his head against a stone—with Dick and Peggy looking helplessly on. Mason would remember the torture of hauling Marcus's lifeless body out of the creek for the rest of his days. Where was the grace and forgiveness that day? Why hadn't a boundless Heavenly love spared that life?

"Marcus wasn't much older than these boys," Holly offered. "Maybe it was just too hard then. But they could use the help and I'm sure one of these families might make a connection."

"It's a splendid idea, Mayor Evans," Curtis Brooks agreed. "Everyone gains. I commend you."

Pauline's smiles were few and far between these days, but the woman managed a terse, strained one at the compliment. Mason had to agree. She'd earned it with some mighty creative thinking. She really was doing Robert's memory proud.

"I think we may have our solution, then." Miss Sterling smiled. "Pastor, can you and Mayor Evans work up a list of suitable jobs and families?"

"I went over the loan applications last night, and I've got four or five in mind already." Pauline pulled a list from her pocket. Mason decided he'd make sure Pauline's name made it onto that list. Her house had taken some damage and with Robert gone, she wasn't able to get the work done herself. She wasn't one to take help quickly, but this was an ideal circumstance to give her a hand without wounding her pride.

"Sheriff, I trust you'll see to the supervision?" It never ceased to amaze Mason how Miss Ward managed to look down on him when he was far taller than she. "We'll need strong men to keep those orphans in line." Did she have to take every opportunity to refer to them as "orphans?"

Mason tried to think of a way out of saying yes, but Holly's pleading eyes stole his resolve. He'd never wanted to run from anything more and yet been so completely unable to do so. "I'll see to them. They'll be no trouble," he choked out, sure that wouldn't be an easy promise to keep.

Miss Sterling steepled her hands. "And then there is the issue of Heidi. She's very handy with a needle and thread, but I don't think a chore crew is the place for her."

"I think I can line up some mending jobs for her. Or cooking and cleaning help." Holly laid her hands on the table. "But there's more. I have something about Heidi I need to discuss." When Miss Sterling gestured for her to go on, she took a deep breath. Whatever it was, the subject was emotional for Holly. Mason wished he were anywhere but in the room watching concern furrow her brow in that tender way she had. "Heidi's confided to me that she deliberately separated herself from her brother at the train's last stop. Up until then, he'd sabotaged every chance at a placement that didn't include her. She felt he'd be better off without her, so she tricked him with the help of some of the other children so that he could be placed."

"That's terrible!" Pauline gasped.

"She believes her scars keep anyone from wanting her. She feels she's too ugly to be wanted by a family. To bear that much rejection, and then give up her brother..." Holly's eyes teared up and Mason found himself hoping the ground would just rise up and pull him under.

"This is the kind of scorn these children suffer. Really, is it any wonder that some of them act out in the way they do?" Miss Sterling looked around the table, catching everyone's gaze. "Can't we do whatever is possible to keep these boys and Heidi from the end of the line?"

Miss Ward took off her spectacles and laid them on the table. "These children are in desperate need of moral guidance. We'll have to be absolutely scrupulous in terms of who is supervising them. It can't be just anyone."

"I'll be glad to see to Heidi's tasks," Holly offered.

"I think it's best I see to that myself," Rebecca declared. "She's obviously very troubled by her situation; I'll want to keep her close." With that settled, the meeting soon drew to a close. Mason watched as Holly headed to the door as soon as the closing prayer reached its "Amen." He watched her go, wondering how it was possible that as awful as it was to be near her, it hurt even more to watch her walk away.

Chapter Fifteen

Two days later, as Mason was coming out of the general store with a new set of door hinges for the chore crew, he stopped in his tracks. Liam was coming out of Doc Simpson's office. Holly Sanders had her arm around the boy's shoulder and his right hand was wrapped in white gauze. Liam was putting on a brave face, but it was clear the boy was shaken. Liam had been hurt? It didn't take two seconds for Mason to ditch his "steer clear of Holly" policy and trot up to the pair.

"What happened?" he asked, bending down to peer at the injury.

"Tom can't work a saw for nothing," the boy growled. "I told 'em not to put him on the other end of that thing. He's not strong enough and he keeps coughing."

Mason looked up at Holly for a further explanation. That was a mistake. The worry in her eyes made his stomach do flips, reminding him why he'd made the "steer clear of Holly" policy in the first place.

"They were cutting fence posts at the Martin place and the saw…slipped."

Liam held up the wounded hand. "I got twelve stitches. What's Tom got for *his* trouble?"

"Tom feels terrible about what happened, Liam. You know that." Holly's hand rested firmly on the boy's shoulder.

Liam rolled his eyes. "He fainted. Fell right over on account of all the blood."

It was then that Mason noticed the bloody smudges all over Liam's pants and a few on Holly's skirts. That poor woman's clothes wouldn't last a fortnight at this rate. "Miss Sanders here, she just stayed cool as a cucumber and tore up Mrs. Martin's apron to wrap around my hand. Mr. Arlington woulda said she was 'battle-tough' if he'd have seen it." He nudged Mason with the shoulder on his good side. "It was gruesome. I thought Mrs. Martin was going to faint herself."

"She was a bit shaken by the whole thing," Holly offered. "It was an awful mess, but Mr. McLoughlin still has all his fingers."

"No thanks to Tom," Liam interjected.

"Any day you get to keep your fingers is a good day." Mason peered at the bandage. "So you've got some whopper stitches under there, huh?"

"Huge." Liam bugged his eyes wide. "I haven't cussed like that since—"

"You cussed in front of Miss Sanders?" Mason cut in, his eyebrows creasing in disapproval. "You know better than that."

"I left the room," Holly conceded.

Mason stood up, hands on his hips. "You cussed so bad Miss Sanders had to *leave the room?*" He nearly growled the question.

"No, she had to leave because she'd used up all her battle-tough and was feeling wheezy."

Mason raised an eyebrow at the teacher.

"*Woozy*," she corrected. "I do have my limits. And in Liam's defense, it was an awfully big needle."

"Huge," Liam emphasized. "Like I said, I haven't cussed like that since—"

"I get the picture." It had become clear Liam was over his pain and ready to milk his injuries for all the pity he could get—especially from Miss Sanders. He'd come to know Liam well enough to see where this was heading. "I guess you'll have to stay after school and study some more while the boys hold up the chore team without you."

Liam looked ready to argue the point, but it was the schoolteacher who spoke up next. "We've thought about that," Miss Sanders offered in a tone that told Mason she'd already come to the same conclusion he had. Evidently even before he had, for Liam seemed sure of gaining extra time at the sheriff's office already. The notion of Liam and Holly in cahoots behind his back was unsettling indeed.

"You get to deputize me for real, just like you said before." Liam looked delighted. Mason swallowed hard.

There were a dozen reasons why Mason didn't have time for this, but the boy's eyes and Holly's apologetic smile wound their way around the last of Mason's resistance. "I was hoping you could take Liam on. An apprenticeship of sorts since he can't be part of a chore team now." Holly clasped her hands behind her back, uneasy around him. Good. It was best if she stayed that way.

"It was my idea," Liam offered, chest puffing up as if ready for a silver star to find its home there.

Mason settled his hat farther back on his head and raised an eyebrow at Holly. "Was it, now?" Holly surely knew Liam's fondness for the sheriff's office; even Mason had begrudgingly come to enjoy the company, unproductive as it was. The "apprenticeship" had other benefits, too: If Beatrice was going to persist in her criminal theories, what better place to sequester the potential ringleader than under the sheriff's thumb? Mason looked at Holly, looked at Liam, and tried to remember why he ought to be irritated at becoming a babysitter.

Glory, but I'm getting soft.

Another glance at the boy only made it worse. No one that young should feel like they were being traded around like livestock. "What if I tell you it was my idea?" he said to Liam. "What you don't know is that I'd asked Miss Sanders and Miss Sterling to release you into my custody even before you went and got yourself hurt." It wasn't true, but Mason couldn't help feeling the boy needed to feel as though *someone* wanted him. Liam had spent the last two days being pawned off to the next available supervisor.

Liam turned and looked at the teacher. "Can I go now?"

"Now?" Mason was thinking this would start tomorrow, not immediately.

Holly turned Liam toward her. "Sheriff Wright may not be ready for a deputy just now." Mason hated how every time Holly said "Sheriff Wright," his mind cast back to that startling moment where she'd called him "Mason" for the first time.

"No, it's fine." He cocked his head in the direction

of the Martin place. "We'll deliver these hinges to the other boys and then you and I need to check out a crime scene."

"A crime scene?" Liam looked as if that were the most exciting invitation he'd been issued in years.

"The Gavins' wheelbarrow went missing the other night."

Holly frowned, exchanging a quick glance of concern with Mason. "Something else?"

"Swiped it right off their back stoop while they slept." He turned to Liam, just in case a flash of nervous guilt crossed the boy's face. It didn't, and Mason wasn't surprised. He couldn't prove anything at this point, but his gut—and maybe just a little of his heart—told him Liam was innocent. "Crafty types, these bandits."

"Not crafty, just crazy," Liam offered. "They don't take anything worth taking. You can't fence a wheelbarrow. You can't fence a fence gate, either, now that I think about it." The boy thought he was being clever, but he'd just incriminated himself by admitting he knew how thieves worked. It was a good thing Beatrice wasn't here. She'd have ordered him locked up on suspicion alone. Holly had the same thought, her eyes darting up the street in the direction of Beatrice's house and her now gateless front fence.

Mason peered down. "And just how would a young man such as yourself know about fencing stolen property?"

"You hear things." Liam was smart enough to catch on to what he'd just done, snapping his mouth shut so fast, Mason though he heard the boy's teeth rattle against each other.

Holly's frown deepened. Mason cocked his head in

the direction of his office. "I think we'd best start right now. You can tell me all you've heard as we walk." He tipped his hat in Holly's direction. "You thank Miss Sanders for her good care of you now and we'll be on our way."

"Obliged, ma'am." The boy had a way of sounding like an eleven-year-old and a fifty-year-old at the same time. Hang it all if that didn't make Mason like him that much more.

Mason kept things quiet with Liam on their walk back to his office. The silence gave the boy—and himself—time to think. After Mason pulled the door shut behind them, he motioned for Liam to take the chair in front of his desk. Mason noticed the wary look Liam gave the pair of prison cells behind them. It was no accident the person sitting for questioning in Mason's office faced those cells—they were mighty effective incentives.

Mason hung his hat on the peg by the door, unholstered his gun, and sat on top of his desk facing Liam. He towered over the boy in that position, his knees level with Liam's skinny shoulders. "How's about you tell me what you're up to." He tried to make his words firm but kind.

Liam's chin jutted out. "I ain't up to nothing."

"You are. Don't take me for a fool, son. I could be your best friend or your worst enemy in all this, so you'd best choose wisely. Now what are you up to?"

Liam's eyes darted around the room before a quiet "Okay" slipped from his lips. Mason crossed his arms over his chest, waiting. "I did fix it so's Tom would nick me, only I didn't figure he'd be such a klutz and near cut off my thumb like he did."

"Why'd you go and do a thing like that?"

"I hate being with those boys. Patrick's nothin' but a big bully, Tom's always whining, and Friedrich—I can't hardly understand him when he does speak, which he doesn't ever anyways." Boys that age could be rough and cruel; the way Liam sank into the chair spoke more about that kind of pain than his hand. "At least in the schoolhouse they couldn't get at each other—and me. I'm glad to be outside, but it's worse in lots of ways."

"So you fixed it so you couldn't work with them, then made sure Miss Sanders remembered how much you like it here, is that it?"

The boy shrugged his shoulders. "Seemed as good a plan as any." Liam wanted to be with him. The way Liam found a reason to show up here nearly every day, was it that much of a surprise? The notion wiggled its way under Mason's ribs to settle there with an uncomfortable warmth.

"That was until Tom nearly cut off your thumb." Mason held out his hand to inspect the bandage. Liam's purple swollen thumb barely peeked out of a neat nest of white gauze. "Can you wiggle it?"

Liam did, but winced. "Miss Sanders said I should thank God for sparing my thumb when I say my prayers tonight."

"Miss Sanders is right." The image of those feisty boys all lined up on their knees at their beds almost made Mason laugh. "You say prayers before you go to bed?"

"Well, Mr. Arlington had different ones than Miss Sterling, but it's much the same thing. I'm not much for that sort of thing, but I go along. Ma'am says we ought to pray for Mr. Arlington's soul, and I figure I owe him that much." He wiggled the thumb and winced again. "Miss Sanders, she told me she prays every morning and every night. Seems a bit much to me, but she's so nice and all." He looked up at Mason. "Do you say prayers before you go to bed?"

Now there was an enormous question—one with an answer that had grown more complicated in the past few days. Mason shrugged, shifting his weight. "Did a while back. My life was different before I came here. Made more sense then than it does now." Was that still true? Mason tried not to ponder that.

"What changed?"

Mason grunted. "The way I see it, this conversation is supposed to be about why you got yourself off the chore team, not the state of my soul."

"They're connected." Liam settled himself in the chair as if he were about to have a man-to-man talk.

Mason didn't even welcome the boy-to-man version of this conversation. "And how is that?" As the words left his mouth, he realized his comment would only invite more conversation from Liam. He should have stuck with a declarative "No, they're not," but the boy had a way of connecting life that hijacked Mason's curiosity.

"Miss Sterling always said if ever I was upset about something, that I should talk to God about it. Mr. Arlington and Miss Sanders said pretty much the same thing."

"That's good advice." It felt disingenuous to be counseling the lad to prayer when he'd barely spoken a handful of words to God in almost a decade, but this wasn't about him.

"It didn't seem so to me. I mean, what's God gonna do about a bunch of orphans way out here?" Liam slumped in his chair, finally looking like an eleven-year-old rather than a sad old man. "He's got more important stuff to fret about than how many times Patrick stuck his tongue out at me when Mr. Martin had his back turned."

So Patrick was taunting him. Just based on how the two boys talked to each other, Mason had already wondered if Patrick's "tough guy" act had started to dissolve into outright bullying. Unless the boy felt more wanted, and soon, it was a distinct possibility. Especially under Martin's watch. The farmer was an upstanding man but not God's brightest mind.

"So," Liam went on as if conversing with the Almighty were an everyday thing, "I figured I'd ask God to send me a good idea for getting out of that. When Mr. Martin handed Tom and me the saw, I took it for the clear shot it was." He spread his hands wide with a grin. "Don't you see? God answered my prayer 'cuz here I am, right where I wanted."

Mason had believed in prayer, once. He believed it worked for other folks on better terms with the Almighty than he. Even so, Mason was pretty sure Liam had things a bit twisted. "Praying for guidance is one thing. Thinking God hands you a saw to half sever your thumb to get out of a little work? That's another thing all together." Mason pushed himself off the desk and headed over to his files to round up some paperwork Liam could do with one hand. There were some receipts the boy could put in numerical order and a stack of notices he could sort by date.

"I like the idea of working here. You and I are the same sort."

"How's that?"

"Smart loners. Men who know our own mind."

Mason could only smirk and shake his head. The kid was one of a kind, that was sure. No other eleven-year-old he had ever met would describe himself as a man who knew his own mind. "Is that so?"

"I still say God did right by me," came Liam's assured voice from behind him, "He knew how much I liked it here and fixed it so I could stay. He must've thought it a good idea, too. Miss Sterling always said God's happy to give us what we ask for if it's in His will."

In His will? Mason turned to stare at the boy. The idea that Liam McLoughlin was sitting in his office at the will of the Almighty pickled his composure. "That's ridiculous," he blurted out. He caught himself, seeing Holly's furrowed brow in the back of his mind. "You conniving out of work isn't God's plan. They're not related. Not one bit. You ought to listen more carefully to what Miss Sanders and Miss Sterling are really trying to tell you instead of making up your own brand of sense." He planted a stack of receipt slips on the table in front of Liam. "Can you count high enough to put these in order?"

The question had the intended effect. Liam looked completely put out by Mason's underassessment of his smarts. "What kind of a fool question is that?"

"Mind your tongue, Liam. Just because we're friends don't mean you can mouth off at me."

Mason hadn't even realized what he'd said until the look in Liam's eyes brought him up short. "We're friends, you and I, huh?" Liam was trying to sound casual, but the glow in his expression gave him easily away.

"I reckon we are. That sit okay with you?"

Liam pretended to think about it, tapping the stack of papers into a neat pile. "That's fine."

"Well, good, then. It's settled." Mason busied himself with his key ring, unable to look at the boy.

They worked in companionable silence for half an hour or so, Liam sorting both piles of papers and Mason pushing through some correspondence with the county seat that was long overdue. It wasn't a half-bad way to pass an afternoon. Liam had already proven he could be of use around the place. Sure, he talked too much, but he worked hard sweeping things out, boxing up things and running errands. Bucky could even take him down to the tracks on Thursday to pick up the registered mail. It'd be his boyish version of Holly's return to the tracks—a chance to do something positive and regular in a place where he'd known fear and chaos. Liam deserved a chance to heal as much as Holly did.

Mason shook his head, annoyed that every train of thought seemed to find its way to Holly Sanders these days. Trying to keep her out of his thoughts only seemed to put her there twice as often.

"Why'd you do that?" Liam asked, putting down the notices he was sorting.

"Why'd I do what?"

"Say Miss Sanders's name like that. Like she made you mad just now."

Had he really spoken Holly's name aloud? "I said no such thing."

"You did. You just said Holly, and that's her name. I hear Ma'am call her Holly all the time."

"I said 'Golly,' as in 'Golly but these shelves are dusty.'" It sounded absurd, but it was the only decoy he could think of.

Liam laughed, completely unconvinced. "You did not. You never talk like that. You said 'Holly.' I heard you. My hand is hurt but my ears work just fine."

"Why would I say Miss Sanders's name while writing letters? That makes no sense at all."

"You know what makes no sense at all?" Liam planted his hands on his elbows, looking like he was about to reveal the decade's biggest secret.

Mason's gut dropped to the bottom of his boots. "What?"

"Why you kissed Miss Sanders the way you did and then don't hardly say a word to her now."

Chapter Sixteen

Mason wheeled around in his chair to face Liam. "What did you just say?" Grown men hadn't shocked him as much as this boy just had.

"I saw." Liam had enough sense to be leery of what he'd just revealed. This would have been the wrong time to get cocky. Mason wanted to slap the boy into a cell as it was.

Keeping his voice very steady, Mason put down his pen and asked, "Saw what?"

"I saw you kissing Miss Sanders something fierce. I knew you liked her and all, and she likes you. What I can't figure is how the two of you have been mad at each other ever since. I didn't think it worked that way."

There were twelve different reasons why Liam had no business saying what he just did. He ought to be taken to task on every one of them, but Mason found himself stumped on where to start. He pulled his hand down his face both to hide his surprise and to give him a moment to think. Then he asked, "You mind telling me how you saw what you *think* you saw?"

Liam gave him a jaded look that said *You're not*

gonna try and deny it, are you?, but was smart enough not to voice the remark. He stuck with a safer response. "I got eyes, you know. I told you, I notice things."

"Noticing something like that—if it happened at all, which I'm *not* saying it did—would put those eyes out on Liberty Street near midnight." Mason leaned in on his elbows, interrogation style. "Midnight on the night Beatrice Ward's gate disappeared."

"I ain't got nothing to do with that," Liam defended. "Honest."

"You just happened to be out counting stars?"

"Okay, I snuck out. Miss Sterling nods off pretty quick. That place is making me loopy, I tell you. I'm not used to being cooped up like that. Someone's always standing over me in there. I had to get out and around nobody else, that's all."

"You snuck out."

"Yeah, but I didn't kiss nobody."

Mason wasn't going to let him get away with that deflection. "You snuck out, nobody saw where you were and things started going missing. That's a heap of trouble from where I'm sitting."

Liam fidgeted in his chair. "I didn't take that stupid gate. And I didn't take the wheelbarrow, neither. I swear!"

Liam might not have stolen the gate, but there was something he was hiding. "Now would be a real good time to tell me the truth. All of it." He kept his voice low and steady, his eyes drilling into the squirming boy.

"Honest! I didn't take anything. Why'd I do something like that when I want to stay here? I saw the gate was still there when I went by Miss Ward's house. I know cause it squeaks in the wind and I heard it."

"Why were you going by Miss Ward's house in the first place?" When the boy sunk down, Mason pressed him. "Fess up, Liam."

"I knew she wasn't living there on account of the roof and I thought it might make a good place to hide. And I thought about throwing a rock through one of her windows. She's awful mean. Only I didn't, okay? I just looked to see how I might get inside." His bottom lip actually quavered, and he pulled his knees up under his chin. "Ain't you ever just needed someplace to hide from everyone?"

All the time, Mason thought but didn't say. "There are better ways. You just gave Miss Ward good reason to think the worst of you."

"Well, I don't think too highly of her, neither. She's always frowning at us, while pretending to say nice things we all know she don't mean. She doesn't want us here, even I can see that. We're gonna end up in Greenville, and if no one wants us there then it's back to New York—right where we started, 'cept this time we'll know for sure that we're orphans because no one wants us." He swiped his good hand across his eyes. "I hate sleeping in a corner of the schoolhouse. I hate learning subtraction. I hate Patrick and I hate how Mr. Arlington's gone."

A lot of hate for so small a set of shoulders. Who wouldn't want to hide from all that? Mason got up from his desk and came around to squat next to Liam, who'd folded himself up into a tight little ball in the chair. "There's a cave down by the creek behind Mr. Miller's smithy shop. It's dark and cool and quiet even when the sun is scorching. I go there when there're too many folks around me. Maybe you and I can go some time. There's good fishing there, too. Anyone ever take you fishing?"

The boy looked up and rolled his eyes. "Nobody fishes in New York."

Mason found himself acting shocked, playing along just to pull the boy's spirits up. "So you're telling me you're nearly twelve and never been fishing? Is that legal?"

He watched a little bit of the weight come off the boy's shoulders. "How would I know? You're the sheriff."

"Oh, that's right. We've still got a formality to do here." Mason stood up. "Only I can't deputize someone who's stolen from anyone in Evans Grove. You absolutely sure you're telling me the truth? Honest?"

Liam straightened up. "Honest."

Somehow, Mason realized this scrap of a boy had probably never been believed since his parents were gone. He'd spent the last few years having the whole world assume the worst of him. And yet he'd still managed to believe he'd somehow come out on top—the exact opposite of the bitterness that always seemed to seep over Mason. "I believe you."

The words transformed Liam's tense features, and for a frightening moment Mason feared the boy would throw himself into his arms. "Thanks," Liam said roughly, cocking his head to one side and leaning toward Mason but not moving out of the chair.

"Okay, then." Mason went around his desk and pulled open a drawer. He suspected he was breaking half a dozen rules in doing so, but a kind of defiance surged up from somewhere under his ribs as he pulled a star badge out from the box in the back of the drawer. When he held up the "Deputy" badge, Liam's eyes bulged wide. "Stand up, young man."

Liam shot out of the chair to stand soldier-straight. He whipped his hat off as an afterthought, as if this were an official ceremony, and Mason felt a smile curl up out of his gut and spread across his face. "By the authority vested in me by the state of Nebraska, I deputize you as…" he fished for a suitably important-sounding title, yearning for Holly's fancy vocabulary, "Interim Assistant Junior Sheriff."

The boy's chest swelled with pride, and Mason fought a surprising lump in his throat. "First order of business, Interim Assistant Junior Sheriff McLoughlin, is a very serious one."

"Yes, sir." The boy fairly beamed—a complete turn-around from how he'd entered the office.

"Fishing."

Holly was walking back from her rare afternoon off, taking advantage of the volunteer chore team leaders keeping the children occupied to go down by herself to the creek to gather wildflowers for pressing. It felt like she hadn't had an hour to herself since Newfield, and her spirit needed time in God's creation to untangle all the knots the past two weeks had put there. She'd let Mason's actions put those tangles in her spirit, and expecting Mason to untangle them was like asking the creek to rise up and apologize for flooding the town. Clearly she was looking for restoration in the wrong place.

She picked her way through the woods behind the creek, following the trail she always used, the one that ran past the tiny cave where the schoolchildren always imagined pirates to hide out. Pirates in Nebraska! How wonderfully illogical a child's imagination could be, free of all grown-up sensibility.

"No, over there," came a man's voice. "Cast your line in right in front of that rock where the patch of shade falls. Yes, right there. You're a natural." It was Mason's voice. And then again, not. The voice belonged to Mason Wright, but it had a tone she'd never heard from him before.

"I still don't think this'll work." Liam's voice made Holly stop and crouch down in the bushes. "Who'd ever want to eat a worm?"

"A hungry fish, that's who." With a start, Holly realized the sound she was hearing was Mason Wright laughing. She'd never heard him laugh, ever. She'd actually wondered from time to time if he was able to show that kind of happiness.

"My pa used to promise me a fishing trip. Back before he got sick, back before…everything." Liam's voice was so matter-of-fact, Holly nearly gasped. That poor boy spoke as if dead fathers were as common as fallen leaves. Then again, to an orphan, weren't they? *Father, grant these boys homes here in Evans Grove!* her soul pleaded silently to Heaven. Moving slowly, she pushed aside a branch so that she could see the pair.

They made an idyllic picture, sitting against a tree by the creek with a pair of fishing poles. Mason had his hat off, giving her a good look at his handsome face. She'd never seen him relaxed like that—he always looked to be twisted tight with some struggle she couldn't see. What would his unguarded smile look like? What did he look like asleep? Holly hated how these thoughts popped up like improper daisies, troublesome and unwelcome in her efforts to put Mason out of her heart.

"Do you miss your pa much?" Mason asked.

"Some days it's awful. Most days I just try to be glad I knew him at all. Lots of the other kids have no folks that they can recall, so I suppose what I remember is better than nothing at all." Holly leaned her cheek against the branch, feeling her heart break for Liam's terrible gratitude.

"I know some folks in Evans Grove who could learn a lot from you," Mason said, rebaiting his hook. "Bitter, nasty types who can only see the bad that's happened to them. You're smarter than they are; don't forget that."

Holly wondered if he saw the irony in his own words. As far as she could tell, there weren't too many souls carrying more bitterness that Mason Wright.

"Come on, now, Sheriff, there ain't nobody thinks highly of me back there. You and I both know that." Liam said it as if such a thing were completely acceptable.

"You're wrong on that count." Holly would have preferred Mason shout that instead of saying it quietly like he did.

Liam jiggled his line in the water. "'Don't matter. The girls? When we were on the train, they needed to believe all that fairy-tale stuff, all those finding good homes stories Ma'am and Mr. Arlington fed 'em. And maybe it'll really work out—kinda has, 'specially for little Sasha and the others. But me, I know what's what. I got too many scrapes and scratches on me to ever clean up cute and homey. I done things. Not here, but you and I both know I weren't no angel in New York. That sort of thing follows a man wherever he goes."

Mason shifted to face the boy. "Liam, you talk like you're ninety years old instead of eleven. You got your whole life ahead of you to make something of yourself. Men have started off with less than you and made great things of themselves. Mostly 'cause they were smart, and by gum, you're smart as a whip."

"Not if you look at my last mathematics paper. Or if you ask that lady who keeps trying to make me sit still in church."

Mason laughed again. "Mrs. Turner? She's the pastor's wife; she has to do that. Come to think of it, she's still trying to make *me* sit still in church. Hasn't worked yet."

Holly tried to swallow her giggle at that, but she ended up coughing instead.

"Who's there?" Mason's voice was back to the sharp bark she knew, and his gaze snapped to the branches that moved as she pulled back.

There was no use. He was probably already on his feet, maybe even with his gun drawn. Holly stood up. "Me."

"Miss Sanders!" Liam's surprise had a funny, too-knowing twist to it. As if he'd suspected her of being there the entire time. "What are you doing way out here?"

Mason's eyes narrowed as Holly stepped into the clearing. "I was just about to ask the same thing."

Holly held out her basket meekly. "Picking flowers for pressing. Forget-me-nots grow up over there."

The sheriff's dark eyebrow lifted in a "how long have you been eavesdropping?" arch, broadcasting his doubt. "Flowers."

"The children do study botany, you know." Holly

hated how she could feel her cheeks reddening. "But mostly, I like them for decoration."

"Girls," Liam lamented. Holly found herself half glad he didn't say "Women." "Sheriff Wright's showing me how to fish. Says I'm a natural, only I think if I'm so great I ought to have a fish by now."

Mason's eyes darted everywhere, annoyed and exposed. He was most certainly a man who did not care to be snuck up on by anyone, least of all her. He set down his pole, but didn't say anything.

"Seems to me fishing isn't always about catching fish," Holly offered. "My pa said it was as much about thinking time as anything else."

Liam ran his good hand down the length of his pole. "I could see that. A man needs time to think."

Holly managed a nervous laugh. "You really do talk like a ninety-year-old man sometimes, Liam." She regretted the remark, for Mason's scowl told her it revealed how long she'd been spying. She tried to switch the subject. "How's your thumb?"

"It's getting better. I'm glad to be here rather than on any chore team. And this cave is a nifty spot."

Now it was Holly's turn to scowl. "Is Sheriff Wright teaching you new places to hide?"

"No," Mason countered, looking straight at her. "But someone else seems to have learned how to sneak around."

"Did you follow us here?" Liam asked with a smirk Holly didn't like.

"I expect I was here before you," Holly was glad to report. "I heard you on my way back into town." She gave Mason her strongest glare. "I couldn't for the life of me figure out who it was I heard laughing."

"Very funny," Mason said, his voice pitched low in annoyance as he turned to pack up the fishing gear.

"She's right. You hardly ever laugh." Liam settled his hat back onto his head. "I reckon today's the first time I heard you, now that I think about it." He winked at Holly. "It's an odd laugh, don't you think?"

"Liam…" Mason growled as he reached down to retrieve the empty fishing bucket.

"Not at all." Holly found herself winking back. "Startling maybe, but not odd."

Liam took two steps back and hurled himself over the creek toward town. "Why don't you two talk about it while I head back," he called as he pulled out of the sloshing water. "I'm done here."

Both she and Mason began to yell after the boy, but he was long gone. Mason said a handful of choice words as he snatched up the remaining gear. "Sorry," he apologized, "that boy gets the best of me sometimes."

Holly picked up a bandanna that must have fallen out of Liam's pocket. "He gets the best of all of us, I think." She handed the bandanna to Mason. "You were kind to take him up here."

"The boys have been rough on him." He caught her eyes for a moment. "He cut his hand on purpose to get out of the crews. You know that."

"I do," she said quietly. It had been bothering her since the "accident." "All this seems especially hard on him, but I can't work out why."

He balked at her. "You can't see why?" Holly didn't like the way he made her feel as if she were missing the obvious.

"No. He wasn't even in the clearing when Mr. Arlington was shot."

Mason pushed his hat back on his head. She'd come to realize he did that when he was about to launch into a lecture, and she wasn't sure she was ready for one. "That's exactly it. He wasn't there to prevent it."

"That's absurd. He was the one who ran for help. We might all be dead if he hadn't….if you hadn't…" The shivers still hadn't stopped coming whenever she dared to think about that day. "He saved us as much as you did."

Something went through Mason's eyes—a shimmer or a shadow, it was hard to say which—at her mention of his saving them. "Not *all* of you."

"How can that be his fault? My goodness, he's a boy. He didn't hesitate when I sent him off the tracks, even though it was dangerous. He was brave. He couldn't have stopped Mr. Arlington's death. He can't think it's his fault. It makes no sense."

"You think this is supposed to make sense? That any of this will ever make sense?" Mason put down the fishing gear. "Liam is clever and he's been looking out for that group since the beginning. Those other boys, they have no idea how many times Liam's connived their way out of trouble or hardship. They may be bigger or older, but Liam's been the leader all along. You saw how he marshaled them back from the clearing, kept everyone moving and calm."

"I did. He was wonderful."

"He was making up for the fact that he wasn't there when it really counted. It's not math, Holly. It won't add up in nice little rows. The fact that he was out getting help won't ever erase the fact that he wasn't there when the shot was fired. Ever."

"But…" It was dawning on Holly that Mason wasn't

just talking about Liam. He carried the same burden—
only twice as fierce—for what had happened to his
wife. She took a step toward him, her heart twisted in
compassion. "Mason…"

He backed up. "So now every time those other boys
make a jab, he feels it twice as hard. Is it any wonder
he did whatever it took to get away from them? Foolish as it was, I can't say I wouldn't have done the same
at his age. Maybe worse."

He was so terribly hard on himself. "Well, then I'm
grateful he has you to turn to. He needs an understanding ear."

Mason just harrumphed—the way he always did
when she tried to compliment him—and picked the
fishing gear back up.

She wasn't going to let this go. "You understand him
in a way no one else does. I think God knew just what
He was doing when He sent you into Liam's life. You
said some wonderful things to him just now."

He grunted again, pushing his hat brim back down
to hide.

"You're important to him. He looks up to you so
much. You're a hero to him, you know that?"

"I'm no hero. I'm just doing my job."

She smiled. "Sheriff-Deputy fishing trips are part
of your job?" Why was it so hard for him to admit he
enjoyed spending time with the boy?

He looked around the small spot. "I thought I'd made
it clear we ought not to spend time together."

"But Liam enjoys—"

"I meant you and me," he cut in. Holly could almost
feel that wall he'd built around himself thrusting up be-

tween them, choking out every connection they managed to make with each other.

It wasn't fair how easily his eyes could hurt her. "I didn't come looking for you."

"No, you only hid in the bushes and eavesdropped."

His tone made her feel like some schoolgirl being scolded for peeking. But he was right. She could have easily walked on by. "Why must you be so mean?"

Mason never answered. He simply growled and pushed past her to walk straight into the creek, as if the cold water on his boots was preferable to one more minute in her presence.

Chapter Seventeen

Rebecca's smile at the Selection Committee meeting the next day could have lit up the county. "I'm delighted to say the chore team idea has been successful. This afternoon, Margaret and David Holland have asked for Friedrich to be placed in their home."

"Margaret heard Friedrich sing on Sunday while she played piano for the choir, and David became fond of the boy when they fixed the Hollands' back steps," Reverend Turner added. "With their son now off to school in Colorado, it was a perfect match."

"Well, why didn't they step up earlier?" Beatrice seemed eager to pull down the buoyancy of the moment.

Holly wouldn't let that happen. "He'll be so happy," she said, picturing the grin that would be plastered on the boy's face. "When can we tell him?"

Rebecca held a pen over the papers that formalized the agreement. "If the committee approves, we can tell him right away."

"We approve!" Holly exclaimed, then looked around the table, "Don't we?"

Curtis Brooks and Mayor Evans said "Of course!"

at the same time, which made everyone laugh. Even Beatrice gave her consent. Holly felt sure an essential corner had been turned.

The only person not beaming was Mason. Since the day at the creek, he'd become even more sour and withdrawn—at least, around her—and Holly hadn't thought that possible. Liam never stopped talking about how much he was enjoying his "deputy" duties. It seemed impossible to her that the frowning man before her who'd scowled at her whenever they met could be the same man who meant so much to Liam. She looked square at him. "You don't agree?"

"Oh, no, I think the Hollands are a fine spot for Friedrich." He sat back in his chair. "I'm just wondering how to break it to the boys that are still left. And Heidi. How do we tell them no one's stepped up on their behalf?"

"I've thought about that," Rebecca replied. "I've asked Charlotte Miller if she'd be willing to host the remaining children for a picnic dinner while Friedrich settles into his new home tonight. The boys have been fascinated by Mr. Miller's shop, and it will give them and Heidi something fun to do away from the schoolhouse."

"That's a splendid idea," Pauline said. "Do you need the committee's help?"

"Actually, I was hoping you and Mr. Brooks would come as well. Reverend Turner has offered to see to gathering Friedrich's things and we'll need some extra hands if the boys get rambunctious. For the most part, we've been able to tire them out between school and chores, but you never know what a little cake can do."

Did Mason notice that he and Holly had been ex-

cluded from this event? Beatrice, even though she hated
to be excluded from anything, seemed genuinely relieved not to be involved, but Holly couldn't help feeling
hurt. She bumbled her way through the rest of the meeting, which was mercifully short, until Mason cleared
his throat.

"I'd like to bring something before this group." He
looked uncomfortable, shifting in his chair.

"Have you caught one of those boys committing a
crime?" Beatrice looked far too pleased.

"No, and I continue to believe they aren't involved."

"Well, then, who is taking things?" Beatrice's eyes
narrowed as if the whole thing were Mason's fault.

"I don't know yet, Miss Ward, but I assure you, when
I find out, you'll be the first to know."

Mr. Brooks cleared his throat and leaned in between
them as they eyed each other fiercely. "Sheriff, you said
you had something to discuss with the committee?"

"You all know I went to Greenville earlier to tes-
tify against the train bandits. Well, I received a wire
from Greenville today. Three of the men have been
found guilty of felony theft and accessory to murder.
I doubt it will surprise any of you that these were men
wanted for a collection of other crimes as well. As for
the leader, Arlington wasn't his first murder. So as it
stands, three of them will go to jail downstate and the
leader will hang."

A silence fell over the room. "When?" Rebecca
asked, her face pale.

"Tomorrow."

Holly felt the familiar chill of fear that stole down her
spine whenever she remembered that day. That man had
shot Mr. Arlington as if it meant nothing. He'd pulled

the trigger as easily as swatting a fly. The memory of the callous look in his eye still made her shiver.

"I was wondering," Mason continued, "what you wanted to tell the children."

Beatrice sniffed as if this required no consideration. "We tell them what the scripture says: That the wages of sin are death and that justice always prevails."

Reverend Turner held out a hand. "I think we ought to be a mite kinder than that."

"To children who may be committing crimes of their own?"

Rebecca squinted her eyes shut, Mason sat back in his chair and Holly groaned. "*Especially,*" Holly emphasized, taxed to her limit to be civil to this cruel old woman, "to children who have witnessed a terrible crime."

"What these youngsters need is a sharp warning," Beatrice countered.

"What these youngsters *need* is someone not thinking the worst of them at every moment." Mason stood up from the table, towering over the group until he pushed back and walked over to face the windows. He was fuming. So was she, for that matter, but she'd managed to contain her anger whereas Mason looked as if he'd boil over any minute. This man was capable of a fierce loyalty, and it was clear Liam—and perhaps all of the children—had come under that protection. She'd felt that loyalty for a moment at the tracks and then again in brief glimpses since then. Its fierceness had grasped some part of her that wasn't ready to let go of Mason, no matter how mean he'd been.

"Seems to me," Curtis Brooks said in a conciliatory tone, "the children need to know they can count on justice doing its job. They should know the men were punished, but perhaps we can spare them the crueler details. And they should be reminded that in these parts, we don't condemn someone until we have proof they are guilty."

"And even if they are guilty," Reverend Turner added, "good Christians are commanded to show mercy."

Mason made a loud *hrumph* from over by the window.

"I think we all have things to do before this evening's dinner," Mayor Evans said, closing the little gray notebook she used at every official meeting. "Rebecca, why don't you and I walk over to the schoolhouse? I've some more ideas for chore teams and we can talk about which families might still be convinced to take the remaining children."

As the meeting ended, Holly broke a promise to herself and went over to stand beside Mason. His grip on the window frame was white-knuckled, the panes reflecting his deep scowl. "Thank you for defending the children."

He didn't say anything for a moment. "They've suffered enough. I've no mind to let Beatrice add to it with her rushes to judgment."

"Do you think the boys are taking things?"

He turned, his shoulders falling in resignation. "I can't rightly say. Liam swears to me he's not taken anything, and I believe him. But he has been sneaking out, and who knows what the other boys have done." He leaned against the wall, his expression falling into a pained reluctance. After a glance around the room to ensure it was empty, he continued. "He was out on Victory Street that night."

"What night?" Then Holly suddenly swallowed, grasping his meaning. She felt herself glancing around, not wanting another soul to hear this conversation. "Oh."

"He saw us."

"Oh." Holly couldn't quite fathom what to do with that information.

"So did Miss Sterling. You know that, don't you? She shut the door just as I...left."

In that moment, Holly decided no matter how much it hurt, she needed one question answered. "Why *did* you kiss me?" She'd been stunned that night, and then wounded, and then angry and then confused. And now? Now she didn't know what she was except that it was driving her plum mad how facts wouldn't line up. It hardly seemed to matter that it was a mortifying question. He'd already hurt her and embarrassed her and a dozen other things besides, so what was one mortifying question if it gave her some peace?

He turned, eyes wide. "Why?"

"Yes, why did you ever kiss me in the first place?" He shouldn't be looking at her like that. He was the only one with an answer to that question. She certainly didn't know why he'd kissed her the way he did when she'd barely been able to get the time of day from him. "It can't have been my gift. You returned it. Worse than returned it, you ripped it. You *ripped a book*. You had to know how offensive I would find that." She'd spent so long being hurt about it that now she found herself demanding an explanation. She lowered her voice and was surprised to find herself glaring at him. "You kissed me, and then deliberately hurt me. You've been nothing but mean to me since. And I want to know why."

He shifted his weight, scratched his chin even, but did not speak.

Holly planted her hands on her hips and stood her ground. "I believe I'm entitled to an explanation."

He made a noise like a laugh, only deeper.

"Well, I do." Her voice pitched too loud, and she clamped her mouth shut but narrowed her eyes at him.

He practically growled. "You never stop, do you?"

That wasn't much of an answer. "What kind of a question is that?"

"I could say the same of you." He lowered his voice. "What kind of a question is 'why did you kiss me?'" He nearly hissed it, as if he didn't even like repeating the words.

She was not leaving until she had an explanation sufficient to quiet the storm in her head. She hadn't any dignity left to lose. "I admit it's unconventional, but in my experience men do not kiss women…that way—" she was flushing just thinking about the intensity she'd felt when he held her "—and then be so hurtful and dismissive."

He turned away from her, pacing the room. "'In your experience.'" His parroting held just enough befuddlement to keep from being cruel, but it stung nonetheless.

How like him to hit the exact point of her weakness. She hadn't much experience at all—almost none. The last man—boy, actually—to kiss her had done it on the worst kind of dare. One of those hideously mean classmates at Miss Ogilvie's School for Girls had promised Matthew Batten a kiss if he persuaded Holly to kiss him first. She could still hear the snickering of their amusement as they ducked from behind the tree where the boy had given Holly her first true kiss. Her "experience" was as a pawn in some girl's grand mean game of hard-to-get.

Holly felt her confidence sinking fast, forcing her straight to the point. "Evidently, I made some error in trying to be kind to you, to show you God's mercy. That mercy which you seem to find so…" she couldn't think of the word, but settled for "…intolerable. Because you've gone out of your way since then to make it clear that you don't wish to be anywhere near me, I need to know—why did you kiss me?"

Mason ran his hands through his hair. At least with his hat off, she could see his eyes. "Hang it all, you really want me to answer that, don't you?"

He seemed so tall, glaring down at her. "I'm not in the habit of asking idle questions. I can't make sense of what you did, so I have no choice but to ask you to explain yourself."

"It's not something I thought out." Mason squared off at her. "Look, this is exactly why you and I should stay away from each other. You drive me to fool notions, Holly Sanders. You are the most…confounded woman!" A door shut somewhere in the church and he brought his voice down to a whisper again. "I kissed you because…you were looking at me with those big eyes, saying dreamy things, all sweet and…" One hand went to the back of his neck, and his expression changed completely. "You have no idea what you did, do you? You really don't have the slightest notion." He turned away, pacing. "This is exactly why I can't be around you."

He saw this as her fault? "I was trying to be kind."

"Kind? You could kill a man with that sort of kindness. All high hopes and soft words."

"I was trying to show you how I feel."

"Great guns, woman, do you think I have *any* doubt about how you feel? You follow me around like some kind of puppy, thinking all kinds of good about me when any fool with half a wit would know better. I've told you what kind of bad I am. I think I did a mighty fine job of showing you. And still you won't wake up. I'm bad news, Miss Sanders. Wise up and steer clear."

"I don't see why my trying to understand makes me—"

Mason threw his hands up in the air. "There is nothing to understand!" He stormed past her, then turned to face her one last time. "Forget it ever happened. Forget whatever you think I am, because you couldn't be more wrong." He made no effort to hide the fury in his eyes. "Go away, Holly. Stay away. For crying out loud, hear me this time and *stay away*."

Chapter Eighteen

"Miss Sanders, are you feeling all right?"

The wire clerk peered over the top of his spectacles at her, seeming to doubt the stiff smile she mustered up as reassurance. Not that she would admit how Mason Wright had rattled her. And anyway, Heidi's fate was more important than any sheriff's grumble-some irritation. How dare he make her feel the way she did! "Yes, Jason, I'm just a bit tired, that's all. It's been a long week."

"You need another form?" She'd had to ask for another form twice already. Her brain just did not want to make polite inquiries at the moment.

"No, I'm quite fine. I'll just need a minute."

She took a deep breath and tried again: *Inquiring about orphan boy Jakob Strauss STOP Placed by Orphan Salvation Society in Glenwood, Iowa, to Robinson family STOP Sister here in Evans Grove Nebraska STOP Reunion possible? STOP*

Reunion possible? Did she have a right to make so bold an inquiry? She imagined that most people would question what a child Heidi's age knew of family ties.

But Holly knew that this young, scarred girl had made a very grown-up decision, made a sacrifice few adults would embrace. It hardly seemed fair to cut her off completely from the brother she'd tried so hard to help. Was it bold? Yes. Did it feel like setting something right in a world where too much had gone wrong?

Yes, Holly told herself as she signed her name to the form and pushed it across the counter to the clerk. Too much in Holly's world refused to make sense lately, and this was one of the only things where she could clearly see her next step.

The next day, Holly went straight to Rebecca the minute Heidi and the boys were settled into their chore teams. The reply telegram she'd received this morning had been burning a hole in her pocket since the wire clerk brought it over, but this wasn't the kind of news she could share around the children.

Rebecca was leaning against one of the benches on the town square, looking exhausted. Holly hesitated, not sure if the news in her pocket would make things better or worse for the OSS agent. "We've got to get you a room at the hotel, Rebecca. You can't keep sleeping at the schoolhouse like this. You're not getting enough rest. Why don't you let me take one night a week? Then you wouldn't even have to worry about the hotel. You could sleep in my bed. We can get volunteers to take some of the other nights."

"It's just hard…alone. Stuart was a grumpy old man some days, and I used to wonder how on earth he had enough compassion in him to leave his wife and daughter alone to do these long trips, but he was a partner. A second set of hands, even on his worst days."

"You're not alone. Amelia and Charlotte and I? We're here to help you. And the rest of the committee—you know they want to help any way they can."

Rebecca pinned a strand of hair back up into place. "I'm not so sure about Miss Ward's intentions."

"Don't mind her." Holly sat down beside Rebecca. "She just…well, she's difficult and opinionated."

"I've met less difficult and opinionated mules." A small smile crept across the woman's tired face. "And I haven't met that many mules." She sighed. "She means well, I do understand that. It's just that she can be so… so…"

"Downright mean?" Holly leaned in and offered.

Rebecca laughed. "I was trying not to put it so sharply."

"We're all sort of used to her bluster. Pauline Evans said to me once that she believes fighting with Beatrice Ward is part of the glue that holds Evans Grove together. I don't think she's half wrong on that. Beatrice is loud but mostly harmless. Even Sheriff Wright said, 'she's all roar and no claw' the other day."

Rebecca raised an inquiring eyebrow. "And how is the good sheriff? Don't think I haven't noticed how you two avoid each other lately. You never did tell me how you built your drawbridge."

"It wasn't a bridge of any kind. It broke into a thousand pieces and fell into the moat, that's what happened, but I don't want to talk about that."

Rebecca turned to face her. "You sure? Both of you look miserable. He practically scowled the entire meeting and he's been avoiding the schoolhouse like he'd catch something if he came near."

"I have much more important things to discuss."

Holly pulled the telegram from her pocket. "I've had a telegram from the selection committee in Glenwood, Iowa."

"Already?"

"Well, it seems there's a reason they wired back so fast. Jakob has disappeared. He ran away the second night he was in Glenwood. He'd been inconsolable from the moment he learned Heidi was back on the train."

Rebecca came to the same instantaneous conclusion Holly had. "He's run away to come find her, hasn't he? He always was protective of her, like nothing I've ever seen." Concern furrowed her brows. "That's got to be eighty miles from here." Her eyes scanned the rough, bare landscape to the east, as if she could see Iowa from their shady spot on the town square. "This is no place for a city boy on his own, even a smart one like Jacob. I can't bear to think what's become of him." Rebecca's hand went to Holly's arm. "We can't tell Heidi."

"I'm glad you see it that way. It'd only make things worse. She feels like she's sacrificed herself so he could have a better life. If she finds out he's in danger on her account—and I suppose we don't know for certain that he is—she'll be heartbroken."

Rebecca's sigh was enormous and heavy. "She's already heartbroken. She's been through so very much, so young." Both women cast their gaze in the direction of Gavin's General Store, where Heidi was helping Mrs. Gavin sort through seed packets this afternoon. "After losing her parents in the fire that gave her those scars, her brother was all she had. It broke her heart to let him go. I keep asking God why he saw fit to allow so much suffering in her short life. I haven't gotten an answer."

"I've had a bit of a go-round with God on that very

subject myself." Holly shrugged her shoulders. "Too many good people—even young ones—lost their lives in the storm and the flood. There was a week where I went to a funeral every single day. After a while, you get so filled up with the hurt you can't see the good even if it's right in front of you." Holly's hand found her handkerchief in the pocket next to the telegram and she thought about how she'd had to hang damp hankies over the chair backs every evening in her room that week. So many tears. Far too many.

"There is good, you know," Rebecca offered. "Tom's made wonderful improvements in his reading and Lizzie wrote her name the other day—even if the Zs were crooked, they were lovely Zs." She caught Holly's eyes. "You're a very gifted teacher, and the children adore you. I don't know what I'd have done without you on that awful day." Rebecca folded her hands. "I'm actually glad we're here. I think you were right when you said you were sure God delivered these children to Evans Grove. If only I could get Patrick and Liam to see it as clearly as I do."

Rebecca's tone told Holly what she'd already guessed when the boys were overly tired and quarrelsome last night. "They snuck out again, didn't they?"

"For a whole hour. I've been just waiting for someone to come shouting about whatever damage or trouble they've caused. They tell me they're only wandering around exploring, but we both know that's hardly likely."

"I'd really hoped the chore teams would help them get that out of their systems." Holly tucked her feet underneath her and looked at Rebecca. "Do we know if they've actually taken anything?"

"I imagine we'd have heard from Sheriff Wright by now if they had." The pretty blonde woman returned Holly's gaze with a sly smile. "And then again, maybe not. He has such a soft spot for Liam, even if he'd never admit it in a million years."

"He does at that, but I doubt even that would stop him if he felt the boys were stealing." Holly smiled as she recalled Mason's inability to hide his grin around the boy. "Mason Wright isn't the kind of man to play favorites—especially where the law is concerned. As a matter of fact, I expect he'd come down extra hard on Liam if he caught him—probably gave him an earful already about keeping out of Beatrice's suspicions."

Rebecca rose and dusted off her skirts. "Well, it hasn't worked. No doubt something new has gone missing and we'll hear tell of it soon if there's not talk already." She hugged her arms to her chest. "Time isn't our friend here, Holly. I was sure once Friedrich was placed, some of the other families would step up and take the other three in. I know they should stay. They belong here, not in Greenville, or back in New York. But we can't wait for families forever."

Before the sun came up Saturday morning, Mason was stepping into the saddle and heading west toward Greenville. It was a long ride, but he needed the time and space. It would have been easier to take the train, but Mason wasn't fond of the notion of heading back to the tracks any time soon. Tracks meant Holly and Liam and all the things that had begun poking themselves into his neatly boxed life.

His neatly boxed, woefully lonesome life. For a man who claimed to enjoy his solitude, he was coming to care too much about the wrong people. Lately it felt like every day found a new way to shake up his spirit, to burst things open that ought to stay locked and hidden. He was too plum fond of Liam for any good to come of it. What could he hope to offer the boy? Liam needed a stable home and family, and he'd never find them while playing shadow to a lonesome lawman. Still, the scraggly redhead was as stubborn as Holly in his belief that they made a team.

Holly. Every time he was sure he'd been gruff enough to put her off for good, she'd come back with some new request. What kind of woman asked for an explanation of a kiss? God in His Heaven must find it amusing that her directness—the very thing he liked most about Holly—would be such a torture to him.

And that God in His Heaven—if He really was the way Mason thought of Him—also knew justice must prevail. Debts must be paid, sins must be punished. Holly could cling to mercy all she wanted, but she wasn't riding into Greenville to watch a man hang for his crimes. The world required order and balance. Dead men—and dead mothers—could never be revived and that's why killers had to hang.

Almost against his will, Mason's memory recalled the one place dead men could be revived. There was one man who hadn't let death be the end. His hand found its way to his shirt pocket, where he'd carried her inscribed page from that book of Psalms. Christ had been in his life once, before his terrible lapse in protecting Phoebe. Christ had extended forgiveness to a convicted criminal right next to him on the cross, hadn't He? Why had that fact come bubbling out of his memory? He was sure Holly would quote it as evidence of the "forgiven future" she offered.

She was sweet, but she was naive. Today's destination only proved such a thing wasn't really possible.

"What's wrong?" Holly opened her door an hour later to find Mary Turner standing with an alarmed look on her face.

Mary pulled her shawl tighter against the early-morning chill. "It's Charlie Miller."

Holly pulled the door open farther and ushered Mary inside. "What's happened?"

"He's dead. He'd been working all day repairing damage to the shop and then having the picnic. Charlotte confided in me that he wasn't very happy about the prospect of so many children in his yard, and he complained of not feeling well that evening. He was out of bed when she woke this morning, but it wasn't unusual for Charlie to be in the shop early. She went to fetch him home for breakfast and found him cold on the ground."

"That's horrible." More death. It hardly seemed fair. "How is Charlotte? Sasha?"

"James is with them now. Doc Simpson was with them earlier, but he left with Charlie's body so they could tend to it away from the house. No one wants Sasha to see too much." The woman shook her head, *tsk*ing. "Poor Charlotte. I'm so glad God saw to give her little Sasha so she wouldn't be alone in all this."

"She's not alone," Holly declared. "She has us. We'll all help her get through this." Holly finished putting her hair up in a bun and grabbed her shawl. "I can't stand the thought of another funeral."

"James said the same thing. He said 'I've prayed over

too many fresh graves,' when Bucky Wyler came and got him this morning."

"Bucky?"

Mary's eyes teared up. "Both he and Mel Hutchinson arrived at the shop at the same time and found Charlotte standing over the body. He was stopping by before work to ask Charlie to help him build a cradle. Seems Cindy's expecting. It's so sweet and so sad."

Mel, Charlie's apprentice, was a kind man. He and his wife had taken Lizzie into their home. But it was Bucky who was closest to the wheelwright. Charlie wasn't a social, gregarious man, but he and Bucky had struck some kind of chord in each other since the flood. A sort of father-son relationship had sprung up between them, as Charlie had no children and Bucky's pa was lost in the flood. Now, it seemed Bucky would be a father with no father to guide him. "Poor Bucky. Poor Charlotte." Holly's mind went to Bucky's other friend, Mason.

Mary sighed and wiped her eyes. "I thought about finding Sheriff Wright next. He and Bucky are friends, aren't they?"

"He's not here." Holly felt the weight of death pressing in all around her. "He went into Greenville early this morning to attend the hanging of the railroad bandit." Death upon death. Death compounding death. Death to repay death. It all seemed like such a fruitless waste. She hugged her arms to her chest. "A baby. I can't think of anything Evans Grove needs more than a new baby." She patted the hand of the pastor's wife. "Thanks for coming, Mary. You head on home now. You look as if you've been up for hours. There's no school today so I've plenty of time to tend to Charlotte and Sasha."

Holly walked up to the door of the Miller house. The chore team had just painted it earlier this week. How many times had Mason sent Liam over to Charlie's for nails or hinges or whatever as the boys worked? Holly looked down the street toward that smithy shop, imagining its glowing forge now dark and mournfully quiet.

Reverend Turner pulled open the door. "I'd say 'good morning,' only it's not so good. Charlie was quiet, but he worked hard. Honest men are always hard losses for a town like this."

"And we've lost so many." Holly felt like this last one tipped the scales from "hard" to "unbearable." In a sad bit of practicality, she found herself wondering if Gavin's even had any black cloth or ribbons left.

"Doc left an hour ago." The reverend nodded somberly toward the doctor's office down the street. "It's best I be going now. Dave Holland's agreed to step in and build the casket on account of...well, you know."

She did. Everyone in town knew that Charlie Miller was the man to build caskets when kin died in Evans Grove. He'd always managed some sort of decoration on the lid nails so the caskets looked dignified and pretty. That was until the flood, when it was all he could do to build them fast enough for the onslaught of bodies. Now not only was there no Charlie to help Bucky build a pretty cradle for his bride's new baby, there was no one to bury Charlie Miller in the dignity he'd given everyone else. Holly looked up into the gray sky, thinking it ought to just open up and rain sorrow on the whole world today.

"Miffanders?"

Holly found a smile somewhere down in all the gray, pasting it on for the little girl who rushed up to her as she stepped into the Miller home. Never quite able to get her tiny mouth around Holly's name, Sasha's "Miffanders" had become a charming joke between Charlotte and Holly. She pulled the girl into her arms. "Hello, sweetheart. How are you doing?"

"Mama sad." She said it in the innocent, incomprehensible way a child grasps catastrophe.

Holly gave Sasha an extra tight squeeze. "Of course she is, darling. We all are."

She stepped farther into the small but homey single room of a house where Charlotte sat at the table with a vacant face. Charlotte was usually an energetic, get-things-done kind of woman, but today she sat quietly. "Hello, Holly." Her voice held no emotion. "You're kind to come."

Holly eased into the seat across from Charlotte. "How could I not? You've been such a help to me and the school. Even last night, giving the picnic for the children like you did."

That brought a response from the woman. "It was lovely to have a yard full of children like that. Charlie said the noise alone would wake the—" She stopped, unwilling to finish the morbid metaphor under the circumstances. "It was loud. But a wonderful sort of loud."

"Why don't I make us some tea?" It seemed a feeble way to stave off the gray of the morning, but when Charlotte made no objection, Holly lit the stove.

There came a knock at the door. "A bit early for condolence calls, but why don't you let me get it?"

Holly returned to the door and pulled it open to find Mel Hutchinson. He doffed his hat, awkward at the intrusion. "Mrs. Miller?"

Sasha had climbed up into her new mother's lap,

and Charlotte looked up from fussing with her braids. "Yes, Mel?"

"I'm not sure that it matters much at the moment," the lad said with his hat twisted in his hands, "but there's something you should know."

"What could be so important now?" Holly whispered.

"I was just out back in your shed and, well, lots of Mr. Miller's tools are missing."

Chapter Nineteen

The wind whipped Mason's hair Tuesday afternoon as he stood with his hand on Bucky's shoulder beside the fresh grave of Charlie Miller. There wasn't much weeping at Evans Grove's funerals anymore; the entire town was plum grieved out, weary of piling fresh sod onto new caskets. After so many in March, this one felt like a last cruel trick. As if God up in His Heaven was taunting that death still marched on and He wasn't through yet. For a man who hated funerals, Mason Wright had been to far too many of them lately.

"Did you find out any more?" Bucky said as they walked away from the ceremony. He and Mason had been trying to solve the mystery of the missing tools, but had only come up with Mel's vague recollection that most of the missing tools weren't in the best of shape.

"It's as if someone went to the shed looking for the broken ones rather than take the best tools from the shop." Mason caught Liam's eye as the children filed back to school. He made a mental note to talk to the boy later, for he looked rattled by the loss of Charlie. All the orphans who had been at the picnic dinner looked stunned by Charlie's death. Poor little Sasha.

"And nobody knows anything about Mr. Gavin's wheelbarrow or Miss Ward's gate," Bucky added, "Except that they were broken, too."

Mason narrowed his eyes at Bucky. "Broken gate, damaged tools, broken wheelbarrow. Someone scavenging for scrap metal maybe?"

"I thought of the same thing, except Gavin's wheelbarrow was mostly wood. And why not take the bigger, better tools if you were looking for metal?"

"Something's up." Mason settled his hat back on his head. "I don't know what, but I aim to find out before Miss Ward gets any more ideas."

Bucky scratched his chin and stared back at the tiny gated cemetery they'd just left. Sadly enough, the forlorn square of land just east of town was already near full. "Charlie told me Mayor Evans came to him last week to see about building new fencing to make a larger cemetery. I gave him a hard time because he made some crack about being glad he'd left room for his own spot near Gloria."

Mason had found it odd to be burying the man beside the grave of his first wife now that he was remarried, but he remembered the days of longing to be laid to rest beside Phoebe when his time came. A man's grief never made good sense. "He's gone too soon." Justice seemed overrun by death these days. Order and balance seemed gone; the bandit leader's hanging had left a sour taste in Mason's mouth on Saturday. And to come back to news of Charlie's loss? Well it just left Mason wondering how folk hung on to any faith when the world seemed out of kilter like this. He'd walked through life these past two days like he was groping in the dark. His soul—if he still had one—felt like it was dragging the weight of Beatrice's gate, Charlie's tools and Gavin's wheelbarrow all together while swimming against the floodwaters. He was going under, and he didn't know what to do about it.

"Sure is a shame." Mason hadn't heard most of whatever Bucky just said. The words just sort of washed over him as he watched Holly Sanders kneel down and offer comfort to Liam. "Charlie weren't never much for young'uns, but he was starting to take a shine to that little girl." Bucky went on. "He never said so, but I could tell." Cindy came up and put her arm around her husband, laying her head on his shoulder as Bucky put his arm protectively around his new wife. "I was planning on asking Charlie to be our baby's godfather, you know." Bucky's voice broke just a bit on the last word. "Planned on asking him that very morning."

What was the point of so much pain? Mason thought. How was he supposed to tell younger men like Bucky— or even Liam—to stand tough and make something of themselves when only more pain waited for them later in life?

"He'd have been happy for us," Cindy said. Her hand stroked the bit of a belly Mason recognized as the beginning of pregnancy. Phoebe's hand would always do that when she was sad or worried, as if the new life offered some kind of comfort from the inside. When Bucky kissed the top of Cindy's head, Mason felt it happen again; the numb emptiness that had always been his companion was giving way to the slow burn of loneliness.

It was a dangerous transformation that had overtaken

him the night he'd had dinner with Bucky and Cindy. It had been his undoing that same night when he kissed Holly. It had near swallowed him whole on the ride to Greenville. He was lonely.

He watched the teacher now from the safety of several yards out. Her hand cupped Liam's chin and offered a sad smile. She tenderly checked his still-bandaged hand, patting it softly while the boy nodded. It still stunned him how he could feel the sky in her blue eyes from here, framed as they were with wet lashes. She didn't seem to drown under the weight that was pushing him down, even though they'd both been surrounded by so much pain. For a moment—an unguarded, careless moment—he let himself wonder if the Bible she clutched fiercely to her side was the thing that held her upright.

The thing she'd tried to give him. Beatrice used scripture like a weapon, but hadn't Holly tried to use it as a lifeline? Had she seen him drowning and tried to throw him a rope? It had stuck in his head—the jumble of thoughts on his ride to Greenville proved as much. Now there was a disturbing thought. Was it faith, rather than the sheer hunger of a man next to a woman, that had pulled him to her so strongly that night?

The wind shifted, and Liam turned in Mason's direction, catching his eye. Holly's glance followed, and Mason felt the yards between them vanish despite neither of them moving. An actual panic crept up his backbone as she made her way across the stretch of grass with Liam. It felt too precarious to be near her anymore, and yet he seemed constantly aware of where she was whenever she was within eyesight. Like a storm he could feel coming but couldn't stop.

"Hello, Bucky, Cindy. I hear congratulations are in order. That's wonderful, really wonderful." She used the tone of voice Mason had come to recognize from the train tracks as her applied cheer. Once he'd found Holly too continually cheerful. Now he knew that her sunny disposition was a tool for her, a bridge of sorts over patches of pain or weariness. He found it highly irritating that he could now hear when she was truly happy and when she was putting on her cheer the way he pulled down his hat—to hide.

"We're so excited," Cindy said looking up at Bucky with a newlywed's wonder in her eyes. It hurt—it physically hurt—to see so much hope and joy right there before him.

Holly held out a hand. "As well you should be. I can't think of better news. My ma always said 'a baby is God's reminder that the world should keep on,' and that's the best message for Evans Grove. A patch of happiness is just what we need."

"I feel like we got a whole acre of happiness," Bucky said with a smitten grin. He looked down at Liam. "Hey there, Deputy McLoughlin. Congratulations to you, too."

"It ain't real," Liam said, cocking his head to one side.

"'Course it's real. Sheriff Wright don't mess around when it comes to the law. He takes his partners seriously and it's serious work."

"Which is why," Cindy said, hugging Bucky, "Mr. Wyler won't be wearing any badges any time soon, Sheriff. My baby needs his daddy home every night for supper and no gunfights." Cindy's unwillingness to let Bucky take the deputy oath despite his excellent marksmanship had been a bone of contention in the past, but now with a baby on the way, Mason knew he'd be working alone for the next year unless someone with the right skills came along.

"I'll do my best, ma'am," Liam said, tipping his hat. "If you don't mind, though, I might get a few pointers from Bucky if he ever has the time." He grinned up at Cindy, charming her the way Liam charmed everyone.

"Obliged," Bucky said. To Mason's growing discomfort, the three of them walked off in conversation leaving him and Holly alone. The silence stretched out heavy and enormous.

She brushed back the strands of hair the wind whipped across her face, turning for a moment toward the fresh grave. "I can't believe Charlie is gone." After a moment, she turned to him, pushing out a breath while she clutched the Bible to her chest. "I'm sorry," she said. "I shouldn't have said what I did the other day."

He'd picked the fight the last time they were together. *He'd* turned her question—direct as it was—into an argument and stopped just short of accusing her, and *she* was apologizing? Did she have any idea the pile of debt, the mountain of unearned mercy she heaped on his head every time they were together? "Don't apologize." It came out wrong; barked like an order rather than the release he'd meant. Glory, but her eyes tangled his tongue. "It's not necessary," he backpedaled, but that only came out worse. Even out under the wide-open sky, he felt trapped in tight next to her, pinned to his faults by the weight of her regard.

Charlotte Miller walked up to Holly, and Mason seized the opportunity. "Sorry for your loss, Widow Miller. Charlie was a good man. Miss Sanders." Quick

as civility would allow, he tipped his hat to the two ladies and walked off toward where the others were heading back to town.

"How are you holding up, Charlotte?" Holly hardly
needed to ask; the woman looked worn and thin.

"Widow Miller," Charlotte repeated, looking after
Mason's quick exit. "I can't quite get used to that."

"I imagine it's a title no woman ever gets fully used
to wearing." She held her elbow out for Charlotte to
grasp. "I'll try to stick to 'dear Charlotte' if it will help
you feel better."

"My favorite title right now is 'mama.'" Holly was
pleased to see a whisper of happiness cross the woman's
pale face as Sasha waved to her mama while walking
toward town with Amelia Hicks. "Sasha has been such
a comfort to me. I thank God every night He sent her
into my life right now."

"It has to be such a blessing," Holly agreed. "Sasha
is a darling girl. I look forward to having her in class
next year."

Charlotte turned to grasp Holly's elbows. "I *need* her.
I know God sent her to me as comfort through all this."

"God knew exactly what He was doing. You'll be a
wonderful mother, Charlotte. The two of you will be
fine." That wasn't exactly true. Holly had heard Beatrice
talking to Miss Sterling, asking if the OSS would consider it proper for a widowed woman to foster a child.
But that wasn't what Charlotte needed to hear. Holly
would hold off on telling her for now, and just pray that
the issue would be resolved soon. "Take your little girl
home, eat something and then both of you try and sleep.
I'll stop by toward dinner and see how you're getting

on. Don't you dare come by the schoolhouse tomorrow. We'll manage without you just fine."

The widow's clothes whipped in the wind, hanging on her thin frame like mourners' crepe. The woman looked more placid than she did sad. *Shock does strange things to people*, she thought to herself, remembering how outgoing she'd become in the wake of the train attack. The world—her life, her town, her friends— had just about turned on its ear in the last two months, as if God had taken the entire universe and shaken it like the snow globes Mama used to keep on the mantel at Christmas. *Lord*, Holly prayed as she watched Charlotte reach down and scoop little Sasha up into her arms, *I know You've planned how all the pieces will fall, but it's hard to see from here. I can't see where I fit into all this. I can't tell if I'm following Your Spirit or going my own willful way. Hem me in. Hem all of us in with Your protection. Give me eyes to see where to go from here.*

With a last look at the sad addition to Evan's Grove's already-too-full cemetery, Holly turned and headed for home.

Liam burst through the door a half an hour early, panting as if he'd run the entire way from the schoolhouse. "She's after me!"

Mason wasn't thrilled about school yard games of tag extending to his office. He'd been angry and irritated all morning, having slept poorly. Come to think of it, he'd been angry and irritated all week. He wasn't in the mood for Liam's theatrics today. "Who's after you?"

"Miss Ward. And she's mad as a hornet." The boy was actually looking around the room for places to hide.

Now, Beatrice Ward mad as a hornet wasn't exactly

a rare thing around these parts, but Miss Ward out to get Liam could only spell disaster. For a second, Mason actually considered hiding the boy, or at least locking him in a cell for protection. By the time he could consider the foolishness of these thoughts, Beatrice Ward had pushed his door open and stood fuming in the center of his office.

"I have endured enough!" she huffed, hands on her hips and eyebrows nearly dug into the bridge of her sharp little nose. "These urchins must go. That one," she said, pointing to Liam, "most of all!"

Mason moved between the two of them. "Why don't you tell me what's gone on, Miss Ward, and we'll see what can be done."

"He's stolen from me. He's stolen from half of Evans Grove, I'm sure we'll discover."

"I did not!" Liam countered from behind Mason. "I never took nothing. I only looked."

"So you admit you were at my home last night. Looting from the unfortunate, were you? You lawless little—"

"Hang on there," Mason cut in. "Miss Ward, why don't you sit down."

"I will not sit down." Beatrice crossed her hands over her chest in a defiant gesture. "I will not sit idly by while our dear little town is overrun with thieves. Thieves who don't belong in our homes."

"As if I'd ever want to live with *you*," Liam snarled.

"That's enough," Mason raised his voice over the pair of them. When the room fell silent, he turned to Liam. "Were you at Miss Ward's house yesterday?"

"Last night. Prowling around after dark, he was." That old woman had no need of weapons with the ability to shoot a look as dark as she could. Even Mason felt a small shiver at the level of disdain in her glare.

Her accusation could only mean one thing. He looked at Liam. "Did you break your promise to me?"

"You knew he'd escaped before? And you did nothing?" came Beatrice's shrill voice from behind him. Mason held a hand out behind him to quiet her while his eyes bored into Liam's fearful ones.

"I was goin' crazy in there. Tom and Patrick were yelling and Heidi was crying and Ma'am was pacing the room all worried." Liam swallowed hard. "It was like I couldn't even breathe."

"So you snuck out again." This was not good news, not at all.

"Well, well," Beatrice gasped behind him. "So he has you charmed now, too. That little miscreant has everyone feeling sorry for him when all he wants to do is rob us when our backs are turned. Greenville's too good an end for that boy, I tell you. He belongs in prison. He's no better than that gang from the train, he is."

Now she'd gone too far. Mason whirled on her. "Miss Ward, I'll thank you to hold your peace." He stalked over to her, wielding every inch of height he had over that bitter old woman. "A woman of your standing ought to know better than to—"

The slam of his office door stopped him short. Mason turned back to find his office empty, Liam's hat on the floor, and the boy long gone.

Chapter Twenty

Mason wheeled on Beatrice Ward. "What is wrong with you, old woman?" Her shock registered a bit of his own, but hang it if that woman hadn't just driven him past his final shred of composure. "Where in that Bible of yours does it say you can treat a child like that?" Mason pushed past her to thrust his head out the door, but he already knew what he'd find. If there's anything Liam McLoughlin excelled at, it was turning invisible.

"I could ask the same of you!" she yelled. "You evidently knew that boy was sneaking out and yet you did nothing. Have you even questioned him regarding my missing gate? Or are you too fond of him to see him as the criminal he is?"

Mason found himself torn between the need to run after Liam and the need to finally give Miss Ward a piece of his mind. "As a matter of fact, Miss Ward, I did." He wanted to snarl the words at her, but forced a civil tone into his voice. "He came clean with me about finding your house a very good place to hide, but resisting going in on account of you being on the Selection Committee and all."

"Every smart criminal works an angle, Sheriff Wright."

"Liam McLoughlin is not a criminal." He ground it out through gritted teeth. "Whereas I have tossed Vern Hicks and his bottles off your porch four times since the storm and I don't hear you calling to run him out of town. How do you know it isn't Vern who's made off with your gate?"

She started in on some version of a defense, but Mason decided he would hear none of it. She wasn't worth the breath it'd take to argue with her. "Good afternoon, Miss Ward," he cut in to her tirade as he grabbed his hat off its hook by the door, not even listening to whatever it was she was spouting at him. "You'll forgive me if I don't see you out."

Holly rushed out of the school yard as fast as she could manage, shouting directions to Cindy and Bucky Wyler as to how to gather the students into their afternoon chore teams. When Beatrice had asked to have a few words with Liam, she never imagined it would turn into the fiasco that ensued. She'd gone back into the classroom to get some papers, and come back out to Liam running down the street and Beatrice shouting after him. With Rebecca off visiting Sasha, Holly couldn't just leave the children and run off after Beatrice and Liam, no matter how bad things looked. The ten minutes it took for Cindy and Bucky to arrive dragged by like hours until she could head off after whatever war had broken out between the young boy and the old woman.

Sure Liam would run straight to Mason, Holly ran down Victory Street to find the sheriff turning and peering in several directions. "Where is he?" she called, panting from the run.

"He's run off. That nightmare of an old woman scared the pants off him and he ran." Mason cursed under his breath and then cupped his hands to call out, "Liam! Liam, where are you?"

The only reply was Reverend Turner coming down Third Street. "Has Liam gone off?" The reverend picked up his steps to meet Holly and Mason where they were standing.

"He's run away, Reverend." Holly scanned the horizon but knew better. Finding Liam would be difficult given how well the boy knew how to hide. She turned to Mason. "What on earth did Beatrice say?"

At that moment, Beatrice came stalking out of Mason's office, furious. "I spoke the truth. That boy is trouble and you all are too weak to see it. I have proof now that he's been sneaking out at night from the schoolhouse, just like I said from the start. I saw him with my own eyes. It's no wonder things have gone missing all over town. He's stealing. He's been stealing all along."

"Now hold on a minute, Beatrice, those are serious accusations." The reverend held up one hand to quiet Miss Ward down.

"Accusations is right," Mason growled. "She sat in my office and told him he was no better than the man who hung in Greenville this week."

"Beatrice," Holly gasped. "You didn't say that."

"Well, no one else will." Beatrice sniffed. "No one else seems to see what's happened to this town since those orphans came here. I had to speak my piece."

"Right to his poor, frightened face you did. What a

fine, upstanding thing to do." Mason stabbed an angry finger at Miss Ward.

The reverend stepped between Beatrice and Mason. "Miss Ward, have you been to your house this morning?"

"I can't live there, you know that. The roof's been shore off the east end." She threw a sideways glance at Mason. "Evidently, it's an excellent place for hiding, though."

"Yes, but have you been there this morning?" The reverend started walking in the direction of Beatrice's house, motioning the group to follow.

"Where are you going?" Beatrice asked, nearly trotting to keep up with the reverend. "Pastor, I can't see what any of this has to do with that boy's behavior."

"You will. That's actually why I was heading toward your office, Wright. All of you, come!"

With a quick glance at each other, Mason and Holly took off after Reverend Turner and Miss Ward.

"Pastor Turner," huffed Miss Ward as they dashed down Liberty Street, "I demand to know what's going on here!"

"I wish I knew," the reverend called back as he turned past Mayor Evans's house on the corner, and led the group up the block of Second Street to where they could see for themselves.

Beatrice Ward was actually speechless.

"Good gracious!" Holly could barely believe it, either.

"Well, I'll be hanged myself," Mason said in utter shock. "Who'd do that?"

There, affixed to the fence in perfect working order,

was a new wrought-iron gate. Right down to the swirly letter "W."

"And that's not all," the reverend said. "I just came from the Millers' where Mel told me a new set of tools was found sitting on Charlie's shop porch this morning. And a new wheelbarrow showed up at Gavin's, too."

"Are you saying everything that was stolen has been returned?" Holly couldn't believe what she was hearing.

"Of course," Mason said so slowly Holly could actually hear his mental gears turning. "Everything that was taken was broken somehow. It wasn't stolen, it was replaced—with improvements."

"That's not possible," Beatrice said.

"Nevertheless, there it is." Reverend Turner clasped his hands. "There's your new gate, right in front of us."

"Liam could not have done this." Mason straightened up, pushing his hat back on his head. "Don't make me stand here and argue with you, Miss Ward. Even you can see this clears him."

"Well, I…"

"Enough, Beatrice. You were wrong." He took a step toward her, making Holly gulp.

"We don't know who…"

"You were wrong about Liam." Mason was practically standing over her now. "Admit it."

"Why don't we concern ourselves with this later?" Reverend Turner stepped in, gesturing Mason back from his stance. "It seems to me right now we ought to be finding Liam."

"Yes," Holly agreed. "Why don't we split—" She stopped speaking, for Mason had turned and begun running down the street toward his office without another word. She stood for a moment, mouth open mid-

sentence. That man never waited for anything once he
made up his mind. "He can't have gone far," she said
to the reverend and Miss Ward, but it felt like an unnecessary afterthought. No one doubted, by the way
Mason ran, that the sheriff would get his man. Or, in
this case, his boy.

An hour later, Mason ran around another corner,
watching the sun dip lower in the sky. The boy was in
none of his usual hiding spots, nor had any of the other
children seen him. Mason turned in a slow circle, rack-
ing his brain for options, hating how panicked he felt.
When had Liam come to mean so much to him?

Think, Wright, think. What does your gut tell you?
Liam wasn't ready to run very far; Mason's instinct told
him that. Besides, anyone serious about skipping town
would head for the train tracks, and while Liam was
frightened and feeling rejected, he wouldn't go back to
a place with all those horrid memories. He'd go somewhere he felt safe, somewhere nearby but still distant
from all the accusing eyes of Evans Grove. He'd said
Beatrice's house made an excellent hideout, but he'd
never go there after what she'd said. He'd go somewhere with good associations. The schoolhouse? No,
he'd have heard from Holly if he was hiding somewhere
near there. He didn't seem the type to hide out near the
church, and the hotel was too busy. He'd want someplace calm. Someplace small and maybe even dark.

He'd go to the cave.

Of course! Mason nearly whacked his forehead with
his hand. Why hadn't he thought of that earlier? He
turned on his heels and ran up Fourth Street to the foot-
bridge that led over the creek. Liam had to be there.

Mason didn't want to consider an alternative. The thought of losing Liam—and losing him to the lie that he wasn't wanted here—made Mason crazy. He wasn't the kind of man who liked needing anyone, much less an eleven-year-old boy. But how to convince the lad Beatrice's sharp words weren't how everyone in Evans Grove saw him? *Show me how.* The burst of prayer startled Mason as he cut through a grove of trees just north of the cave. He hadn't felt this far out of his depth since the night Phoebe died. In some ways it was worse: there was no remedy for Phoebe's loss, nothing to be done but mourn. Now, this loss could be stopped—but only with the right words.

And words were the last thing Mason Wright was good at. Words were Holly's realm.

Why hadn't he taken Holly with him to find Liam? He knew the answer to that, and liked it less than his growing affection for Liam. He couldn't contain himself around her, not with the storm going off in his chest right now. *You've got to help me,* Mason prayed, too desperate to worry what his new habit of praying might mean. *I can't mess this up. I need You to give me the right words.*

"Liam?" Mason started toward the clearing where they'd been fishing. By some cruel joke, he found himself behind the same outcropping of bushes where Holly must have hid when she listened. Some of the forget-me-nots she'd been gathering were spilled on the ground, withered. He stared at them while he listened for sounds of Liam, his mind imagining Holly in a field of the flowers, sunlight catching the colors in her brown hair. He'd never loathed silence more.

Moving slowly, Mason stepped into the clearing,

studying the grass on the creek bank for signs of a visitor. There was a scrape of mud to his left, the damp side of a rock recently overturned just beyond it. *He's here. Thank You, God, he's here.* "Liam, come out."

No response. Then a quiet scraping sound from inside the cave. "I know you're here. I'm glad you're here and not gone." Mason sat down on a rock, laying his hat beside him in the lengthening shadows. "I don't believe what Miss Ward said. No one believes that."

A twig snapped from beyond the dark opening of the cave.

"We can prove now it wasn't you who took those things. Whoever took Miss Ward's gate replaced it last night with a new one. And Mr. Miller's tools, and the wheelbarrow from Gavin's store. You couldn't have done that."

A pair of puffy eyes became barely visible in the cave shadows. "I could've."

Thank You. Mason felt one corner of his mouth turn up, right after his entire body let go of the tension that had gripped him for the last hour. "Is that so?"

"Could be." The boy's body shifted into view from the mouth of the cave. He had a big swath of mud down one arm, and one pant leg was soaked. He sniffed and wiped his nose on his clean sleeve.

"You bought Miss Ward a new gate just like her old one? And blacksmith tools? And a wheelbarrow?"

"I could have managed it."

Mason shifted toward the boy, who moved farther into the light but still hadn't left the mouth of the cave. "I expect you could. Only you didn't take any of those things, because you're not a thief."

"Miss Ward sure thinks I am."

"Miss Ward is dead wrong."

"But I am a thief. I did steal, back in New York. Get hungry enough, and anyone'll figure out how to steal food."

It clawed at Mason's gut that the boy had learned those kinds of lessons. How dare the world let this boy want for anything ever again? He'd had enough misery for three lifetimes, let alone less than a dozen years. "That's not the same. Those men on the train? They didn't need what they were taking. Wanting something because of greed isn't the same thing as wanting something for survival." He tried to draw Liam out by looking straight into the boy's red-rimmed eyes. "You're not them. You're not anything like them." Oh, how he wanted to strangle Miss Ward for ever making such a cruel comparison. That woman was twelve kinds of mean some days.

"Nobody wants me here."

The boy's wounded tone wrapped itself into a tight little ball Mason felt at the back of his throat. "That's dead wrong, too."

"No, it's not. Miss Sterling and Miss Sanders, they've tried real hard to get someone to take me in, but you and I both know it ain't worked."

"I'd take you." It leapt out of Mason's mouth, ridiculous as it was. "They wouldn't let me, I'm sure, but if they did…"

"Why won't they?" Liam stepped out of the cave with a heartbreaking eagerness.

How to explain this? Mason pulled his hand across his chin, reaching for the words. "A boy needs a mother and a father. I don't have that kind of life."

Liam took two steps toward Mason. "I like your life."

The boy looked positively bedraggled, and Mason was surprised he had to squelch the urge to swallow the lad in a hug.

"I do, too." That suddenly felt like a lie. He'd come to hate his life lately, mostly because two people had stuck themselves so far into it that all the lonely spots stuck out like thorns. "Only it's not..." He found he couldn't finish the sentence. "It's not what the OSS thinks you ought to have."

"How come they get to choose?" Liam's words were defiant. He must think the whole world didn't give one fig what he wanted. That was a poor way to live at any age, much less eleven.

Mason groped for the right response. "Someone your age can't always see what's best. You got your future to think about."

He moved his hat, motioning to Liam to come sit on the rock. When the boy eased himself down, Mason allowed himself to rumple Liam's hair.

"My future," Liam mocked, mimicking Beatrice Ward's righteous tone with alarming accuracy. He turned to look up at Mason with eyes so cynical they looked out of place on his young face. "C'mon, what kind of future have I got?"

Something fierce roared up out of Mason's chest. "You got every kind of future, that's what. You're smart and young and you got more energy than twenty of me, and that's just for starters." He wanted to take the boy and shake him, make him realize how much good was ahead of him despite what fools like Beatrice Ward chose to believe.

Liam wasn't buying it. He leaned on his knees with slumped shoulders, wiping the mud off one hand. "I can't subtract, I got no parents, no money and no prospects and I'm a thief. I done too much wrong to end up with some nice family. I belong on my own, alone. I don't need mean ol' Miss Ward to lay that out for me. I can see it all by myself."

Mason grabbed the boy's shoulders. "Don't talk like that. Don't you dare let them make you feel that way. Your future is yours, not anybody else's to take. Yours. And I don't care even if you stole every day of your life in New York, you don't have to live like that here. You get to choose how it goes from here on. No one ever has to be alone, ever. No matter what they did."

Liam looked up at him, and Mason felt the weight of his own words come back around to hit him full force. *No one ever has to be alone, ever. No matter what they did.* Did he really believe that? His memory cast back so fast and so clearly to the inscription Holly had written that Mason almost had to blink and shake his head. "Around these parts," Mason choked out, feeling as though he'd lost complete control of whatever was going on here, "we believe everyone gets a forgiven future. What's past is gone, as long as you're willing to make the next part right." He put his arm around the boy, feeling a wave of warmth as the bony shoulder leaned into him.

"That's just you. You and I, we understand each other." There was the "old man" voice Liam so often used. Mason was delighted to see it come back, annoying as it was.

"No, it's not." Mason reached into his pocket and pulled out the inscription page from Holly's book of Psalms. Had this moment been the true reason he'd been unable to throw her heartfelt words away? No, there was more. They were true words, but they were also Holly's words. There might have been a time when he thought that inscription would be the only part of her he got to hold on to, but he was starting to see how wrong that was. "Take a look at this." Mason carefully unfolded the thin paper to reveal the delicate, swirly handwriting:

"To Mason,

Who believes himself lost, but isn't.

God's eye never wavers,

A forgiven future always waits,

And the true heart knows a true hero.

Holly"

"All that's the same for you," Mason told him. "You think you're lost—done for—but you're not. If God's got some kind of plan for the likes of me, He sure must have one for you. I done worse things than you by far, Liam. More than you know." It was like some tight cord around Mason's chest had finally unraveled. He felt like he was taking his first deep breaths in years, and the words kept spilling out of him. "Only I'm just figuring out I don't have to be alone, and I'd rather you didn't spend years on your own like I done. The way I see it, we both got futures right here, and we'd best get to them. It'd be a waste if we didn't, don't you think?"

One corner of Liam's mouth began to curl up in the familiar impish smile. Somehow, that boy had managed to sneak into Mason's dark, closed heart and crack it wide open. "I know what I think," the boy said wryly.

"What's that?"

"I think Miss Sanders is stuck on you something fierce to write something so fussy." He looked at the ragged edge. "What'd she write it in?"

Mason couldn't stop his smile. "A book."

Liam's eyes popped. "You tore something out of a book? A book of Miss Sanders's?"

"It wasn't my best idea."

"No foolin' there." Liam watched him fold it back up and return it to his shirt pocket. "Why'd you do something like that?"

"A dumb notion. I wanted to hurt her 'cause she cared about me." He raised a knowing eyebrow at the boy. "Sort of like running away from folks who want you to stay." Mason ruffled his hair again, wondering again how this scrap of a boy could manage in the space of a few days to peel years of guilt and punishment off his spirit. Actually, he knew the answer. Liam had managed it because Holly had done much the same thing. The pair of them, he realized, were an unstoppable force.

The pair of them. All three of them together.

With one more look into Liam's eyes, Mason saw the whole thing line up in perfect order. The train, the boy, Holly, all of it. No matter how hard he tried to push it away, God had sent him the things that could heal his life. Holly's relentless insistence that he had a future allowed him to show Liam his. The astonishment at the perfection of it all was matched only by his fright that he'd nearly managed to throw all of it away.

"What's the matter with you?" Liam asked, eyebrows furrowed. "You look all funny all of a sudden."

"I just figured out something really important, that's all."

"Just now?" Liam moaned in his "old man" voice. "Just *now* you're figuring out you're sweet on Miss Sanders, too? Didn't you know that when you kissed her?"

That boy was far too clever for his tender years. "Funny enough, I didn't."

"Well, that *is* dumb."

Mason snatched his hat off the rock. "What's dumb is you and I sitting here yakking away while a whole bunch of folks are over there worrying about us. What do you say we head on back and set things to rights?"

Chapter Twenty-One

"What is wrong with that man?" Beatrice looked off after the figure of Mason running down the street. "I don't see why we can't just let God's will take its proper course here."

"Now, Beatrice…" Reverend Turner placated.

"God's will?" Holly balked. "You think God would permit us to make a young boy feel as though he's not wanted? Over something that isn't even true?" Holly could normally write off Beatrice's judgmental nature to the woman's abrasive personality, but this got under her skin.

"A bad seed is a bad seed. He might not have stolen my gate, but I'm certain he's stolen before. I'm sure the reverend would agree with me that we can't have Evans Grove's children exposed to that kind."

"I have to say I'd…" the reverend started in.

Holly had no interest in hearing his opinion. She squared off in front of the old woman, not caring how her voice raised right there on the street. "*That kind* of boy ran for help two weeks ago into an unfamiliar town and saved my life. *That kind* of boy has looked out for

his companions and worked hard at his studies. *That
kind* of boy has put up with your cruel attitude long
enough, Beatrice Ward. So help me, *that kind* of boy is
staying in Evans Grove if I have to take him in myself!"
Holly had always viewed facing down Beatrice Ward as
not much different than facing down the bandit's gun
barrel, but a surprising new strength now roared out of
her heart. If there was one thing she knew, it was that
each and every one of these orphans had become dear
to her and was worth fighting for.

"You couldn't!" Beatrice sniffed, insulted. "Why, a
woman alone couldn't possibly hope to raise a child."

"I'd find a way," Holly shot back. "Would that you
could find a way to show them the kindness and Christian love they deserve."

"Now, ladies, let's all try to…"

At his words, Holly turned to the reverend. "I'm
going to try and find Liam before he does something
rash. He's had his feelings terribly hurt, and Heaven
knows what he'll do if he's frightened enough. I'm going
back to the schoolhouse to see if he's taken any of his
belongings. I'm going to pray for his safety the whole
walk back and I'll kindly ask you to do the same."

Holly turned toward the schoolhouse without a single
look back. *Forgive me, Father*, she prayed, still shocked
at the strength of her words, *but that woman annoys me
so!* Half of her wanted to dash all over town, peeking
into every shadow until she found Liam's wide brown
eyes. The more sensible half of her knew he was too
skilled at hiding. He wouldn't be found until he wanted
to be. The best thing she could do was to be waiting
when he ventured forth from his hiding spot. And pray.

She was praying for Liam, and for Mason to find

Liam, when Rebecca came out of the schoolhouse. The look on her face told Holly Liam was still nowhere to be found. "I haven't seen him since he took off with Miss Ward behind him. Holly, what's happened?"

"Beatrice accused Liam of stealing. Of being behind all the things going missing around town. Oh, Rebecca, he's run off."

"To the sheriff's office?"

"No," Holly countered, "he ran off *from* there. Beatrice was dreadful, evidently. Even to me she said the most horrid things about the children. Even after Reverend Turner told us the missing items have turned up replaced."

"Replaced?"

"Yes, someone has repaired Charles's shop tools and left the Gavins a new wheelbarrow, and even fixed Beatrice's broken gate." Holly looked at Rebecca. "How could she be so cruel when someone has shown her such a kindness?" She stopped walking, realizing the school yard was empty. "Where are the children?"

"It was chaotic after you left, so Mrs. Turner took them to the church parlor. She said something about needing a hall swept, but honestly, I think she was just inventing something for them to do. I started looking for Liam when you didn't come back, but didn't know what to think when I found the sheriff's office empty." They reached the schoolhouse door, and Rebecca pushed it open. "Is Sheriff Wright looking for Liam?"

"Yes." Holly shut the door behind her. "I was terrible to Beatrice, Rebecca. I said the most dreadful things to her."

"She has a habit of bringing that out in people, I think." Rebecca paced the floor. "Where could Liam be?"

"Anywhere. You know how good he is at hiding. He's snuck out more times that we realized, and Beatrice knows that. She called him a bad seed." Holly looked up at the woman. "He's not a bad seed. You know that. He's come through so much; they all have. Evans Grove needs to be their home, I know it."

"They know it, too, Holly. They know how much you care for them, how you'll fight for them to stay. We'll both fight for them to stay." Rebecca pressed her fingers to her temples. "We've got to find him. Why don't I go talk to the children and see what I can find out? Some of them must know his favorite hiding spots. You should stay here in case he comes back."

Holly flailed her arms in frustration. "I can't just sit here."

"Of course not." Rebecca laid a hand on Holly's arm. "You can pray. Pray as hard as you can that one red-headed boy comes home where he belongs." With a quick hug, the OSS agent turned and headed out the door in the direction of the church.

Holly turned agitated circles around the empty room. The silence hung heavy and choking. The room had become so continually boisterous that the lack of noise felt unnatural. Devoid of life. Holly fell into a desk chair— Liam's desk chair—and sunk down, laying her head in her hands. *I'd take him, Lord. You know that. If that's what all this was for, to bring Liam into my home, then make a way. I'll be strong enough if You stand by me.*

Mason would stand by Liam, too, even if he still kept a rigid distance from her. "I'd thought it so dreadful when he ignored me," she told the empty room, "but this is worse." Bad as it was, she'd endure it if Liam had Mason in his life, for there could be no doubt the boy did something to the sheriff's hardened heart. "Something I was never able to do," she told Liam's desk as she ran a hand down one side. "Oh, I can't stand here and wait. I've got to do something."

She had to go look. Frustrated, Holly rose from the desk, dashed to the door and pulled it open.

Mason stood before her.

"He's fine. I found him."

"Thank you, Jesus!" Holly closed her eyes and sank against the door frame, relief flooding her features. Mason fought the urge to put an arm out and steady her. Glory, but he didn't know how to do this. The whole walk back he'd been trying to form words in his head, but his mind went blank at the sight of her.

She put her hand to her chest as if her heart were pounding. He knew the feeling. "Where is he?"

"I found Miss Sterling outside the church as we went by. She wanted a few words with the boy." Mason was pretty sure Liam's next hour wouldn't go nearly as well as the one he was hoping to spend. Miss Sterling looked like she had more than a few choice words for the boy, despite her clear relief that he'd been found safe and sound.

"You didn't bring him here?" For a moment, Mason was annoyed she was so preoccupied with Liam when he was standing in her doorway, but then he remembered Holly had no idea what he was about to say. She couldn't know how much he'd changed in the past hour, in the past day, in the past two weeks.

"I wanted a few words with you."

He must have been trying too hard to hide his smile, because she turned and walked into the schoolhouse as though she were expecting a lecture. "Yes, I know we've been horrid to each other lately," she began, "but you seem to bring out the most dreadful stubbornness in me. You've simply got to see how much you mean to that boy. You're always storming off without answering anyone, I don't see how—"

There was nothing for it. Before she could work herself up into a dither, Mason grabbed her hand. Holly spun toward him, mouth still open midword, startled by his sudden touch. She was so perfectly, simply beautiful just then. Strong and filled with all the wonder he was sure he'd lost. She'd never, ever stopped pushing through toward him, and evidently God was right behind her, pushing toward him as well. It was such a release, such a new grasp at life to take her hand and pull her toward him. This was no torrent of impulse as his first embrace had been. This was a deliberate, willful response to the grace he'd ignored for so long.

"Mason?"

It was a sheer delight to watch her stumble back into using his first name. He slid one hand around the tender curve of her waist, watching her eyes go wide like a new foal. "Thank you." He wanted a flood of words, some bunch of adjectives to match what he was feeling, but those words were the first and only ones that came to mind.

"For?" The breathless, surprised quality of her voice danced down his spine.

"For never giving up on me. For being stubborn and…" he tried to remember the long word she'd called him, the one that meant bullheaded and uncooperative "…recalcitrant." He pulled her in an inch closer, enjoying it when the hand that had been on her chest turned to lay against his. He'd thought this would be so hard, but it was so easy. Like letting go of something he'd fought for ages—which wasn't that far off, was it?

Her brows furrowed, delightfully confused. "That's not the meaning of the word. You must mean…"

Mason let go of her hand and brushed his thumb over her soft pink lips. Nothing he'd ever touched felt softer, and the smile he felt when she fell silent seemed to spring to life out of every dead part of him. "Let me put it this way." He let his lips brush against that softness, feeling her breath catch at the contact. The hand against his chest fluttered, and she made the most delightful noise of astonishment. Had he just now come to love her? Or had he loved her all along and denied it?

Holly stiffened for a moment, and Mason felt a bone-deep stab of regret for the way he'd rejected her after the first time they'd kissed. He never again wanted her to fear her welcome in his arms. Then, somehow sensing his feelings, she softened and melted against him. Mason tried to let his touch say the thousands of things he couldn't find words for, to extend to her the endless grace she'd given him. When she fully softened, when her hands wandered up his chest to wrap around his neck and pull him close, Mason thought he'd drown in the sensation. It felt like the whole world welcomed him back to life in the circle of one woman's arms.

When he finally pulled back, the two of them dragging in lungfuls of air as their foreheads fell together, Mason felt the pieces of his broken life slip neatly into a whole again. "Forgive me," he whispered, his eyes falling closed at the world-tilting wonder of it all. "I've hurt you so much. I thought if I hurt you enough, you'd stop coming after me and I wouldn't have to risk my heart ever again. I thought making you hate me would stop me wanting you. I was so wrong."

She looked up at him. "You've... All along? I didn't imagine it?"

"You're too clever for me to hide it." Mason shook his head, running one finger down the delicate waves of hair that framed her face. "And beautiful. So beautiful."

Now it was she who shook her head. "No, I'm not."

He held her face in his hand. "You are. Can't you see it? Can't you see how I've looked at you all this time?"

Holly pulled back. "You've hardly looked at me. Why, before all this business I couldn't get you to say two words to me." Her words were sharp but her smile could have filled the room twice over.

"I didn't handle that very well, did I?" He laid a half-dozen tiny kisses on her forehead, feeling like twenty tons had slid off his weary shoulders.

"I should say not." He found her schoolmarm scolding endlessly endearing. Mason couldn't remember the last time he felt anything close to playful. Her face grew more serious. "So when you kissed me that night, it really was a moment of weakness."

"I suppose it's closer to say I couldn't fight it anymore. It was so wrong of me to make you feel as though that was some fault of yours. I've been so awful. Please forgive me."

Her smile told him she did long before her words. "Plain old me drove the sheriff to awful behavior? How amusing. I ought to be ashamed of myself."

"You ought to be proud of yourself. You've never wavered, never faltered in your faith, or your faith in me. I think you loved me back to life, Holly Sanders.

You kept thrusting my forgiven future in my face until I woke up to realize it was there."

"The book?"

"It was the beginning of all of it. You scared me to death with that gift. When you came out and said what you felt, it was as if I couldn't pretend it wasn't there anymore. I'm sorry I punished you for that. I am. I'll replace the book, I promise."

She traced his jaw with one finger, and he felt the touch go through him like a lightning bolt. How had he ever hoped to fight something so powerful as this woman's love? "You don't have to replace it. I kept it. I wanted to throw it into the creek that night, I confess, but I couldn't. Now it's only missing a page."

Mason reached for his shirt pocket. "No, it's not."

Chapter Twenty-Two

Holly could barely get a deep breath, and her knees felt as if they would go out from underneath her at any moment. She was sure she'd search for a hundred years and not find the words to describe the look in Mason's eyes right now. It was as if every feeling he'd held back over so many years was bursting out from behind his smile. A smile that was for her. *For her.* While she wanted to ask him endless questions about whatever it was that had made this glorious transformation in the man, she was conscious of the moment's singular wonder. Too many words might ruin it, and she wanted to remember this time forever.

"I kept it," Mason said as he pulled the page from his shirt pocket. She recognized it immediately, feeling as if she could float right up and sparkle in the sky like a star. "At first I didn't know why." He unfolded the small thin page with a reverence she could feel— as if her heart unfolded with the paper. "Then I knew I'd keep it because it was the only part of you I'd ever get to have."

"You've had my heart for so long. Don't you know

that?" She ran her hands across the edge of the page as he held it.

"I didn't deserve it. I hadn't ever let go of all that darkness, and I couldn't drag you into it. I wouldn't do that to you."

"But now?" She already knew the answer. The Mason before her had no more darkness weighing him down. The storm that had always brewed behind his eyes was gone, leaving in its wake a stunning blue gaze—the clear eyes of a man at peace.

"I remembered a wise woman's words about a forgiven future. I told them to Liam, but I suppose I told them to myself, too. He was so hard on himself. And then I realized he's just like me. When I wanted him to reach for his future, I realized I had no business asking him to do that when I wouldn't myself." Mason's hand stroked her hair, and Holly felt certain she would dissolve of sheer happiness. "That night when I kissed you…"

"I did kiss you back, you know," Holly surprised herself by being able to tease him.

"Boy, did you." He smirked like a schoolboy. "But that night, I read that book. All of it. In there was a man who was as tangled up as I was. Who felt all the darkness I knew. Back then, I felt like the forgiveness in that book wasn't something I could have. Now I know it's been there for me all along. That's what you've been trying to show me, why you gave me the book, isn't it?" His hands moved to clasp hers, warm and strong. "I've been such a fool. I want that forgiven future, Holly, but only if it's our future, not just mine." He brought her hands to his lips and kissed them with a tenderness she'd never dreamed he possessed.

"I want that, Mason. It's all I've ever wanted." She took his face in her hands, marveling at the perfect angle of his jaw, reveling in the clarity of those eyes that had been hidden from her so much. And then it was she who kissed him. A confident, courageous kiss. An invitation to life and love and all the grace God had for them to share.

She nearly laughed when Mason pulled back and exhaled. She had the power to stun Mason Wright with a kiss. What an astounding thing that was. For this one moment, Holly luxuriated in the things she had resigned would never be hers. Feeling beautiful. Being loved by a man she loved. There couldn't be a thing the two of them couldn't conquer, not if God had brought them together now.

Mason held her by both shoulders, suddenly serious. "I love you, Holly Sanders. I imagine I have for a long time. Only now I need you to be brave and courageous." He shook his head, starting over. "I already know you're brave and courageous. You've shown me in a dozen different ways. Only now there's something we need to do, you and I."

"Yes?"

"We need to make a family. Holly, I want to marry you. And I want us to adopt Liam. Not just an OSS placement—a real adoption, to make him really our son. That's the family I want to make. Not just because of Liam, but because I see now this is what God had in mind for all of us all along. He brought us together, and brought Liam to us."

Holly knew there was no sense in holding back the tears. How many times had she daydreamed of just that?

Seen some endearing spark in Liam's eyes, had it remind her of the lack of spark in Mason's, and crafted a dream of what they would be like as a family? Hadn't she had that very dream as she watched Mason and Liam at the creek, felt a pang of envy at the father-son relationship they seemed to have? While she wanted all the children to stay in Evans Grove, there was no question that it was Liam who had stolen her heart. Right after Mason, that is.

"Crying is a yes, right?" He shifted his weight, nervous. Mason Wright, nervous. The world really had turned upside down. "That's a yes?"

"It's a hundred yesses. It's a thousand of them."

Mason picked her up and twirled her around the room, laughing as his hat tumbled off his head. A full, clear laugh she felt down to her toes now dangling in the air. "I love you, Mason," she whispered into his neck as he whirled her, feeling the reaction surge through his chest and the strong arms holding her tight. "I've loved you for so long."

Mason set her down, pushed out a breath and then bent down on one knee. "Say you'll love me forever." He took her hand, and for the first time ever, he looked up at her instead of the other way around.

"Longer." Holly bent down and kissed him. He laid his head against her waist, his breath deep and labored. She ran her hands through his wondrous dark-blond hair and sent a prayer of deep gratitude to the God whose grace had finally released this man from his exile. "Mason?"

He looked up at her, and somehow she managed to love him even more. "Yes?"

"When should we tell Liam?"

He grinned, looking all too much like the boy who would soon complete their family. "I think now sounds perfect, don't you?"

For the longest time, secrets had been dark and heavy things pressing down on his chest and making Mason feel lonesome. Now, as he and Holly tried to walk casually toward the church steps, secrets felt wild and energetic, pounding with urgency to get out of his chest and be shouted to the world. Mason knew his life had changed when he walked right past Beatrice without a mean thought. She stared at him, perhaps at the silly grin he knew he must be wearing, but said nothing.

His smirk widened when he heard Holly laugh softly once they'd passed. They'd both been angry at Beatrice's accusations, but now her sourness seemed so inconsequential. Mason stole a sideways glance at Holly, fighting the urge to take her hand.

"I know I said we should wait to tell everyone," she whispered, one hand fiddling with her skirts, "but I'm not sure I can keep it in."

He knew the feeling. "We just need a day, like you said. To let Liam get used to the idea." Mason pulled his hat down and stuffed his hands in his pockets to keep from reaching for her. "Although it won't be much of a surprise. He knew, you know. Spotted it right off. He saw us kiss that night."

Holly's hand went to her mouth, and she stared toward the church. All the children were sitting on the steps, listening to Liam tell some rousing tale. The boy probably was making his hiding out to be some grand adventure instead of a few hours in a damp cave.

"Rebecca encouraged me to be brave enough to tell

you how I feel. She made it seem so easy." He followed her gaze as it rested on the tall and elegant city woman, who couldn't be more different than his lovely, simple Holly. "I thought I could be confident like her." Her voice was wistful. "How foolish I was."

"Holly. Holly," Mason repeated her name until she turned and looked back at him. "I've no eye for any high society airs." He gazed at her, letting his eyes hold her if his arms could not. "And believe me, I was charmed. Dumbstruck's more like it. You could have knocked me over with one breath when you gave me that book. I could hardly breathe for wanting to kiss you." He paused for a moment, needing her to understand how she'd moved him that night. "I fell for you so hard that night I was scared to death. I'm still a mite spooked by it all."

"It is a powerful thing, isn't it?" She smiled, and for the first time Mason wondered who was the stronger of the two. "Big enough for three, I expect." Her gaze flicked down as her cheeks flushed, and she tucked a strand of hair behind her ear. What he wouldn't give to be that strand, brushing her rosy cheek. "I can't wait to tell him."

"Then let's stop standing here and go tell him." He started toward the church, but said to her, "I'm warning you, though. I'm going to have a bit of fun with this. I reckon it may be the last chance I have to get the upper hand on that boy in a long time."

Stuffing his smile down inside, Mason lowered his voice until it rumbled like thunder. "Liam McLoughlin!"

Liam's head jerked up as every head on the church

steps turned toward Mason. He was pretty sure he saw the boy gulp. "Sir?"

"I'll need a word with you. Alone." The mumbles of the other children told him he'd succeeded in giving the impression Liam was in serious trouble.

Liam didn't look too eager to come away from the protection of his companions, but Miss Sterling raised him by the elbow and motioned for him to walk forward. The boy pulled his cap from his head, trying to look penitent, perhaps, and shuffled forward.

Out of the corner of his eye he caught Holly turning away. Good. She could never hold her feelings in, least of all now. Her "shunning" likely scared the boy more. "I didn't do it," Liam pleaded. "You know that. You told me so."

"All the same, I have serious business with you. Very serious business."

Liam simply nodded.

"There are going to have to be some big changes around here. I need to know you're willing to step up and make them."

Twisting his cap in his hands, Liam said, "I'm up for anything. I'm willin' and ready."

Mason pointed to the ground just in front of him. "Come on over here close. What I got to say isn't the kind of thing everyone can hear."

Liam seemed to think this spelled his doom, moving forward with eyes down and shoulders slumped. Mason felt a small surge of victory at finally rendering the boy speechless.

"You are not to repeat to anyone what I'm about to tell you. You are to stand silently and listen. Understood?"

"Yes, sir."

"And you are not to move or any such thing. No matter what I say. Eyes down, son."

Liam complied, looking worse than ever.

"I can't. Mason, we can't do this with everyone watching." Holly's voice came whispering behind him, pitched high with tension.

He turned to her, and she looked as if she'd come apart at the seams in a matter of minutes. The woman had too much joy bottled up inside her to hold it in. Mason nearly gave in to a soft laugh, realizing he'd asked for too much composure from a happy woman about to deliver happy news. "We could just let the whole world know right now."

"Know what?" Liam looked understandably stumped.

"Not yet!" Holly nearly squeaked. "He needs to hear first."

"Hear what?" Liam's eyes shot from side to side, panicked.

Mason cast about for a quick solution. Opting for the closest place out of the public eye, he pointed toward the church doors. "Inside. Now." He was sure his gruff voice wasn't doing much to mask the smile he was having trouble hiding. This was entirely too much fun. Glory, how long had it been since he'd had anything close to fun?

Grabbing Liam's elbow for effect, Mason started for the church doors, only to have Holly dash ahead of him. Doubly puzzled, Liam glanced up at him, but Mason kept his eyes forward and walked as fast as he could manage. Now that he thought about it, a church was the perfect place to deliver his news.

* * *

Holly pushed through the church doors, relieved to find the sanctuary empty. She let out the breath she'd been holding, wanting to shout for all the happiness cooped up inside her. Unable to face Mason or Liam, sure she'd give the ruse away, she perched on one of the back pews and faced forward.

"Exactly how much trouble am I in?" Liam's voice came squeaking as she heard Mason and the boy come in behind her.

"Let's just say your life will never be the same after I get through with you today."

"Miss Sanders, you're not gonna let him hurt me, are you?"

"Relax, Liam, I'm not out to hurt you." Holly peeked back to see Mason take the boy by both shoulders. He angled Liam so that he was facing back, giving her a clear shot of Mason's face over the boy's head. She swallowed a laugh when Mason actually winked at her. It was as if her sheriff had become a whole new man in the space of an hour. "You need to listen up good to what I'm about to tell you. Understand?"

Liam nodded.

"You're clever, so it should come as no surprise to you that Miss Sanders and I...well, we have strong feelings for each other. Feelings we haven't been...well, let's just say things have been a bit tangled between us."

"I'll say," Liam replied, "but you mind telling me what—"

Mason held up a hand. "It'd be best if you let me finish, son. This gets a mite complicated."

"Yes, sir."

Mason, suddenly remembering he was in church,

pulled his hat from his head and handed it to Holly. Something about the gesture touched her so deeply she was glad to be out of public view, afraid she might actually cry. She clutched the hat as if he'd given her a bouquet of roses.

"Now, then. Your little escapade earlier today brought certain things to light, and while I do not *at all* condone you hauling off like you did, there have been some…happy consequences. Miss Sanders and I, well, we finally figured things out. Not to put too fine a point on it, but I've asked her to marry me, and she's said yes."

Liam's head whipped around so fast she thought the boy would fall over. Eyes bugged wide, he raised an eyebrow in stunned inquiry, and she nodded. It was so wonderful not to have to hide the mile-wide smile anymore. It felt like she might not stop smiling until Christmas at this rate. "That's great," the boy said slowly, still trying to piece together what this whole charade had to do with him.

Mason reached for Holly's hand and drew her to his side. "It certainly is. Only the way we see it, things still aren't quite right. Truth is, we were hoping you'd come on board. Stay here."

"Well, sure I'd want to stay here. I've always wanted to stay here, you know that. Only I don't see how…" The idea slowly began to dawn on him, and Holly felt a tear slip down her cheek as the boys eyes grew big as saucers. "You mean…?"

"We're asking if you'd like to be part of our family." Holly said, squeezing Mason's hand.

Liam's mouth was wide open. "No foolin'?"

"No fooling." Mason finally let the smile play full

across his face. "Not just placement, but a right and proper adoption in front of God and everybody." If Mason was a handsome man when he scowled, he was surely the most handsome man God ever created when he smiled like that. "If that's okay with you, that is."

"Okay? Good grief, Sheriff Wright, I thought you was gonna wallop me, not take me in."

"So that's a yes?" Holly asked, reaching for the boy.

"Absolutely!" He spun in a small circle, his hands on his head in total bafflement. Mason pulled her close and planted a delightful kiss on top of her head. "I don't think I got enough yesses to say yes to that." He looked up at Holly. "So you're gonna be Mrs. Sheriff Wright?"

"As fast as we can make it happen, Liam. These things take a little bit of time. There are lots of things to work out, but I've no doubt God will clear a path faster than you and I could ever imagine. The important thing is we'll be together—a true family—as soon as we can manage it. Can you wait?"

"I'll wait as long as you want." He thought about that again. "As long as it's not too long."

Holly opened her arms, and Liam tumbled into them, nearly whooping until the three of them laughed and embraced in more joy than Evans Grove had seen in a very long time.

Suddenly, Liam scrambled free and scratched his head in thought. It was such a treasure to watch him take it all in. "Hey, I'm gonna be Liam Wright, aren't I?"

Mason tussled his hair. "If that's okay with you."

"Are you kidding? Now I can say I'm 'Wright' all the time."

Mason's laugh was rich and deep. "How did I know you'd find an angle? In less than ten minutes, even."

Liam pondered the whole thing for a moment, his face turning from that of a conniving imp to a tender little boy's. "This is for real?"

Holly's heart swelled as she watched her sheriff— the lonely man who'd kept the world at a distance— pull his new son close in a powerful hug. "Absolutely," Mason said, catching a glance at Holly. "It's real. This is your home now."

"Wow." Liam stepped back and looked up at them, his happiness lighting his face. "Can I tell everyone?"

"Why don't you let us take care of the telling," she replied. "I imagine this will come as a bit of a shock to some people."

Liam stroked his chin, scheming. "Seems simple to me, but okay. In that case I'd better get back out there. If we stay too long in here, folks'll wonder what's up." He looked at Mason. Then he reached into his pocket, pulling out the deputy badge Mason had given him. "You want me to make up a good tale, tell everyone you gave me a fierce talking to and took away my badge?"

"You kept it, even though you were heading out of town?" Rather than be angry, Mason seemed charmed by the idea. When Holly remembered he'd kept her inscription page, it was easy to see why. Pocketing the badge with a smile, Mason said, "I'm glad you wanted to keep it. And I'll keep it safe for you until you get promoted."

"Promoted?" Liam asked, fetching his hat off the floor where he'd dropped it in the commotion.

"To 'son,'" Mason answered, and Holly felt the lump in her throat double in size.

Liam's chest puffed up. "Interim Assistant Junior Sheriff Liam Wright." He planted his hat on top of his head. "I like the sound of that." As if the shift of his entire world were that simple, Liam thrust his hands in his pockets and walked back out of the church.

Tucked together alone in the back of the quiet church, Holly felt as if God smiled down on the launch of her new life. "'Interim Assistant Junior Sheriff Liam Wright?'" She looked up at Mason as she leaned into him.

His arms slid around her with ease, as if they had always belonged there. "I was reaching for your way with words."

Holly looked up into the surprising peace of his eyes. "Is this for real?" she asked, borrowing Liam's words, feeling as dumbstruck as the boy.

His answer was a kiss so powerful it stole her breath and reason. When she finally broke away, gulping in air, Holly cocked her head to one side with amusement, "Mason Wright, kissing in church?"

"I'm just showing God how much I love you." He feathered a hand across her cheek, and Holly felt the tingle spread all the way to her toes. "I do, you know. Even if God had to go to great lengths to shake me into realizing it. It was your faith in me that brought me back to mine. And to you. The way I see it, I ought to kiss you in church every Sunday."

Holly wondered if her world could hold any more happiness. "My favorite kiss might just be the one that comes right after 'I now pronounce you man and wife.'"

"I don't know about that," whispered Mason, pulling her close, "I plan on you having a couple of dozen favorite kisses before that."

* * * * *

Dear Reader,

It's the human condition—we always think we know what's best for us. What is God's best for us, however, is often His deepest surprise—and maybe His strongest lesson. Most times, we're never as quick to forgive ourselves as God is eager to wipe away our sins. That's when God tenderly sends the clear vision of those who love us to remind us of our worth in His eyes. Friends in faith can always pull us from life's ruts and shadows, don't you think? Mason and Holly receive far more than they ever hoped for by trusting in God's plan even when they cannot see the outcome. And there are more happy outcomes to be had in Evans Grove, so be sure to read the next two books in the series. As always, I love to hear from you at www.alliepleiter.com or P.O. Box 7026 Villa Park, IL 60181.

Allie Pleiter

Questions for Discussion

1. Have you ever faced a danger as dire as Holly's? How did you react?

2. Has God ever laid a problem at your feet and helped you to realize the blessing hiding behind it like Holly does with the orphans? How did it change you?

3. Do you have a Beatrice in your life? What are her positives? What makes her hard to deal with? How can God change your attitude or the relationship?

4. Rebecca says she's "plum prayed out." When have you felt like that? What revitalized you?

5. Was Pauline smart to invite Curtis Brooks onto the Selection Committee, or was she inviting trouble?

6. Have you ever felt Holly's certainty about a challenging project like placing the orphans? What did it make possible?

7. Do you agree with Mason's tactic of forcing Holly back to the tracks? What would you have done in his place? In hers?

8. Mason says "duty isn't honor." Do you agree or disagree?

9. Curtis Brooks says "times like that bring out the best in some but the worst in others." When have

you seen disaster bring out the best in people? The worst?

10. What would you have told the children about the bandits hanging?

11. Have you ever "built a drawbridge" to someone in pain like Holly does? What happened? Would you do it again if given the opportunity?

12. When have you gone to church feeling "hollow and frail"? What helped to restore your strength?

13. Could Mason have done anything other than give the book back with the page ripped out? What would you have done in his place?

14. Holly believes that "as long as she could find some sort of use for this pain, she could endure it." When have you felt this way?

15. Do you think "one doesn't even need a home to be homesick"? Has it happened to you? Is there a homesick heart in your world who could use your comfort?

COMING NEXT MONTH
from Love Inspired® Historical
AVAILABLE MAY 7, 2013

THE COWBOY'S CONVENIENT PROPOSAL
Cowboys of Eden Valley
Linda Ford
Ward Walker thinks he's doing Grace Henderson a favor when he rescues her from a saloon, but she's been hurt too many times to trust the handsome cowboy. Can Ward convince her that he loves her despite her past?

THE MARRIAGE BARTER
Orphan Train
Christine Johnson
Recently widowed Charlotte Miller will do anything to keep the orphan placed with her—even marry the bounty hunter who's threatening to take her child away.

HILL COUNTRY CATTLEMAN
Brides of Simpson Creek
Laurie Kingery
Escaping a romantic scandal in England, beautiful aristocrat Violet Brookfield arrives in Texas and falls for rugged cowboy Raleigh Masterson. But is love enough to bridge the distance between their two worlds?

THE PRODIGAL SON RETURNS
Jan Drexler
As an FBI agent, Bram Lapp denied his Amish roots for twelve years, but an assignment forces him back into the Plain world where he meets Ellie Miller. Could Bram be the young widow's second chance at love?

LIHCNM0413

REQUEST YOUR FREE BOOKS!

2 FREE INSPIRATIONAL NOVELS
PLUS 2
FREE
MYSTERY GIFTS

Love Inspired
HISTORICAL
INSPIRATIONAL HISTORICAL ROMANCE

YES! Please send me 2 FREE Love Inspired® Historical novels and my 2 FREE mystery gifts (gifts are worth about $10). After receiving them, if I don't wish to receive any more books, I can return the shipping statement marked "cancel." If I don't cancel, I will receive 4 brand-new novels every month and be billed just $4.49 per book in the U.S. or $4.99 per book in Canada. That's a saving of at least 22% off the cover price. It's quite a bargain! Shipping and handling is just 50¢ per book in the U.S. and 75¢ per book in Canada.* I understand that accepting the 2 free books and gifts places me under no obligation to buy anything. I can always return a shipment and cancel at any time. Even if I never buy another book, the two free books and gifts are mine to keep forever.

102/302 IDN FVXK

Name		
	(PLEASE PRINT)	

Address		
		Apt. #

City	State/Prov.	Zip/Postal Code

Signature (if under 18, a parent or guardian must sign)

Mail to the Harlequin® Reader Service:
IN U.S.A.: P.O. Box 1867, Buffalo, NY 14240-1867
IN CANADA: P.O. Box 609, Fort Erie, Ontario L2A 5X3

Want to try two free books from another series?
Call 1-800-873-8635 or visit www.ReaderService.com.

LIH13

"I won't lose my daughter. I'll do anything to keep her."

He flinched and looked away. "I'm sorry. I tried my best."

"I know." She boldly grasped his arm, forcing his gaze
back to her. "Thank you." The time had come. "Will you
help me again?"

Confusion clouded his expression. "How?"

She opened her bag and pulled out the wallet. "Charles
left me some money. Whatever Mr. Baxter paid you, I'll
pay double."

He pulled back. "It's not that simple."

"Of course it is."

"No, it's not. The Orphan Salvation Society has an agreement with Greenville. If the judge rules that the children must
go to Greenville, then I have no choice but to take them."

Charlotte shook her head. He didn't understand. "I'm
not talking about all the children. I'm talking about Sasha."

Instead of walking away or shouting at her, he spoke
firmly. "There's nothing I can do to help you keep Sasha."

"Yes, there is."

He stared at her. "No, there's not."

"You can marry me." The words exploded down the street like gunfire.

He didn't blink. Not one muscle flinched except that tick below his eye. Dear Lord, he must think her mad.

"For money," she added, lifting the wallet. "I'll pay you double, triple. I'll give you all I have." Tears threatened, but she refused to let them surface. "I don't want anything from you. You don't even have to live here. I just need to be married long enough to legally adopt Sasha. Once the adoption goes through, you can move on." She shoved the wallet at him.

He held up his hands and backed away.

"Please help me." The words came out strangled, and for a moment she feared he didn't understand. She held out the wallet again. "Please."

Don't miss THE MARRIAGE BARTER
by Christine Johnson, available May 2013 from
Love Inspired Historical.

Love Inspired HISTORICAL

In the fan-favorite miniseries
Cowboys of Eden Valley

LINDA FORD

presents

The Cowboy's Convenient Proposal

Second Chance Ranch

She is a woman in need of protection. But trust is the one thing feisty
Grace "Red" Henderson is sure she'll never give any man again—not
even the cowboy who rescued her. Still, Ward Walker longs to protect
the wary beauty and her little sister—in all the ways he couldn't
safeguard his own family.

Red desperately wants to put her tarnished past behind her. Little by
little, Ward is persuading her to take a chance on Eden Valley, and on
him. Yet turning his practical proposal into a real marriage means a
leap of faith for both...toward a future filled with the promise of love.

Available May 2013

www.LoveInspiredBooks.com

LIH82963